ELEXIS BELL

WORLD FOR THE BROKEN

THE APOCALYPSE IS NOT FOR THE FAINT OF HEART.

World for the Broken

Elexis Bell

The apocalypse is not for the faint of heart.
And neither is this book.
Seriously.

If you're easily upset, read something else.

"If everyone took the high road, it would just be called the road."—Jeremy Johnson

Chapter 1

Christian

Snow crunches beneath feet, not far from my aching head. Dazed, I wonder how I could have let someone get so close. I try to lift my face from winter's blanket, but the world threatens to fall out from under me with even the slightest movement. Head pounding, I struggle to center myself. Holding as still as humanly possible, I strain my ears to pick out the size of my newest *friends*.

A trickle of warmth slips through my hair, dripping over my scalp and down my forehead. It's almost pleasant, except for the little voice in the back of my mind telling me that it shouldn't be there. As if for emphasis, a cold wind sweeps over my back, the only part of me visible above the snow. Warmth has no place here.

I remember how to open my eyes, lifting my head as I do so, and see red swirling before my gaze. The ground tilts and whirls, mixing melting snow and blood in psychedelic patterns. I slam my eyes shut once more, letting my head fall to the ground. My face splashes in the watered-down blood.

My blood.

Another foot breaches the snow with a crunch. The danger that I'm in screams back into focus, so loudly my skull aches with it. Or maybe that's just the head wound talking.

Fucking get it together, Christian.

I growl inwardly, but I'm excited that I can piece even that together amidst the agony bursting across my scalp.

Are these more of The Wolf's men, come to finish the job?

Then, it all comes back to me, hitting like a ton of bricks. Tate, Jesse, Karen…Are they safe? I don't know, don't remember much, and that scares me.

We'd been on the run, having escaped Breyerville two and a half days ago with The Wolf's Fangs dogging our heels every second. Poor Tate, just four years old, was terrified to fall asleep, as were we all. He'd only done so to the tune of Karen's voice, singing a soft lullaby, nearly whispering through choking fear.

What if The Fangs were close? What if they heard her song?

What if they found us?

Then, the blizzard hit and made our tracks impossible to miss. The Fangs found us within a day of the first flakes falling. The scene bursts across my eyelids, like some horrible version of the instant replay used in sporting events back before the war.

We'd just stopped so Tate could go to the bathroom, which took an unfortunate amount of time given the layers the poor kid was wearing, and we were about to set off again. Not that we really knew where we were going.

Just…away.

Away from Breyerville and the brothel Karen was forced into. Away from The Wolf and his cronies, demanding payment and tribute from all locked within his stupid walls. The walls we all helped him build, back when he seemed like a decent human being, someone we could trust to help lead us through the end of the world.

Funny thing about the apocalypse, that. It brings out what's hiding underneath the surface. Given time and power, The Wolf revealed his true nature, evil incarnate.

The Fangs found us unaware. Karen and Jesse had been arguing again, with Jesse lobbing some new unfair accusation at his poor wife. I'd been a little worried, thinking I may have to step in again and…calm my brother down.

Tate clung to his mother, burying his face in her legs. Her hands covered his ears, trying to spare him the worst of the argument, even as he shielded his eyes with tiny hands.

We heard the gun go off, loud and close. Instinctively, instantly, I ducked. A habit I wish I hadn't had the opportunity, or the need, to cultivate. Another crack and a bullet meant for me sailed over my head.

A third shot was attempted, presumably to correct their mistake in thinking I wouldn't drop to the ground. But the hammer fell, and the gun merely clicked. Empty. Luckily, they haven't figured out how to reload their own ammo.

Before my eyes, my little brother fell. With a small hole in his forehead, blood trickling from it, Jesse landed in a crumpled heap. Thankfully, he was facing the sky. I'd rather Tate remember his father's dead eyes than the state the back of his skull must have been in.

Four Fangs rushed us, giving me no chance to mourn.

One ripped Tate from Karen's grasp and threw the kicking, screaming little boy into the snow. Heart racing, all thought gone from my mind, I threw myself upon The Fang whose boot hung in the air, poised above Tate's head, and we went flying into a snowdrift.

I righted myself first, climbing atop the man, and pummeled him with everything in me. Rage filled me and boiled over. I remember the blood splattering across my face, some my own as my knuckles tore open a bit more with each hit, but mostly from The Fang, a dirty looking man with five o'clock shadow on his entire head. His hood fell back, and the scarf that covered half his face was soggy with blood.

Below each eye, the tattoos of fangs marked him as a bona fide member of The Wolf's Fangs. The quality of the first tattoos meant he'd been a member for a while. Since before they ran out of traditional ink a year and a half ago and had to start making their own. Since before the legitimate tattoo gun broke a year ago, and they had to do it the old-fashioned way. He'd been a Fang for at least a year and a half. Maybe longer.

The number of fangs tattooed beneath his eyes, rimming the socket, denoted how many times this particular Fang had bitten for his master. Four beneath one eye, and five under the other. Nine times, he'd killed for The Wolf.

Another Fang followed, crushing snow beneath sprinting feet, leaving the other two struggling to contain Karen's fury, all 5'4" of it. They shouldn't have separated mother and child. Swearing and screaming and flesh-hitting-flesh rang out behind Christian, with Tate crying in the snow not far off to the right.

"Stay there, Tate!" I screamed, sending another fist into the face of the man who would have killed my nephew.

Anger almost got the best of me, and I momentarily lost track of the assailant approaching me at full tilt. As the Fang beneath me faded, head lolling to the side in death, I sprang to my feet. I spun, just in time for another Fang to barrel into me, a palmed blade ready to sink into my flesh.

Back down into the drift I went, and this time, I didn't come out on top. The Fang hadn't expected me to turn, so his blade merely gashed my side, rather than digging in. Unbelievable luck.

Twisted up in the cloth of my jacket, the spin also jerked the knife from my assailant, sending it flying off somewhere. A miracle.

But that's where the good news ended.

With something clenched tightly in his fist, packing it for rigidity, The Fang landed a solid blow, unfortunately, located squarely on my temple thanks to the awkward way we landed.

I nearly passed out then and there, retaining only enough consciousness to hear Karen scream out, "Stop! I'll go with you if you just stop! Leave my baby alone!" Tears choked her voice, but it carried, nonetheless. All motion stopped, even the man sitting atop my chest stilled, unafraid of his seriously dazed victim.

"Please," Karen begged. "Please, just…we won't cause any more problems. Just…don't hurt him." I heard her slump to her knees, heard the rustle of fabric, and Tate's whimpering as she pulled him to her breast.

I saw the grizzled Fang standing behind her spit into the snow, mostly blood. Bright red gashes lined his face, leaking openly. He jerked his chin up at the man on top of me, and my chest got lighter as The Fang heaved himself onto his feet.

Karen's hands clutched at her son, pressing him tightly against her. Her pale face was rosy with the cold, and her long, black hair tumbled in a tangled heap, spilling free from the hood of her jacket, partially concealing Tate from view. Between her hair and his too-big jacket, I couldn't see the boy's face.

Rather than walking away, my assailant turned toward me. With black eyes rimmed with seven fangs and a cruel smile lurking beneath them, he pulled his foot back and slammed it into the left side of my head.

I remember the pain, arcing through every synapse, filling every cell of my body. I remember curling onto my side, watching through eyes barely open, clouded with the blood that dripped into them, as Karen and Tate were led away, sobbing. All our packs were gathered up and taken, as well.

Now, lying broken in the snow, the reality of their absence wallops me, leaving me breathless and gasping.

They're gone. All three of them. Jesse is dead. Karen and Tate…who knows. Will they kill Tate? Or use him against Karen to keep her pliable?

Disgust burns within me at the thought, simmering beneath the icy hands of agony as they steadily rip my heart to shreds.

And what of me?

I'd been so sure I would die, even as I slumped sideways, rolling onto my stomach. The snow fell around me, sapping the warmth from my body. When darkness took me, I thought it the end.

But now, shockingly gentle hands roll me over, and the ground tips beneath me. Stomach roiling, I worry

I may vomit, but manage to hold myself together. Barely. My eyelids flutter, stars exploding in my vision.

A shadow takes form, just beyond the starbursts. A woman.

Brilliant red hair tumbles forward, hanging in loose waves just above my face. A gloved hand pulls the scarf down from her nose and full mouth, revealing pale cheeks flushed with cold. Meanwhile, surprise registers in her shining emerald eyes. Turning her head to the side, she speaks in a voice that sounds a hell of a lot like salvation. "He's alive."

She leans forward, no doubt getting her pretty hair dirty with the blood that coats my face as the delicate strands brush my skin.

"Can you hear me?" she asks, very gently.

I nod. Sort of. The motion upsets my already spinning equilibrium even more, and my eyes fall shut, robbing me of the sight of her.

"Please," I murmur.

But what could I ask? Please save them? Please help me?

She owes me nothing. She and her companions will likely take whatever they can from me, from Jesse's corpse, from the body of the Fang that I killed. They'll desert me, likely take the shirt from my back.

Why wouldn't they?

Before I can ask her anything, the darkness claims me again.

Chapter 2
Chloe

Jackson and Grant lug the half-conscious man along and follow me into the forgotten farmhouse, made even lonelier by the sheer size of the place. Blinding light floods in through the windows, reflected and amplified by all the snow.

Closets hang open in the hallways, and drawers are pulled out of side tables in the living room. A grand fireplace overlooks the living and dining rooms, once the centerpiece of the home. Now, it stands like a silent sentinel, guarding over a place to which no one intended to return.

The occupants, like so many, gathered their valuables and whatever they thought would help them and fled, seeking their family members or government shelters. Back when people thought that was a good idea. Back before the government completely collapsed beneath the strain of the third world war, and the shelters became denizens of filth and chaos and death.

Before New York was nuked. Before Chicago, St. Louis, Houston, Miami, Los Angeles, and pretty much every other major city was bombed into oblivion, thankfully with regular bombs. Troops even made landfall on the west coast, with some making it as far inland as Utah before they were finally overcome. From what I gathered before the news stations gave up and the grid went down, most European countries came out worse than any in North America.

Either way, the economy collapsed. Chaos ensued. Panic ran rampant. Everyone went into fight or flight mode, taking and killing and running.

The former occupants of this farmhouse doubtless did exactly that, running to government relief agencies in search of food, medicine, or the means to find loved ones. With everything going on, no one went to work. Electricity, phones, and the internet, vital parts of life before…became extinct.

No one kept them up. Suddenly, they didn't seem important. Not with opportunistic thugs seizing control of cities and terrorizing the populace.

Checking in with friends on social media didn't matter as much without any food to take pictures of. Shopping in stores freshly looted or burned, only to reach a register that didn't work because the banks had been robbed or the phone lines were down and the credit card machine didn't work…

Somehow, it lost the thrill it held before.

Every abandoned home we come across makes me wonder what happened to the people who lived there. Every occupied home makes me worry.

So, why was I so ready to help this man, so clearly slotted for death?

I decide to save that question for my turn for watch and spread a throw blanket, dusty with two and a half years of disuse, over the couch. The smell of mildew greets my nose as I plop a pillow down on one end, and the guys lower the Sleeper onto it.

Hope he isn't allergic to mold…

Surveying the wound on his head, likely from something blunt, I wonder if his body could withstand the abuse of an allergic reaction. I don't know the extent of his injuries just yet and can't be sure what he can handle.

Slipping out of my wool hoodie, I toss it on a chair and pull the coffee table closer to the couch. I sit down on the hard, dusty wood. Gently, I probe the sleeping man's legs and arms, checking for any broken bones. I find none.

Behind me, Grant shifts uncomfortably, and I roll my eyes.

"Why are you even bothering?" he asks petulantly.

I don't justify it with a response. Not out loud.

Because we can't be the people who leave someone to suffer and die?

I know Grant only helped carry the man to the side by side, affectionately named S. S. Deadweight, and then to the farmhouse because he didn't want me touching him. Seeing me do exactly that, regardless of his effort, clearly stings.

Not that I care. I've told him I'm not interested. And I'm pretty sure he's been sleeping with Becky back home, anyway. He needs to get over this. Besides, what did he expect? I have a little bit of training as a veterinarian, enough to stitch this guy up and set any broken bones he may have.

"Here," Jackson says, handing me a wet cloth.

He must have used some water from his canteen. If there weren't a ton of ice falling from the sky, I might have scolded him, insisting I could use a dry cloth, just as well.

I thank my brother, and he pulls Grant's attention away. They focus instead on lighting the hearth and checking cabinets for any cans that haven't burst from the heat that surely built up in the house during the summers since air conditioning went by the wayside. Silently, I thank him for freeing me from the yolk of Grant's gaze.

Wet cloth in hand, I set about wiping away the freeze-dried blood in search of any additional cuts that need stitched, then use one of my remaining antiseptic wipes. Wary of waking him, I start with his hands. The knuckles are split. They'll need wrapped, but they should heal on their own.

I pretend I don't notice the strength clearly held within them, unsure whether the reaction in my stomach is fear that he could wake and wrap them around my neck...Or something else. Callouses cover his hands, and I briefly wonder what he did before.

Rummaging through my pack, I pick out a clean linen strip, tear it in two, and wrap his hands. I opt not to tie his hands together, hoping he'll still be somewhat uncoordinated if he wakes.

Judging by the state he was in when we found him, he likely has a concussion.

Digging out a flashlight stocked with the only batteries I have with me, I pull his eyelids open. His left pupil, on the side he got hit, is dilated far more than his right, shielding the majority of his beautiful blue iris.

When he spoke earlier, he said "Please," but it came out rather slurred. He also looked like he wanted to vomit, not exactly the reaction a girl wants. Then, he barely woke on the way here, despite the cold and the unfortunately bumpy ride.

Definitely concussed.

Now...the part that might wake him.

I clean his face and his scalp, pushing his shaggy black hair out of the way, partly wishing for scissors or a razor to get some of it out of the way.

He groans but doesn't wake.

An unfortunate patch of his scalp has been ripped up in a bloody semi-circle. All in all, it could be worse. It'll need several stitches, but it doesn't look terrible.

"Alright…guy," I say, wishing I knew his name. "Please, don't try to strangle me."

Med-kit out, needle prepped and poised, I hesitate. Jackson and Grant make all manner of noise in the kitchen, rummaging through cabinets, grimacing at the cans which didn't survive and the mess they made in death. I wonder briefly if it would be better to wake this man to keep from startling him awake or just hope his concussion keeps him under, beyond the reach of pain.

Deciding to try the latter, I set to work. After a couple of stitches, he groans and groggily tries to shake me off. The motion of his jerking head apparently upsets his balance, because he stills rather quickly, hands racing up to cover his eyes.

"Oh, god…" he murmurs.

I need the light to stitch him up but know it must dig at his eyes like claws. I sit patiently, waiting for him to gather his thoughts. When the bandages on his hands register, he squints at them, confused. He looks around, and his eyes find me.

Somewhat awkwardly, I say, "Hi."

"Uh…what…" His words are slow, clearly strained. He blinks several times and stares at me. "Who…are you?"

"My name is Chloe. Chloe Tucker," I answer. "And you?"

"Um…Christian. Jacobs. Christian Jacobs." Still astonished, his scrunched-up eyes never leave mine.

Partially to check his faculties, partially out of curiosity, I ask, "Can you tell me how old you are?"

The question is unexpected, but he responds with little trouble. "30. Why?"

Just three years older than me.

"Well," I say, "here, let me finish stitching you up. You took a bit of a blow to the head." With a smile to soften the words, "Just making sure you're still all there."

Chuckling, then regretting the motion of it, he says, "Never really was."

"Seems your sense of humor is still there," I say. "Any other injuries I should know about?" I probe, noting the yellowed remnants of a bruise encircling his right eye.

Punched by a leftie, roughly a week ago? Maybe a bit longer?

"Not that I recall," he says and winces as the needle bites in.

I almost laugh at the concussion joke, but think better of it, saying only, "Not that you recall?" Sarcasm drips from my words.

"Yep," he groans through gritted teeth. The suture tugs at his scalp as I tie it off, and he jerks a bit. His hand drops to his side. "Fuck…"

"You ok?"

"Just remembered something," he answers, gingerly lifting his hand from his side, "Dickhead back there stabbed me."

"Alright. I guess I'll stitch that one up, too," I tease, wary of my own lightheartedness.

Why should I be so casual? I don't know this guy.

Another stitch brings a sharp intake of breath, hissing through gritted teeth. But he holds still this time.

"I know," I gentle. "Stitches kinda suck ass. It's better than walking around with your scalp flapping though."

He chuckles, careful to keep the movement contained to his chest rather than his stomach, and is apparently made less dizzy by it this time. "I could see where that might be inconvenient."

His words are still slow, but slightly better.

The magic of adrenaline, perhaps.

"So…" I begin, hedging as I work my way into the elephant in the room. "What happened?"

He sighs, then groans with the renewed sting of the needle. "Running," he says, finally. We sit in silence for a minute, and Christian says, completely disheartened, "It didn't work."

"I saw…" Silence descends upon us once more as I finish stitching his scalp.

I help him sit up, unzip his jacket, and push it back off his shoulders in a move far more intimate than it was originally intended to be. My hands slide down his muscled arms, guiding the fabric down over the sleeves of his shirt before helping him lean back onto the couch.

I tell myself that the heat in the room is simply from the fireplace, crackling away behind me. *Not* from the way his eyes hold mine. *Definitely not* because of the way his gaze dropped to my lips right before I sat back up.

Christian slides his shirt up, revealing a tight lean stomach with a gash marring his right side. He rolls to face me, careful to keep his face turned upward so as not to lay on his freshly tended scalp.

Whether feeling pressured to explain because of the help being offered to him or simply to avoid the still air, thick with tension as my gentle hands clean his side, he eventually goes on. "We were in Breyerville, before. We lived there. Jesse, Karen, their son, and I."

Another deep breath.

"Jesse, my brother, worked construction with me. Karen was a pre-school teacher. They saved and saved, bought the business…doesn't matter, now." He closes his eyes as my needle bites into his side for the first time and goes on, "The Wolf's second-in-command, Billy, liked Karen. They threatened to beat Jesse and me, to…" his voice breaks. "The Wolf threatened to kill Tate. He's just four."

Christian's eyes open and find mine. I listen with rapt attention. I saw the fang tattoos on the face of one of the dead men back where we found Christian and assumed The Wolf was in this, one way or another. The other man had no such markings.

Must've been Jesse.

My heart drops, recalling the massive swath of tramped down snow leading away from the scene. I remember no female bodies, no tiny icy corpse.

They took them back with them.

Christian begins talking again, and I go back to work, eyes reluctantly deserting his so that I might do so. I stitch quickly, determined not to let my hands linger upon him.

"Karen agreed to join his filthy brothel if he'd leave us alone, but that just meant him and all his fucking Fangs were using her, beating her. She's so nice, so sweet…But she got quiet after that. She came home, bruised and battered."

Christian's eyes are haunted.

After tying off the last suture, I reach out a hand and lay it upon his cheek without fully comprehending my actions. He holds very still, and I don't quite know how to interpret that.

Not that I'm given much chance to wonder.

"Look who's awake," Grant grumbles from the doorway of the kitchen.

I look at him, staring daggers. I roll my eyes and glance, far more softly, at Christian. Pulling my hand away, I say rather awkwardly, "Sorry." I set my needle aside, resolving to sanitize it via fire and say, "Well, you're all good, now."

"Yeah," he says. "Good as new." Christian struggles to sit up, and I help. As soon as he's upright, he holds his head and whispers, groaning, "Mistake…"

I nod. "Probably."

***

Dinner is a quick affair, spread out across a small table, hastily wiped clean of dust. A few cans of vegetables warmed by the fire and a pack of exceedingly stale chips, split between the four of us. Jackson sits beside me. Grant, of course, snatches the chair perpendicular to me.

Across the table, Christian says little, watching us closely. I can only guess at his thoughts. He's lost a lot today, and his mind is likely still swirling a bit with the concussion, or at least aching.

I briefly entertain the idea of asking what he plans to do now but think better of it, opting to save that for when Grant isn't around. All I need is for him to get jealous and try to push Christian away before we have any idea what kind of man he is.

We could use someone skilled in construction. Something is always breaking, be it a fence or a barn or a roof. Something always needs built, whether it's more shelves for a cold cellar or an entire house.

Hell, the Vincent family needs a crib for the babies due in spring. Trent wants more cabinets for his tech stuff. Strong straight winds tore up some shingles at Mrs. Ableman's. And that's just what I can name off the top of my head.

Not to mention my inability to keep my eyes too long away from Christian. Or the fact that his eyes seem to drift my way whenever his mind strays from the terrible events of the day.

Or is that my imagination?

Either way, I didn't want to bring Grant along on this trip but knew we were going close to The Wolf's territory. We needed the extra muscle, in case The Fangs were anywhere near the pharmacy.

Trent's diabetes, while it ensured his safety had there been a draft, means he needs a steady supply of insulin. The tech-savvy little goober is getting low. We're working on learning to make it ourselves, but for now, Trent still has to rely on whatever we can find.

He never hesitates to help though. He's wired up solar panels at a few houses, providing lists of what he needs whenever trips out of town are made. He deserves for us to take the risk out here, and the pharmacy allowed us to stock up on some vitamins and antibiotics.

But it meant going close, too close apparently. Had we reached Christian any sooner, we very well could have died right alongside Jesse. Or maybe we could have saved them all, knocking out a few Fangs in the process.

Crunching a few chips, I long to be home. I want to break into some of the strawberries in my cellar. I want to eat some of the bread I baked just before we set out.

"Shitty chips," I mumble.

The tension in the air dissipates, if only for a moment, and we share a quick laugh.

"Not exactly fresh, are they?" Jackson says, eyes softening. "We'll have to make some good ones when we get home."

"Speaking of going home," Grant segues, glaring at Christian, "Where are *you* going?"

The air thickens, instantly.

Chapter 3
Christian

Rushing in to salvage the situation with green eyes glittering, Jackson suggests, "You could come with us, provided you don't turn out to be a dill-hole. We've got another stop to make, so we'll have time to find out." He smiles, as light and cheery as his bright blonde hair.

"You told Chloe earlier that you worked construction. Seems pretty handy." Jackson pauses, eyes twinkling with the pun he just made. "We could set you up in a house, get your garden started come springtime."

"I…um…" I stammer. "I should really go back for Karen and Tate."

"Well, problem solved," Grant says, words dripping with acid. "Though it does mean we wasted our time, *and our sutures*, since you're walking back to your death." His dark eyes glare at me.

Chloe stares down at her food, actively avoiding eye contact as she says the one thing no one can argue with. "You're not exactly in any condition to go back for them."

"Doesn't matter," I say. "I can't just let them suffer." My eyes focus on her, willing her to meet my gaze, but she doesn't look up.

"Then be smart about it," she says, shoving a few more barely-crunchy chips into her mouth.

"There aren't really any smart options for me here," I admit, shaking my head and instantly regretting it. My headache intensifies.

"You don't know Chloe," Jackson whispers, almost conspiratorially, leaning closer. An awful lot of comradery, considering that we just met. "If she's saying this, it means she's thought of something you haven't. She likes rubbing that sort of shit in, drags it out, makes you earn it."

Looking at her brother as if to say, "Are you kidding me?" Chloe shakes her head. "Oh, shove off, Jackson. I do not." She rolls her eyes and throws a chip at him.

Jackson catches the chip in his mouth with a smirk. "Saw it coming before you even picked it up," he teases.

"You might know me a little too well," she says and stares down at her plate.

Munching away at salty green beans, I watch her. I can practically see her mind drifting to some far-off place. Her face falls, even as a sad little sigh escapes her lips.

With a physical effort, she seems to stuff her feelings down deep. She takes a heavy breath and steadies herself. Finally, she looks up, clearly hoping her momentary lapse went unnoticed, only to find Jackson and Grant preoccupied with their food.

No such luck with me. My eyes lock on hers, paralyzing her. I have questions but don't ask. I have no right. But I want to, and that troubles me. I can't let myself be drawn in.

Karen and Tate need me.

I glance around the table at these strangers. I'd worry over their intentions toward me, but honestly, if these people meant to hurt me, they could've done it long before now. They could've let me die in the snow.

But no.

All I have to worry about is my own resolve.

"Come back with us," she says. Grant starts to butt in, so she speeds along, cutting him off. "We've got one more stop to make in the morning, then we're heading home. That'll give us time to see if we still want you along. We have to get some things back there, as quickly as we can. Come with us, wait out your injuries. When you're healed up, good as new, we'll bring you back here."

A stupid little smile twists Grant's features, but he has the grace to hide it with his food. It's enough to make me wonder about him though. Jackson merely looks at his sister, wonderingly.

"You'll still be outgunned, outmanned…but you'll be able to think clearly. You won't have any obvious wounds they can exploit." Poking a bit of fun, she adds, "Maybe you'll even be able to sit up on your own without almost puking all over the place."

Habit pulls my hand up and through my hair, making me wince sharply. "Son of a bitch…" I mutter, eyebrows rising as I close my eyes.

"My point exactly," Chloe says and scoops the rest of her vegetables into her mouth. Her chair slides back as she rises to her feet and circles the table.

I hear her approach, but purposefully keep my eyes shut. She's too distracting, especially without that big hoodie drowning her in wool.

Dropping into the chair beside me, she says, "Here, let me see if you tore anything loose."

Leaning forward, I brace my elbows on the table, resting my forehead on my hands. Even that hurts, so I lift my head again, groaning.

And I can't help it. I look at her.

Skin glowing with the warmth of the nearby hearth, she may as well be an angel. Eyes like a pure meadow sparkle in the flickering light, alternating between openness and shadow. Red hair like fire burns around her face, falls just below her collarbones, and leads my eyes to the scooped neck of her black shirt and the curves beneath it.

She scoots in close and pulls one leg up under herself in the chair. Her knee brushes my leg, and a stupid thrill skitters through my body. I close my eyes to hide it.

Then, her hands are on me, gently turning my head, tipping it forward. Her expert fingers push my hair aside, and a single lance of pain shoots through me, breaking the moment I thought we were having. A sharp intake of breath. The gritting of teeth.

"Sorry," she whispers, leaning closer to get a better look.

"Tell me I didn't screw them up too badly…"

The prospect of redoing the stitches makes my stomach turn, and my dinner, somewhat better than what I've been eating recently, threatens to make a second appearance. Somehow, I don't think it'll taste as good the second time around.

"I'll have to redo a couple of them." An apologetic smile graces her lips.

Her hands desert my poor abused scalp, one falling to her lap. The other simply drops down to the middle of my back, electrifying my skin.

"Finish eating. I'll get my med-kit," she informs me. Standing, she trails her hand over my shoulders as she leaves the room. "I'll be in here, so…When you're done…I need to wrap them, anyway."

She pulls the strips she cut from the living room curtains from their pot of water, freshly boiled for some semblance of cleanliness, and hangs them by the fire to dry.

I watch her. I almost decide to forget the food and follow her, immediately. Even though I know the stitches will hurt like hell, I want her hands on me, again.

It's been a long time since I've been with a woman, that's all. Hell, it's been years.

But deep down, I know there's more to it than that.

There's something more to *her*.

Before, when she was joking with her brother, something came over her. Darkness moved behind her eyes, and I wanted to know why. I shovel food into my mouth hurriedly.

Granted, everyone has their demons, now.

That doesn't dispel my curiosity, though. Rather, it makes me long to know the beasts that plague her nightmares even more.

"So," Jackson speaks up. "What'll it be? Are you coming with us?"

Looking up, I frown. I have to admit, Chloe has a point. I'm not fit for what I need to do. Hell, between my own stupid habit and Chloe's gentle prodding, my head is pounding. I'd stand a better chance of getting them out of Breyerville if I wait.

But what will Karen and Tate have to endure in the meantime?

"Do you mind if I sleep on it?" I ask.

I can't let the distraction of a pretty girl throw me off course. It just so happens that this mesmerizing woman also talks a lot of sense.

Jackson merely nods and goes back to his food. Grant finishes his, stacks his plate with Chloe's, and glares openly at me.

Okay, then...What's his *problem?*

Finally downing the last bite, I wobble into the living room, still mildly unsteady. I make it through the stitches and the wrapping without fussing too much, but my head sets the world to spinning, again.

Eyes closed and one foot off the couch, planted flat on the floor, I try to stave off the dizziness and the pain as Chloe's nimble fingers set to work on my scalp. I listen as she sterilizes and stows her med-kit, and Grant and Jackson settle into bedrooms in the back of the house.

The light tread of Chloe's footsteps leads to a nearby chair. I hear the brittle thing creak as she sits down. Part of me wishes she had sat on the edge of the couch, her hip brushing my side. I want her hand on my chest, want her lips on mine.

"Ugh," I mumble, accidentally aloud. Inwardly, I scold myself.

This is what I'm thinking about?

Karen and Tate are back in that hell hole. Jesse, asshole that he was, is dead. My baby brother...and I'm here, warm and cozy and this, THIS is what I'm thinking about?

"Are you ok?" Chloe asks, having heard only the small grunt.

Jesus...

"Yeah, sorry. Just…thinking." I spare her the details, very much doubting she'd like my train of thought.

She doesn't pry, thankfully. For a few minutes, we listen to the crackle of the fireplace, enjoying the heat that soaks into our bones. Chloe adds a log, and her silhouette draws my eye for an instant.

Redirecting my eyes to the ceiling, I say, "I don't think I thanked you earlier, for saving me. I really appreciate it." The words seem lame and ineffective, at best.

"Despite what Grant may say," she begins, laboring over his name, "it's no problem."

A yawn catches me unaware, stretching my words, "Why aren't you going to sleep?"

Contagion forces Chloe to yawn, as well. "Don't do that," she laughs. "I can't be yawning. It's my turn for first watch."

"I'll do my best," I chuckle sleepily. The long day catches me all at once, tugging my eyelids downward.

Has it really only been a day?

The fiasco with The Fangs did happen rather early in the morning…

I can't be sure how long I was unconscious before they found me, or after, for that matter. Slippery thoughts of time glide between my fingertips, pulling away from me as sleep comes to take their place.

Chapter 4

Karen

I wake in my ramshackle apartment, once nice and new, now rundown and coated in a layer of soot and grime that will never come out.

Just like me…

Jesse and I bought the condo when our business finally turned profitable. The construction company was nearly in shambles when we took over, but effective money management and aggressive marketing turned it around.

So much for that. None of it matters, now. The only good it's doing me now is that we splurged and got a unit with a fireplace, a luxury at the time, now a matter of life and death. I shiver thanks to the freak storm which chills the air, the storm that doomed our escape from hell.

Rolling out of bed, I groan involuntarily as my bruised arm smacks the side table, the only wooden piece of furniture yet to be broken down for firewood.

"Should have burnt it first," I grumble, careful not to smack anything else with my arm.

The bruise there is new, easily forgotten until it's bumped. Billy, The Wolf's right-hand man and biggest Fang, came to visit last night at The Wolf's house, the house he stole from Christian.

That man is a terrible excuse for a human being. His insides are nothing but filth and decay, almost to the extent of The Wolf, himself.

Even if I submit, which I always do now having long since learned that I can't overpower these barbarians, he still pins me. When he wants a challenge, he merely pins my arms with his own.

Last night, he chained my ankles to the legs of the kitchen table, forced my face down upon it, and with cuffs linked by dog chains, secured my hands together beneath the table. He made sure to punish me for trying to escape.

The Wolf watched, for a while, before taking his turn.

A tiny sob wrenches its way free of my throat as I meander out of my room and stir the embers in the fireplace, tossing in a chair leg. A deep sigh puffs out my ample chest, one of the things which got me dragged into the filthy grasp of the Wolf and his Fangs in the first place.

My chest, my hair, my height, my eyes. My smile.

The one I never use anymore.

I never resented my body, before.

I never knew Billy, or that I resemble his mother, either. The mother he beat to death when he was 17. A chill rolls down my spine as I wonder if I'll meet the same fate as that poor woman.

I force myself into the kitchen and pull open the lone remaining cabinet. Three cans of vegetables, two granola bars, a half-eaten bag of beef jerky, and seven water bottles stare at me. If I'm careful, if I boil enough of the snow, we can make this last a couple of days. Maybe three.

God knows what I'll have to do, with who, to get more. A small shiver runs through me.

In my room, Tate stirs. He never sleeps long after I get up. Granted, he goes to bed at least six hours before me, so it isn't terribly surprising.

I dig out one granola bar and a couple of pieces of beef jerky, listening to my son's tiny feet plodding across the hardwood floor. I count his steps and when he gets close, I paint a smile onto my lips.

Tate, that precious little boy, is all I have left. He's the only connection I have to reality, all that brings me ashore when my mind wants to drift on seas of numbness. He's the only thing in the world that still brings me joy, and I refuse to set a bad example for him. This world is terrible, I know, and I don't pretend it isn't.

But for him, I can smile. For his sake, I won't allow the world to make a monster of me, too.

It doesn't have to be that way, the way it was with his dad. Just because things are more difficult, that doesn't make it okay to let circumstances get the better of you.

For Tate, I can be strong.

As strong as Jesse couldn't *be.*

Tiny arms wrap around my legs, and my son mumbles into my thigh, "Morning, Mommy."

I kneel and hug Tate to me, so tight I fear I may break him. "Good morning, sweetheart."

I hate all that he's seen, all he's been through. My mind flashes back to Jesse's fists and the sound of Tate crying as he listened to my abuse.

He throws his arms around me, and I hide my wincing as his hands land upon a bruise on my back. Pulling back, I smile into his sweet little face.

"Ready to eat? Then, we can work on the alphabet some more."

Behind shaggy waves of brown hair that Tate won't let me cut, his big brown eyes light up, though I can't tell if it's for the food or the learning. He has a healthy appetite for knowledge. My heart leaps, glad that my experience as a teacher will help him.

I glance at the letters we went over yesterday, drawn on the wall in soot.

If only I had a better way to teach him.

My heart cringes at my own destitution.

Chapter 5

Christian

Blinding light comes in around the cut-up curtains, far too bright thanks to yesterday's blizzard. My head throbs and disappointment settles over me.

It was real.

The pain in my head, side, and hands are a testament to that. I want to stretch out but don't. No reason to rip open the stitches in my side. Cleaning the damn things will hurt more than enough, already. Though, Chloe will likely be the one to do it which…helps.

Speak of the devil. Her ever-light footsteps enter the room. "You look like you should be in a hospital," she says with a laugh.

Is that a giggle?

She checks me over and cleans my wounds, but doesn't like what she finds in the process. Early signs of infection fester in the knife wound.

I'm not terribly surprised. Who knows what or who that knife was used on before yesterday. Surprisingly, my head is well on its way to recovery. Apparently, The Fang's boot was cleaner than his knife. Maybe the snowy grass scrubbed the dirt off.

To be safe, Chloe opens up a bottle of antibiotics, a surprising find. In an act of generosity that's even more shocking than the antibiotics themselves, she gives me two. The pills seem so much larger than they are and as I gulp them down, I wonder at how big a role they used to play in everyday life.

"So, you're just giving those to me? And helping me…without expecting anything in return?" I ask, allowing some of my skepticism to show through.

"No. I'm asking for something."

Her response unsettles me and eases my mind at the same time. After all, it *is* the end of the world. Everyone expects something in return. For some reason, I'd just been hoping she was better than that.

Somewhat wary, I ask, "What do you want?"

"Don't make me regret this."

Five very simple words, ordinary in every way and wholly within reason. But something in her eyes makes me believe she's taking a much bigger chance on me than just helping out a stranger in the apocalypse.

A certain sadness lingers behind those sparkling green eyes, clear and oh so painful. It wavers, deciding how much of itself to show.

I put a tender hand on her cheek, and the sadness stills like a deer caught in headlights. "I don't intend to," I say, voice low and entirely too intimate given everything that's going on in my life. But to have said it any other way would've felt wrong.

Chloe holds my gaze for a moment before taking a deep breath and glancing down at her lap. Taking the hint, I back down, lowering my hand. Yet, I'd be a liar if I said my curiosity wasn't piqued.

She helps me sit up and put on my jacket. Jackson helps me to the table for breakfast, more random cans from the cabinets supplemented with a squirrel they caught in a snare overnight.

How out of it was I? I didn't even see them set traps…

I glance out the nearest window and find the sun rather higher than I expected.

How long did I sleep?

Throughout breakfast, they maintain a steady, surprisingly jovial conversation, making me curious just how good they have it wherever they live.

They seem willing to take people in, which implies their community has room to grow. Maybe they'll take Karen and Tate, too.

I can only hope.

Hell, hope is the only thing I have going for me, at this point. I still have to find them, then I have to successfully sneak them out, with 'successfully' being the operative word there.

Not to mention that I'm a little bit broken. Gashed, scuffed, ripped, and bruised. A minor infection. I'm really not in a state to help anyone. Lying on a couch, sleeping away a third of the daylight hours...

Barely able to walk from the couch to the fucking table...

A deep sigh bubbles up within me. Resignation settles over me like a thick blanket on an oppressively hot day.

I can't help them.

Not yet.

When Jackson eventually asks for my verdict at the end of breakfast, I say I'll join them, as long as they agree to bring me back here when I'm healed. I do my best not to let it sound ungrateful.

Chloe mostly hides the little smile that tries to sneak onto her pretty face.

Grant makes no such effort to hide his reaction, scowling quite openly. "Hurt any of us, hurt anyone back home, and you'll regret it."

"Though lacking tact," Jackson begins, glaring mildly at his companion before addressing me, "He's right."

"Just don't fuck up, okay?" Chloe adds with a teasing smile, slipping a bit of squirrel meat into her mouth.

A very serious turn, but it isn't exactly unexpected. They have a lot at stake, obviously. "The only way I would hurt anyone is in self-defense." Then, thinking on it, I amend, "Or to defend someone else."

Jackson makes a show of considering my words, extends a hand, and says, "I'll allow it." His grip is firm, but the smile on his face is soft.

I shake Jackson's hand and return the smile.

He's an odd character.

***

With me loaded up in S. S. Deadweight's little trailer and supplies arranged around me, we set off. The lack of autonomy bothers me, but Jackson refused to watch me struggle into the trailer.

It's a smart set up, really. The little off-roader, previously used on their farm for gathering eggs, hauling food to the pig pens, and such, is electric, so they don't have to worry about bad gasoline. They have a solar panel set up on board for charging it with a cage welded around it to prevent damage.

It makes me wonder even more who these people are.

As we ride, thankfully not at breakneck speed thanks to the newly melting snow, my mind wanders to a day long ago, back before everything collapsed, before the war began. Before Tate was even born.

I'd been sitting in the office with Karen and Jesse at the end of a very long day. Karen was maybe five months along, only barely showing. She never got very big during her pregnancy. We'd just gotten word that the bid we put in for a major job, the construction of a new superstore, had been accepted.

It was fantastic news. It also meant that Jesse was trying to push me into a position as foreman again so he could bring in additional workers, rather than finding an experienced, well-paid foreman *and* workers.

"Sis," I started, rolling my eyes. "Please, tell this buffoon to stop trying to get me to take the Foreman spot."

As usual, she stayed quiet on the subject, concealing a laugh behind the rim of her glass of sparkling grape juice.

Jesse had no such grace. "What? I just want the best for you." The wine we shared that evening mingled with the joy of the new contract, making us laugh giddily. "You'll still be able to build."

"Yeah, you said you'd still build too before you bought Harrison out and…How often are you on-site?" I'd said the same things many times. I knew I'd have to keep saying it until they found someone else who was qualified to fill the spot.

I just couldn't stand the idea of having to sacrifice time working with my hands to direct others on the tasks I'd much rather do myself. I've always loved building and fixing things, ever since I took a woodworking class in high school. Back then, it was an escape, a way to forget the catastrophe that was my home life.

But it developed into a passion.

One which the end of the world robbed me of, until now. These people, Chloe and Jackson and Grant and all the people back in their community, they're my chance to touch base with it, once more.

So long as I survive my attempt to free Karen and Tate.

Chapter 6

Chloe

Through the afternoon, the temperature rises enough to begin melting the blizzard's left-overs. I sit, silently staring out across the flat fields. They've long since returned to wild plains, reverting from the tamed fields farmers painstakingly maintained.

Nearing sundown, Jackson shifts, somewhat uncomfortable. Loaded down and with an extra person sitting where I likely would have been for the return trip, Jackson, Grant, and I are sandwiched tightly into a seat meant for two. Of course, I'm stuck in the middle with elbows digging into both my sides.

Crossing his arms to hold the steering wheel with his hands on the wrong sides, Jackson says, "This is what they meant by '10 and 2,' right?"

Face as straight as ever, I reply, "Yeah, that's how they taught it in Driver's Ed. That way, if the airbag goes off, you punch yourself in the face." I pause, staring at him with laughter in my eyes, and add, "With both hands."

He rolls his eyes, but the three of us share a laugh. In the trailer, Christian rides along, likely unable to hear us, our words lost on the wind.

With the fields becoming a muddy mess, and the road showing itself once more, Jackson meanders over onto it, following it until we reach a small trailer. The fences around it sag, struggling to contain collapsing chicken coops and a small barn perhaps once used for goats. Boards have fallen off the barn, and the door hangs limply on tired hinges. Snow huddles in the shadows, determined to live through the night.

Sadly, the house hasn't fared much better. Mature trees dot the yard all around, bare and skeletal with winter's embrace. They stand tall and proud despite their nakedness. All save one, which lies across the back half of the single-wide mobile home. A streak of white mars its bark. Lightning.

It'll have to do, though.

If we travel much farther, we'll come up on Sawton just as night falls. Not an appealing prospect. Though the darkness of night would shield our eyes from the agony of countless grisly visions, it would leave us vulnerable.

My stomach turns in a mixture of anticipation and recollection. My nose fills with the phantoms of smoke and burning flesh, and I regret suggesting we check the place out. I can still see them, the survivors, with bandanas over their mouths and noses, burning their dead, sobbing as they tossed loved ones on the pyre like unwanted garbage.

Spray painted in bright yellow across the outward-facing walls of nearly every building were the words, "Deadly Flu. Stay Back."

We turned away, unable to risk bringing a veritable plague upon Harville, and vowed to return the next week to trade, merely skipping a meeting. We assumed it would blow over within a week or two.

Several times, Jackson and I returned but were always greeted by the same scene, burning bodies and weeping. Only two things changed. As the weeks went on, the mourners became fewer and fewer, and the pile of ashes grew. Eventually, we stopped trying.

Now, after eight months, thinking it safe, I thought it a good time to check in and re-establish trade. The main attraction is the mill with lumber stacked all around, ready for use. If Christian were to come back to us after going to Breyerville, perhaps we could fix some things correctly.

Climbing out of S. S. Deadweight, I help the man in question out of the trailer. He seems a little better, less wobbly, and helps me tarp the trailer to keep animals and any stray rain or snow out.

Gently, I chide myself for entertaining the idea of him coming back. The odds aren't exactly in his favor. He's setting himself up for a suicide mission, at best, and I'm not quite sure how to react to that.

Seize the opportunity? Or, as per my usual, let it pass, foregoing both the inevitable heartbreak and the need to open up to him? Uncharacteristically, and in spite of everything I know he's dealing with, I feel myself leaning toward seizing, even as I smile at him over the covered trailer.

He smiles back, blue eyes shimmering like sapphires, and my silly little heart goes a-galloping. Inwardly, I roll my eyes, at myself and at the swarm of butterflies flapping away in my stomach.

We walk into the partially collapsed single-wide together, followed by Jackson and Grant, and quickly survey the place. On first glance, the residents appear to have abandoned ship after the tree fell in, but that theory doesn't hold for long.

Two skeletons sit in the corner of the master suite. Their bones have fallen into a heap, and their clothes lie in shreds around them, likely savaged by wild beasts after the couple died. Judging by the patterns on their clothes and the décor throughout the house, an overabundance of faded florals and plaids with signs about the glory of grandchildren, they were old when the world collapsed beneath its own weight.

I can only guess what finally did them in.

Was it starvation?

Surely not, with chickens and goats on the property.

Thirst?

I didn't see a well outside, but that doesn't mean it isn't concealed on the other side of the little barn.

Maybe they froze? Last winter was brutal.

It spelled the end of a great many people, especially the elderly. And the young. By comparison, the winter which holds us captive now seems paltry and weak of will, except for yesterday's blizzard, of course.

No fireplace to speak of, anywhere in the house. On closer inspection, I find a small metal pan near their bones, still stained with soot and relatively undisturbed. The animals must not have wanted to mess with it in the interim. The tattered scraps of a blanket mingle with the remnants of jeans and shirts, amidst a slew of feathers too cleanly white not to have been bleached for use within a fancy comforter.

I hope that, in the final stages of hypothermia, they at least had pleasant hallucinations. Maybe visions of their grandchildren. Closing the door to the master suite, I hope we don't find tiny bones in another room.

A few squirrels scurry about, running from the predators moving into their home. They escape through vents and into cabinets. Bird droppings adorn the tables and counters of the kitchen, as well as basically every other surface near the tree's resting place in the master suite.

The bedrooms on the other end of the house remain closed off though, and aside from a thick layer of dust, are relatively clean. One holds a full-size bed, clearly meant as a traditional guest room, while the other houses bunk beds. The dark blue comforters conceal no tiny bodies, for which I'm immensely thankful.

In short, it'll do.

***

Huddled together on the floor of the kids' room, the larger of the two available rooms, after a modest dinner of dried fruits and jerky from home, we settle in for a game of cards to pass the time before bed. Christian turns out to be terrible at cards, failing spectacularly several games in a row.

Somehow, it proves to be rather endearing. His attempts at bluffing fall far short of the mark, leaving him as open as a book. To be fair, I'm rather good at reading people. I refuse to call it a gift though, being the result of an unbelievably hard lesson.

Don't let it cloud you. Don't let it ruin this. I need to leave the past where it belongs.

Nowhere near me.

He has no place here, in this room, in your head. He deserves the prison cell he rotted in for years, and he deserves whatever death he got after the world...

My thoughts trail off. Something in me knows that he hasn't died, yet.

The truly evil people in the world keep on going, scraping some sort of existence from the bottom of every barrel, exploiting and using whoever they can. In my mind, another flash of that night breaks free from the depths.

The grains of the wood floor as he smashed my face into it, holding me down with a body honed by various sports in high school and college. The single nail that stuck up just enough to dig at my stomach just below my belly button when he ripped my shorts down.

My head slamming into the floor a couple times to keep me docile. The futile efforts of scratching at his arms, his face, reaching behind myself or over my head.

The scream when Mom walked in, having forgotten her purse when she and Dad left for the movies. The sound of panic as he left me lying broken on the floor. The crash that I didn't know was my mother falling, shoved to the ground. My dad's shouts as he tried to fight.

Two loud bangs, another crash. My father falling, weighed down by two lead rounds.

Another bang. My mother.

Another. My side burned with it, rejecting the pain. It was one thing too many, and my flesh revolted against it, refusing to accept it.

His feet crashed against the wood floors, thundering out as he ran.

Blood pooled beneath me. I turned, then regretted it, immediately. My poor parents, mere feet from me…

So much blood.

Vomit streamed from my mouth, scorching my throat.

I don't remember crawling to grab my phone. I don't remember the 911 call, though I listened to it a dozen times during the court case.

Deep breaths…

This won't rule me. I won't let it.

If I let it drag me down now, then all those years of counseling, all those self-defense classes, all the martial arts training, all the hard work piecing myself back together, all Jackson's efforts to help me through it even though he was suffering, too…would be for naught.

I'm better than that, and I know it.

Or as my counselor told me, reminding me that everyone struggles, especially after something so terrible, I *deserve* better than that, and I know that…

Now…

Mostly.

Pushing my demons back into the hell from which they came, I reorganize my face into something resembling a smile and lift my eyes from the hand of cards they'd drifted down to rest upon.

My little moment didn't go unnoticed, though. Jackson and Grant argue over whether a certain hand of cards is better than another, neither apparently able to remember the true rules correctly.

But Christian gazes at me, inquisitive as ever, eyes shining kindness.

I always get lost in them, in the long lashes that frame them. His tan skin, his strong jaw, the lean muscle I know rests beneath that olive-green coat of his, that black hair curling down to his shoulders and begging for my fingers to ramble through it…None of those things hold a candle to his eyes.

His head tips to the side, begging me to speak, and his hair falls across his forehead. The bandage concealed by hair and hood comes into view, and a strand of hair whispers across the barely-there bruising around his right eye, yellow and almost entirely faded.

Thankful for the distraction, I ask, "So, what happened to your eye?"

He furrows his brows slightly, surprised by my train of thought.

Quick as can be, Grant asks, "What do you mean?"

Did he not see it? Perhaps he didn't look quite so closely.

I spare him a glance, then specify. By Christian's dark expression, I know that my explanation is for Grant and Jackson alone, for he clearly hasn't forgotten it. Not for a second.

Unhappy that I've been staring so intently at Christian as to notice such a trivial thing, Grant speaks harshly, like a petulant child. "You know he just got the shit kicked out of him. What more is there to know?"

"This bruise is older than that. A week, week and a half? It's mostly healed."

Jackson leans closer, inspecting Christian in a way I didn't expect. "Make a habit of fighting?" he asks, tone on edge.

Eyes downcast, Christian whispers, "Jesse."

The name is a eulogy in a single word, filled with pain and regret, sorrow and longing, a misplaced joy which long since abandoned him.

Chapter 7
Christian

If I'm honest with myself, I was hoping not to have to recount my fight with Jesse for them. My baby brother…He certainly didn't blossom in the time since civilization abandoned us all. If anything, he backslid, falling right back into old habits.

Realizing they're all still staring at me, waiting for me to speak, I begin, "It was Jesse. He…"

I sigh, watching it play out in my mind for what feels like the millionth time in the past nine days.

"Jesse didn't like Karen taking part in The Wolf's brothel, not that she had much choice. He started getting defensive and insecure. And angry. Now," I pause, struggling for words.

"There's something you need to know about Jesse. Growing up, he was really short. He was 5'3" until the end of junior year. All the other kids picked on him. When he finally hit his growth spurt, he shot up to 6'4". They still bullied him, called him a freak."

I look up at Chloe, knowing the next part will reveal a bit of myself in the process of explaining Jesse.

"He was already an angry kid, even without the bullying. Our parents weren't exactly stable. We didn't hurt for money or anything, they both had good jobs, but they basically hated each other. Every night was a fucking battle. In high school, I took a few woodworking classes. It became an escape. Jesse was still too young for them, though. All he could do was listen to mom and dad, screaming at each other, throwing things, hitting each other…"

"He started lashing out, getting into fights at school any time someone picked on him, which was a lot. He got expelled a few times, but that just meant staying home with *them*."

I feel my vocal cords growing taut, straining over the words.

"Until he got to high school, that was how he let off steam. Then, he started doing some carpentry. It's a great creative outlet. We went into construction straight out of school. I was out a few years before him and moved out as soon as I could afford to. But he couldn't. He was still too young, so I just kept a bedroom open for him. Any time mom and dad were particularly bad, he came over and crashed with me."

Realizing I'm beginning to circle, I decide to land the plane. "Anyway, since The Wolf took over, since we finished the wall, there was nothing to build. No outlet."

I close my eyes and watch Jesse scream at Karen, over and over. I'd just tucked Tate into bed when I heard a plate shatter.

"Stay here," I told Tate and went to the living room, just in time to hear Karen say, "Don't get short with me."

"A poor choice of words," I say aloud.

"That's all it took. She just told him not to get short with her. Tons of people say that, all the time. She wasn't making fun of his height, but he just…" I mumble, speaking more to myself than to Chloe, Jackson, or Grant. In my mind, I watch my little brother do the unthinkable, settling back into his old defensive patterns.

"He hit Karen," I say.

I remember the sound of Jesse's fist smashing into Karen's face, already bruised from The Wolf or one of his Fangs. I remember her falling to the ground, crying, shying away from the man who was supposed to honor her, to cherish her.

The man who was supposed to protect her.

I shouted at him, drawing his attention away from the woman already carrying too many burdens. She hadn't the strength to spare for this one, nor should she have had to bear it.

Jesse and I screamed at each other. He knew I'd be a better match, so he wasn't as quick to throw the first punch. He justified his actions, accusing her of enjoying the brothel, accusing her of being just like the bullies when he was a kid.

I lost it, yelling at the top of my lungs, "I don't give TWO FUCKS how short you were, or how much those assholes picked on you. You do NOT lay a hand on your wife! She's not like them, *you* are."

Unable to face the truth of the matter, Jesse hid behind his fists, once more. But I knew it was coming. I knew, at some point, it would happen. I dodged, mostly, taking only a glancing blow to my right eye rather than a solid hit. It still gave me a black eye, but it didn't knock me out.

The partial miss threw Jesse off balance, which I used. I knocked my little brother out. I held Karen while she cried, hating that she had to endure such pain.

In that moment, the balance between us tipped. She felt more like a sibling than my own brother. Jesse was a stranger to me, a stranger whose entire past was known to me, but whose motives were concealed as he, somehow, turned into the very thing he should've abhorred.

I sat there, staring at Jesse's unconscious form, for several minutes, sleeve and chest wet with Karen's tears, completely at a loss. My hands shook on her back, and revulsion warred with guilt in my stomach, a potent mix ripe with promises of vomit.

Eventually, when her sobbing calmed to regular tears and her entire body no longer shook with violent tremors, I led her into Tate's room. She crawled into bed with her son, calming him down, soothing his fears. She didn't tell him everything would be ok, as she once would have done. Instead, she told him that they would get through it.

Such a simple thing, a change of words, yet so powerful.

She was once so optimistic that I occasionally wondered if she even saw the problems around her. She did, of course, but she hoped her way through them. When an obstacle came up, she hoped for the best. If it didn't happen, she simply laid her hopes upon the next best thing, never truly showing any signs of disappointment.

"Everything will be ok," she would say.

But that night, she didn't.

She told Tate they would get through it. The optimism was still there, but she was blatantly acknowledging the hurdle. The only person I thought stood a chance of escaping the apocalypse with their cheery personality intact…had been broken.

After relaying the bare bones of that evening to my new companions, I say, "I sat up most of that night, thinking about a way to get us out of there. I planned it for a week. I just…" My throat closes over the words. "I didn't plan it well enough."

My heart twists in my chest, contorting itself into painful positions as it tries desperately to get away from the guilt writhing within me. My mind repeats, "They're gone…" over and over until it becomes the default background music of my life.

"I'm sorry, man," Jackson says, gently patting me on the shoulder.

A deep, shuddering breath racks my body, battering every muscle in its path with Jesse's fists. I nod, unsure how else to accept these condolences. When I finally look up, Chloe grants me a gentle smile.

One corner of my mouth lifts, half-heartedly.

Rubbing my face, I say, "It doesn't feel real."

I shake my head as if that would confirm the impossible nature of this situation.

"I keep expecting to wake up, for them not to be gone," I say with longing. "For me never to have met you," the words are filled with regret, and my eyes never leave Chloe's face.

"I keep thinking that, when I go back for them, Jesse will be there, smiling like he used to after he graduated, while we were working together. I keep thinking I'll go to their door, walk through it, and just go back to…before."

"You're probably still in shock," Chloe says. With agony resonating in her voice, she adds, "It can mess with you, pretty badly."

***

The sun sends long fingers of light through the window, waving to say good morning, and urging us to rise with the dawn. I shy away, turning toward the body lying next to me and shielding my eyes. Taking a deep breath, my nose fills with a distinctly feminine scent. Not perfume, no, but definitely something feminine.

Eyes fluttering open, I'm met with a shock of red hair draped over a pale face. Long, dark lashes fan out over Chloe's cheeks, and her head rests upon my left arm. She nestles in closer, burrowing into my chest. For a moment, I'm stunned.

Still half asleep, I don't overthink it. I wrap my arm around her waist and pull her closer. A soft sigh of comfort slips past her full lips, and she nuzzles my neck. Her left arm loops around my waist, skirting past the still-tender gash on my side as she pulls her arm from between us to do so.

As I drift back toward the land of dreams, I thank my lucky stars that there weren't more usable blankets, that it was bitter cold, that there was no fireplace in this little home…that we all huddled under the layers of blankets, together.

On the other side of Chloe, Jackson shifts, throwing an arm up over his eyes. He groans, turning to face away from his sister. The movement prompts her to fold herself further into the warm arms surrounding her.

With a sigh, peace settles into me, and my eyes fall shut.

***

"Wake up, sleepyhead," calls a voice, very near.

A gentle finger traces down the length of my nose, from bridge to tip, moving at a wonderfully slow pace.

Chloe.

The name is an exaltation, singing itself through my mind.

I open my eyes very slowly only to find those brilliant gems she calls eyes inches from my own. The warmth of sleep envelops me, and I find it difficult to keep my lips from moving toward hers. My thumb caresses the small of her back, moving to and fro, having somehow found its way beneath both her hoodie and the shirt beneath it in the night.

"Good morning," I mumble, barely stopping myself from kissing the tip of her nose.

She giggles at my groggy tone and says, "Good morning," very softly. "It's time to get up. Breakfast is ready, and no doubt will be fit for a queen." Sarcasm laces her words. "You won't want to miss it."

Stomach gurgling, I definitely agree. I don't want to miss a meal.

And yet, I don't want to get up. I don't want to leave this room, to pull away from her. If I go out there, I have to face whatever's coming up in this little town called Sawton. If I get out from under these blankets, if I release Chloe from my arms, will she ever be within them again?

If I fully wake, I'll have to withstand the weight of loss, the absence of Tate, Jesse, and Karen. The burden of Jesse's death, the desperate attempt I have to make to save Tate and Karen, all of it will settle squarely upon my shoulders once more.

But here, lying on this old floor, under dusty blankets with Chloe nestled up close, my shoulders are light. I'm free.

The door to the bedroom opens abruptly, thudding into the wall behind it and robbing me of the decision. I crane my neck, looking up and behind myself to find Grant staring down at us with disgust writ plainly across his face.

"Oh my god," Grant spits out, unjustly appalled, and turns on his heel. "Get up," he calls over his shoulder as he walks away down the hall. He leaves the door wide open, letting the accumulated body heat escape the room. Cool, crisp winter air rushes in to take its place.

Chloe rolls her eyes and smiles. "Shall we?" she asks and throws the blankets off herself, not waiting for a reply.

***

The ride to Sawton is uncomfortable despite the warming weather, what with boxes of random shit jabbing into my legs. Before we left the trailer, I positioned a few bundles of fabric near my side, eliminating the potential of a box corner stabbing me in my stab wound. No need for that.

The conspicuous lack of any food outside of what they'll eat on the trip makes me believe that, wherever they live, Chloe's group is self-sufficient. That line of thought brings with it the acceptance that, already, Chloe is more important than anyone else in present company. To me, it's *her* group. Not Jackson's. Not Grant's.

I force my mind back to the food, staring behind them at the dust trail the UTV kicks up.

If they're stable, if they can make it through the winter without fear of starvation forcing them to raid and pillage, if they want only for things like antibiotics and…What the hell is this for?

I run my hand over several lengths of PVC pipe and a small motor.

Anyway, regardless of the purpose of the pipes and motor, if they have time to search for crap like this, they have readily available food and water. If they'll take me, Karen, and Tate in...

It just might be perfect.

I just have to find them.

Cresting a hill, we hit a bump in the road, and the corner of a box digs into my leg, eliciting a groan. A box of...

Craft supplies?

I look into the box and find a few knitting needles, tall thin-walled metal molds labeled as candle molds, wicks, buttons, sewing needles...There are even a few bottles of dye and various scents for the candles.

Another bump, another jab to the leg.

I'll be glad when we get there...

I immediately take the thought back. Meeting new people doesn't typically go well, certainly not so well as it has since I met Chloe. Who's to say the people in this town will respond well to me?

My eyes drift upward to the sky, and I watch as the trees around the road get thicker, eventually forming a closed canopy overhead. The mild winter and the buffer provided by all the other trees have allowed some leaves to come in exceedingly early, and their thick shadows dapple the ground. Saplings edge closer and closer to the road, taking advantage of the road crews' absence, and their roots kick up small patches of asphalt, buckling and cracking it.

After about twenty minutes more of driving down the winding pocked road destroyed by two and a half years of freezing and thawing, we ascend another hill. At the top, Chloe takes a deep breath. I crane my neck around to look forward, peeking through a break in the canopy and don't particularly like what I find.

At the bottom of the hill, in a small clearing amidst a sea of trees, lies the remnants of a small town. Jackson brakes to a stop, and stares.

The outer walls of the buildings are adorned with faded spray paint, "Deadly Flu. Stay Away." Dead, dried-out vines of poison ivy snake up the buildings, partially obscuring the old words.

Several homes have windows busted out. Multiple buildings are reduced to burnt, charred husks clawing at the air. A couple have been partially dismantled to repair the obviously inhabited buildings, all three of them. In the center of town, a huge black circle takes up a good portion of the general store's parking lot.

They may not have much to trade.

I settle back down into the trailer of the UTV.

Pulling forward, we dip back under the canopy, and the temperature drops, making me realize just how warm it was in the sun. I hadn't paid it any mind, but it was substantially warmer than when we left the trailer this morning.

All the way down through the tunnel of trees, I practically shiver. Breaking free of the trees, the temperature shoots back up again.

"Is spring here early?" I ask. "It must be like 45 degrees. We just had a fucking blizzard a couple days ago."

Looking back, Chloe jokes, "Did you forget you're in southern Illinois? Mother Nature does whatever she wants here." Though her words are light, her tone is anything but. Her eyes only briefly leave the disheveled town before her, glancing at me for but a moment.

Did she have friends here? Family?
A lover?

Pulling off her wool hoodie, Chloe tosses it into the bed of the UTV on top of a bow and a quiver full of arrows and grabs her pack.

"Now," she says, "I don't know what we're walking into, here. We haven't had contact with them for a long time. Eight months, I think. May as well be eight years with how things are, now."

She rummages through it and pulls out a small, sheathed knife. She turns to face me, offering the knife to me, handle first. "Can I trust you?"

I nod, wrapping my hand over the handle of the knife. Our fingers brush, so my voice comes out husky when I tell her, "Of course."

Beside her, Grant groans, mumbling, "For fuck's sake." He evidently thinks himself unheard, but really should have spoken more softly if that was the intention.

Over Chloe's shoulder, I see movement.

A man separates himself from the rotting buildings around him, gun at the ready. "Get out, now! Hands up!" the man shouts, expecting no opposition as he walks slowly forward.

Behind him, two other men appear, one with a machete and the other with a crossbow. He only has three bolts, but that's enough to take out most of us without his apparent leader ever wasting a bullet. It doesn't have as much of an intimidation factor as a gun, but a well-placed shot will kill you, just as dead.

Jackson and Grant step out of the UTV, and Chloe follows, exiting on Grant's side.

"Why don't you help Christian?" she whispers.

Grant offers no opposition to her suggestion, making me wonder what they have planned. She and Jackson creep forward, one step at a time, even as the men from Sawton close the gap.

"Terry, Jack, Ben. Long time, no see," Jackson says, quite amiable despite the gun and crossbow trained on him and the machete practically begging for his blood. "I have to say, I expected a nicer welcome than this."

"Welcome? You want us to welcome you?" hisses the man in front. His dark hair flaps about his face in greasy tendrils as a breeze caresses them.

Grant pulls me from the trailer, not quite gently, and whispers, "What's *his* fuckin' problem?"

"Well, maybe not a full-on party or anything so extravagant," Jackson banters, "but a gun?" With a light tsk, he adds, "Aren't we beyond that, Jack?"

"We used to be," the gun-toting man answers. "Before you left us all for dead."

The gap closes, and the man named Jack practically holds the gun to Jackson's forehead.

Utterly nonplussed, even with the asshole with the machete approaching Chloe, his little sister, Jackson's face is placid, if a little confused. "Did you not see the signs left for us on the walls?" he quips. "We were told not to come. We kept trying, for a long time. But we couldn't risk bringing a plague back to our people."

"Excuses," the machete man spits. "You should have helped us."

"I've got this, Ben," Jack shouts, eyes never leaving Jackson. His hand tightens on his gun.

Careful to keep my pace even, I make my way forward. Grant moves too, but at such a pace as to suggest he has no intention of completely closing the gap. In his waistband, I glimpse the handle of a pistol and think I understand.

"Slow down," Grant whispers. "You'll get in the way."

Without looking away from the man pressing a pistol to Jackson's head, watching Jack's face contort with rage as he shouts and screams, I ask, "What?"

"I said, you'll get in their way. Slow down."

Thanks to our exchange, I almost miss it when, after a failed attempt at negotiating the lowering of weapons, Jackson says something that makes no sense. He asks Chloe if they have any apricots back in Deadweight to give the lovely 'Sawtonites.'

"I think so."

In less than the blink of an eye, he diverts the man's gun, using it to shoot the man with the crossbow in the chest. Meanwhile, Chloe breaks the wrist of the machete man with almost no effort. The blade falls to the ground, now useless.

So many punches and kicks follow that I lose track of what's going on. "What kind of ninja shit are they doing?" I whisper, incredulous.

My eyes are drawn to Chloe, even as Grant urges me to get back in the trailer. We try to climb back into the UTV. A few bullets fly our direction, and we opt to duck down behind it, instead.

Peeking out, heart racing and ears ringing, I see Chloe knocked to the ground. My stomach plummets.

I can't watch the murder of another person I care about. I can't lose her, lose these guys. Not them, too.

And somehow, I know that if they're killed, I'll be left alive to suffer. Again.

"No. It's not happening, again," I mumble.

I vault up into the trailer, ignoring the pain in my side. I duck back down, just in case any more bullets find their way this direction. When none come, I spring up to grab the bow from the bed of the UTV and see Chloe flip the machete man, regaining the upper hand. She punches him once, twice, then snaps his neck. He lies beneath her, head lolling.

Meanwhile, the man fighting Jackson lands a solid hit, sending Jackson flying. Jack makes a dive for the machete. His gun is nowhere to be seen. By the time I can string an arrow, Jack has the machete to Chloe's throat, hauling her up by it.

The knife bites in enough that I see a few drops of red running down her neck, even from a distance. Granted, my vision is excellent, but still. It makes me nervous that there's enough for me to see. Enough that she doesn't try to fight her way free for fear that the knife might sink in deeper.

As I line up my shot, I hear Grant whisper behind me, "What the fuck are you doing? You'll hit her!"

"Believe me, I won't." I've been hunting since I was big enough to pull back a bowstring. Grant just doesn't know that.

Standing nearly a foot taller than Chloe, Jack's neck is clearly visible. Makes for easier arrow retrieval than going for the head, and minimizes the chances of bending the shaft. More importantly, I'm confident I won't hit Chloe, thanks to the height difference.

Jackson stops, mid-step and skidding, unwilling to risk his sister's life. Jack calls out the customary, "One more step, and she's dead," line. He issues commands about leaving the side-by-side and all its contents, leaving Chloe, and vanishing. Otherwise, her life is forfeit.

Practically hissing, Grant says, "If you hit her, I promise I *will* kill you."

I take a deep breath, calming my frantic heart. Fingers loose on the grip, left arm beginning to ache from holding the damn thing so long talking to Grant, I aim down the arrow, and let go of the string. My arrow flies true, sinking into Jack's neck. It breaks through the other side, finally stopping at the fins.

Blood gushes and spatters, dappling Chloe's beautiful hair. Shock loosens Jack's grip, giving Chloe the chance to push his hand away from her neck. The machete goes flying, and the man grasps at his own throat. Desperate attempts to hold in the blood fail, and he grows weak with the loss of it.

I knew I could make the shot, but relief still flows through me like a cool river when Chloe steps away from a falling Jack. I drop my head down upon my arm, resting it on the side of the trailer.

I glance up to see Jackson hugging Chloe and inspecting her neck.

"I'm fine," she repeats, over and over, barely audible.

They start walking back, and I leap out of the trailer, adrenaline masking the pain in my side.

When they get close, I recall the spinning kicks and flying punches, and cut off whatever they were about to say, exclaiming with a laugh of immense relief, "Who the fuck are you people?"

Chapter 8

Chloe

Perched on the tailgate of Deadweight's trailer, I stare at the houses Jack, Ben, and Terry claimed for themselves in the center of Sawton. I thank Christian for cleaning me up and for saving my life.

"No problem," he says, smiling sweetly. Then, with a bit of mirth, "Now, we're even, right?"

Spirits decidedly low, I barely manage a huff in response. I wince as Christian runs an antiseptic wipe over the cut on my neck. Grant and Jackson meet in the doorway to one of the houses, one going back in for another box of goodies as the other carries a box out.

The customary, "Ope, sorry. Let me just slide past you," is uttered by both parties.

As I watch them do the dance of trying-to-get-out-of-each-other's-way, I mumble, "It shouldn't have gone this way."

Of course, it would be stupid to leave everything behind knowing that no one here will need it, but I hate it, all the same.

With gentle fingers, Christian inspects the freshly cleaned cut. "Not everyone copes as well as you guys have. People crack under pressure all the time," he soothes. "You did what you had to."

He tips my head to the side and looks closer. "You might need stitches…" He probes a bit, and I clench my jaw. "Probably only one or two, though. Most of it should be fine."

He informs me that he's never had to stitch anyone before, so I tell him how. He sets to work, and I keep my wincing and outcries of pain to a minimum, hoping not to discourage him. I ball my fists on my knees and grit my teeth.

Silence punctuates our interaction, holding back all words and sounds. Even the breeze stills, leaving the branches motionless and quiet.

I hear only Grant's and Jackson's footsteps, my thoughts, and Christian's breath, very near my neck. My mind swirls with regret, pain, and the lure of having him so close.

He finishes, hands deserting my skin and leaving me chilled despite the unusual warmth in the air. A stray thought warns me to be wary of tornadoes, and I hope desperately that Breyerville, high ground that it is, will split whatever may come our way, as usual.

Christian's hands find my arm, whisking my mind away from the weather with a thrill of tingles and a sting of pain. I'd all but forgotten the tiny cut on my bicep. My shirt is torn, sliced through, and he manipulates the tear to see the cut.

"Hang on," I say, pulling the long-sleeved shirt up and over my head. Sitting in a dark green camisole, I feel goosebumps rising on my skin. "Might be easier like this," I say, doing everything in my power to slow my hammering heart, lest it beat my ribs into dust.

For his part, Christian's eyes only rake over me once, and then, he busies himself cleaning my arm. That one glance is all it takes to build a small fire within me though.

"No stitches here," he says, obviously relieved. "Let's wrap you up."

He reaches for the gauze we found in one of the houses and threatens to make me into a mummy. I end up with a gauze scarf and a matching armband. Having found no medical tape, we merely tie it off. It fends off some of the chill in the air until I stand and put my other shirt back on.

Foregoing my hoodie, I slam the tailgate back into place and say, "Shall we help them clean everything out?"

***

As we grab the essentials, food, weapons, and medical supplies, I wonder if we'll need to make a second trip. I load a box of canned food into Deadweight's trailer, eliminating the space Christian occupied on the way to Sawton. We'll have to cram him into the seat, as well. A strange little thrill runs through my veins at the thought of being so close.

More boxes, a few bags of clothes, and a collection of miscellaneous items later, we sit down for a late lunch, carving into the perishables.

The leaves turn over outside, calling out to the sky for rain. Clouds roll in off the horizon, and we light candles to fend off the encroaching darkness. Christian opens his mouth to speak, but a bolt of lightning and a near-immediate crash of thunder interrupt him.

"Grant, open up the garage," Jackson says. "We're going to have to wait this out here. I'll pull Deadweight in." He sizes up the coming storm through the window and doesn't seem to like what he sees.

I follow his eyes, see the mild green tint in the sky. "I was afraid of that," I mumble between bites of rabbit.

Though almost certainly not the topic he would have broached a moment ago, Christian asks, "So, why do you call it S. S. Deadweight, anyway?"

A smile graces my lips as I fondly recall the day Deadweight got her name. Jackson swore the ice would hold, and at first, it seemed like it would. Then, the creaking and crunching started. He was about three feet out into the creek.

"Jackson's dumbass thought she was a boat. He nearly sank her in a creek," I say, laughing.

Not quite outside yet, Jackson rushes back into the room to defend himself. "I did not! There was only, like, six inches of water under the ice. It barely came to the center of the damn wheels," he explains, gesturing to illustrate the amount of water.

We erupt with laughter.

"Nearly sank it…" Jackson mumbles. "Bullshit!"

"We had to dig the thing out of the ice, didn't we? At the very least, you buried her," I jab.

"Look," Jackson says, turning toward Christian and the huge smile plastered across his face. Mock serious, he goes on, "Don't listen to her. She clearly doesn't know what she's talking about."

"Really?" I laugh. "I never sank poor old Deadweight." Looking at Christian, glad for the smile on his face and the deep laughter bursting from him, I add, "You should have seen his face when the ice dropped out from under him. It was perfect!"

"GOD!" Jackson yells, feigning humiliation. "You always embarrass me! And in front of my new friend! Geez!"

I laugh, and he says, "I'm going outside." Pseudo-petulance rolls off his words, and he stomps out like an angry child.

Waves of laughter crash in his wake, settling into an amiable silence as Christian and I eat. When the door to the garage opens and another clap of thunder rings out, Christian speaks once more. A smile still lingers on his beautiful face, as he brings up a topic he has no idea will pull our moods low.

"Where did you learn to fight like that?" he asks.

The words are so innocent, but my smile vanishes instantly. Robert's face, the feel of him on me, the floorboards, my parents dead on the floor, all of it flashes before my eyes. I nearly drop my fork as a sudden wave of anger and self-loathing washes over me.

The fingers of my free hand find their way to the tiny scar on my stomach, thanks to one stupid nail in the floor. Clearing my throat, as if that simple motion could also clear my mind, I remind myself that it's been over a decade.

I shouldn't be so affected by this anymore…

Of course, my counselor always hated it when I talked like that. Rationally, I know the effects of something so…gut-wrenching are far-reaching. Somehow, though, it makes me feel weak to be dealing with it still, and I hate the bastard more for that.

I hadn't expected to have to tell this story, again. I hadn't thought there would be anyone new to tell it to. Everyone in Harville already knows. They remember the court case that dragged on, even in the face of overwhelming evidence, and the outrage at his minimal sentence meant to lessen the impact upon such a *promising* young man.

A deep sick hatred fumes within me at the ignorance of the judge, placing Robert's athletic prowess above my sanity and virtue, my parents' lives, and Jackson's sanity.

Now, I ask myself the same question I asked Christian this morning when I handed him the knife.

Can I trust him?

I knew that giving him that knife meant trusting him with my life. But he came through. Not only did he refrain from turning the blade on me, but he ended up saving my life.

This feels different though, riskier somehow. In my mind, trusting him with my heart holds more potential for disaster. Perhaps because, if you trust the wrong person with your life, you don't exactly stick around for the aftermath.

I look up at him, and he asks, "Are you ok?" Concern laces his eyes, and he waits patiently for an answer.

At that moment, I realize that I want to let him in.

Perhaps it's the deadline looming over our interactions freeing my tongue even as it minimizes the risk of getting overly attached, a bit of preemptive damage control if you will. I open my mouth to assure him that I'll be fine. I almost start to explain.

"You two make me feel like I'm in a hospital, all wrapped up like that," Grant jokes, strolling back in to finish eating.

"A conversation for another time," I say apologetically, and Christian nods his understanding.

Grant rolls his eyes and plops down into his chair.

Jackson walks in, carrying two more candles, just as the bottom falls out of the sky.

Chapter 9

Karen

I tuck my baby boy into bed, our bed. His was cut and burned for warmth, not long ago. Not that Tate liked sleeping on his own anymore, anyway. The metal frame of my own bed provides little in the way of firewood, otherwise, it would have gone that way too, leaving us only a mattress on the floor, until the time came to burn that, as well.

Unluckily, or luckily, a few neighbors starved or were killed since everything fell apart, and Jesse, Christian, and I took anything and everything we could from their condos. I hated every second of it, but did it, regardless.

I push a few strands of hair from Tate's tiny forehead and place a kiss in their wake. He stirs but doesn't wake. I sigh, mourning the life he's to be subjected to.

If only we'd made it further...

The trip back to Breyerville was depressingly short, far more so than I expected. I'd actually thought we were in the clear when...

But bullets found us, followed by the Fangs.

Jesse's face materializes in my mind.

In that last second, mid-argument, his face went placid. I thought, before I saw the crimson blooming from the hole in his forehead, that he'd realized how terrible he'd become. I didn't put it together immediately, even with his blood misted across my skin.

My stomach churns, recalling the relief in my veins when he fell, when I realized what happened. Here, in the safety of my mind, I admit to myself that the man I loved died long before that bullet claimed his body. The man in the snow that day, though he wore the face of my love, my partner, was a stranger. Of course, the relief I felt in that moment was short-lived, quickly replaced by dread and all-consuming terror as the situation dawned on me.

I close my eyes for just a moment, mentally settling into the little boat in my mind, ready to drift into a roiling ocean where mercy doesn't exist, at least for the evening.

A burst of air fouled by too many nights of unwashed bodies floats from the mattress as I push myself up from it, but I don't really notice it. Long past are the days when I registered the scent of my own nightmare-induced sweat and Tate's sweat from being beneath a blanket with his furnace of a mother.

Locking the door to our apartment behind me, I leave my baby boy unattended, something I never expected would be necessary, before. My feet carry my body onward through halls too dark to see, navigating solely by memory. I trail a hand along the chair rail of the wall, find the carved mahogany banister of the stairwell.

Were it not for Tate, I might consider jumping over the banister, falling three stories, and hoping for a swift end. A glance back down the hall, despite the blindness of the dark, reaffirms that I can't do that.

He needs me.

With the railing for stability, I pick my way down the stairs, gearing up my little boat with everything I may need to sail through the night with as little emotional damage as possible. A life raft takes the form of my son's safety. I wrap his future around myself like a safety vest. Memories of my parents, of my career as a teacher, and of my friends provide light amidst the rolling waves, replacing emergency flares.

Outside my apartment building, I thank the stars and the moon for the light they afford me. Without them, the sounds of cats, opossums, and stray dogs rattling the various piles of garbage in the street would be far more unsettling.

With one last look at my apartment building, I shove off. I can almost see Tate, waving to me from shore, beckoning for me to return. But I mustn't. I have no other means to provide for him.

My feet carry me onward, moving toward The Wolf's house, the house Christian, God rest his soul, built for himself. Before. Yet my mind drifts.

I think of the kids from my class as I move past a pile of rubble, once a bank. I hope for their safety while I pull my jacket tightly around myself, pretending not to notice the holes forming in it or the strings dangling from the seams.

At the door to The Wolf's house, with the sounds of screams and cruel laughter reaching out for me, my mind can no longer distract itself.

Through the shredded curtains in the front window, I see my neighbor, Lyla, being slapped across the face. She stands there, shivering in only her underwear, with her bra and clothes forsaken in some disgusting corner. Bruises cover her pale skin from head to toe, all in various stages of healing.

The skinny, lifeless slip of a girl, once a boisterous and confident nurse, stands with her head hanging low, waiting for the next blow. Such a far cry from the cheerful woman she once was, her optimism has been crushed beneath the weight of this new world.

The thug standing over her laughs when a few silent tears roll down her cheeks. He slaps her again, and her head flies to her shoulder. My movement on the steps draws Lyla's notice, and our eyes lock. An uncertain smile lifts one corner of her mouth, and she nods. I see her chest rise with a deep breath, easily lifting her small breasts.

Dingy blonde hair, once pristinely kept, hangs limp in Lyla's face. Wide cheekbones, previously a sign of beauty, now serve as a perfect target for a thousand strikes from calloused and cruel hands. Pulling her lips in, she nods again and faces her attacker. Something shifts in her demeanor and she stands with a bit of determination, though nowhere near what she once possessed.

Meanwhile, the two armed men at the door leer at me, not even attempting to hide their thoughts. Bile rises in my throat, and I dread the things I'll be forced to submit to in the coming hours.

Tate needs food.

Inwardly, I curse the damn rat that got in our cabinet, finishing the last of our food long before we should have run out. A few tears threaten to fall, but I force them back.

"For Tate," I whisper, tightening the straps on my life vest as a huge wave looms over the little boat in my mind. I reach out and turn the doorknob.

Chapter 10
Christian

Rain pounds the metal roof of the only three-bedroom house among the habitable ones, but it isn't loud enough to drown out my thoughts as I lie awake in bed. Though more comfortable than the floor of the trailer last night, I resent it.

The loneliness of being in my own bed, away from everyone, away from Chloe, sinks in. It permeates my bones, showing no regard for the warmth the hearth in the living room spreads throughout the place. Cold fingers claw at my heart, reminding me just how alone I really am.

Fierce winds batter the house, mimicking the chaos within me. Another thunderclap threatens to split my eardrums as the room flashes. Dark. Light. Dark. Light. Dark.

All I see is Jesse's face, a single bullet hole dripping hot blood onto the snow. The protective shell of shock splinters, sliding off of me in bits and pieces, one memory at a time.

I remember playing near the pond in the city park at the tender age of ten, feel the momentary joy of slipping free of our parents' burning hatred for each other, even if only for a few hours. Our aunt and uncle were visiting from Montana and took us for the afternoon, a rare occasion. The smile on Jesse's cherubic face almost would have convinced me that the boy had never known pain.

But I knew better.

A chunk of shell falls away, and the agony of loss begins to trickle in around the edges. Another bolt of lightning, the closest yet, turns the night into a quivering form of day for just a few seconds.

Another memory screams into focus, blurring the ceiling of my dirty room and drowning out the sound of rain and thunder.

Recently graduated, I was enjoying living on my own. My apartment was essentially a shit-hole, but it was mine, and I was away from *them*.

I'd just gotten home from work and was about to clean up. Sweat dripped down my back as I turned the thermostat down. The AC rumbled to life in the vents. It was mid-August, and autumn breezes were nowhere in sight, making for a very long day on site. The air was so thick and muggy that it weighed on us, making our movements sluggish.

As I walked to the bathroom, fully intending to shower, Jesse burst in through the front door, slamming it shut behind him. 16 and angry all the time, bullied at school, treated like shit at home by parents who really couldn't have cared less if they'd tried, he was a bomb just waiting for someone to detonate him.

I'd suggested he take the woodworking class at the high school, the same one that saved me, but Jesse put it off, being stubborn. He didn't want to listen. Junior year, he relented. But school had only just begun. They were still going over proper shop safety. Jesse had yet to begin actually carving or building anything.

Half-falling, half-slamming his small frame into one of two chairs at my kitchen table, he dropped his head in his hands. He screamed and pounded his fists on the table several times, letting out the rage inside him, and I just let it all slide off me, knowing it wasn't meant for me, no matter what Jesse said.

I asked about the black eye blossoming on Jesse's face, careful not to insinuate weakness. It was no flaw within Jesse that caused our parents to beat him, just as there had been nothing wrong with me to make me the target when I still lived there.

That was what broke Jesse.

The care that went into choosing the right words, the concern that prompted me to ask.

The poor boy cried, bawling like a baby. I easily folded him into my arms. Jesse hadn't yet hit the growth spurt that took him from 5'3" to 6'4", and thus still fit comfortably in my arms.

Standing there with my brother's tears, the tears of a boy turned man far too soon, further soaking my sweat-drenched shirt, I hated our parents and all the little assholes in Jesse's class. I assured my brother that it would get better, but even after Jesse finally grew, they mocked him. They called him a freak.

"It'll get better," I told him. But did it?

Jesse slept over that night, sacking out in the second bedroom, just like he did on many occasions before and after that evening.

It was better for a while…

When he started working construction, it was better. When he met Karen, it was better. When they had Tate, it was much better.

But all of that was ripped away. A lump forms in my throat. Jesse never even had a chance at a happy life.

And now, he's gone.

Pain roars in, breaking apart the remnants of the shock which shielded me thus far. It pours in around me, choking me, filling my lungs.

Jesse's gone. He's...dead.

The smile that only rarely peaked out, the little boy that feared more than loved, the man who had a glimpse of happiness only to have it torn from his grasp...

The man who lashed out.

"I never got to say goodbye," I murmur, heart exploding in my chest. "To any of them. I didn't even get to see Tate's face, one more time. And they're gone. They're...gone. Jesse's gone forever. And he thought...he thought I hated him..."

I remember the fights. I remember standing between Jesse and Karen, acting as a dam to hold back the punches. I remember shouting at Jesse, my baby brother, the little boy I swore to protect.

So many nights, I told him that I'd always be there, that I'd always love him. That I'd never lay a hand on him.

But in the end, even I hit Jesse.

Guilt wraps its hands around my heart, choking it, collapsing my chest. I fight it off, knowing I had to do it, I had to protect Karen. She was basically my sister.

"IS," I correct myself. "She IS my sister. She's not dead."

The voice of dread speaks to me, saying, "Yet."

My soul shivers, and I hate myself for thinking such things.

"Jesse thought I hated him," I breathe out into the darkness, voice lost to the beating hooves of horses shaped like raindrops, stampeding across the roof.

I was just so disappointed in how he turned out.

The admission feels like treason.

The boy cowering in the corner of his room, trying his hardest to be invisible, brown hair all a mess and bruises covering his bare chest and back, comes crawling out at my beckoning, as he did so many times in our childhood. But in my mind now, Jesse shrinks back from another fist coming his way.

I'll never get to make it right.

"He's gone." Tears fall down my face, impersonating the heavens. My hands ball into fists.

"I'll never see him. He'll never be happy. He'll never see Karen. He'll never watch his baby grow, he'll never hold him, he'll never smile at his wife over breakfast or have the huge family he always wanted or…"

A sob wrenches itself free of my throat, and I jerk a hand up to my face to stifle it. "Oh god," I mumble through clenched teeth.

Panic scratches at me, digging up patches of skin to crawl beneath. It spins my mind like a top, and the world becomes harder and harder to grasp.

"Karen…Tate…They've got no one, now. They're stuck, in that fucking hell-hole, and they've got no one. She's too sweet, too soft. She won't be able to defend herself. She was already so brittle, so broken, how much more can she take? And Tate…He's just a baby, just four years old. And I'll never see them again. I'll never hold him, I'll never…I'll never see my baby nephew, I'll never hold him again. He's gone."

"They're gone…"

"Oh god, they're gone."

"He'll never know how good his dad could have been, he'll just remember the yelling, and the screaming, and the hitting, and..."

Thunder roars out once more as a flicker illuminates the room. I roll onto my side, caring little for the pain. All I know is that it's one more thing keeping me from them.

"Will he remember me, at all, if I can't get there?" I wonder, tears drenching my face. My nose runs, but I don't care.

I try to figure out how far we've traveled since Chloe found me, but the best I can guess with the snow and the storm holding us back is maybe 70 miles. It stretches out before me like an eternity. We may as well be on the moon.

I have neither the provisions nor the means to make it that far in any sort of timely manner. I know I'll try, no matter what happens. I have to try, but it seems so impossible.

And what if I get there...only to find them dead, too?

My heart stops in its tracks, refusing to beat in a world where none of my family exists. Even setting aside the absolute agony of loss, it would rewrite my entire approach to life.

Without them, what am I? Jesse's the only one who knew, really knew, what our childhood was. Without him, who else can help carry that burden? Who else can understand?

Karen was the closest I could've gotten to another sibling. She heard it all. She *knew* all of it. She cared so much. Once again, I correct my tense, telling myself that she's still alive, that she still knows, she still cares.

And Tate…

Even his name prompts a hiccup of anguish. I choke and sputter over the sound of it as I croon, "Tate, my poor baby…"

Even though he wasn't technically my son, it felt similar. Determined not to have the type of family in which we grew up, Jesse and I vowed to be a part of each other's lives, to be a part of our future nephews' and nieces' lives. We would be there, no matter what. I saw Tate nearly every day, never less than three times a week.

Already it's been longer than I've ever gone without seeing the poor kid.

"Does he fall asleep alone, now? With his mother kept away for the savage Fangs to enjoy?" I nearly puke at the thought, barely able to hold down my gorge. The wracking, wrenching cough-sobs make it unreasonably difficult to stop myself from getting sick.

"What if The Wolf kills them?"

Unholy images of mother and child lying side by side with bullet holes like Jesse's punched through their sweet little faces float into my head, and I know I'll dream about them. I want to scrub the sight from my mind, want to carve my eyes out to get rid of it, but it won't help. It'll haunt me.

The thought of them killing Karen and leaving Tate in their little run-down apartment to starve is a kick to the gut. Dinner once again threatens to make a second appearance.

"They're gone…" I whisper hoarsely, over and over again.

"Gone…I'll never hold Tate, again. Jesse will never smile, again. Karen won't laugh. They're just…gone…"

Brow creased, head shaking as if somehow denying it could make it untrue, could make them reappear, happy and healthy, I sob as my entire world falls to pieces around me. A meek little voice in the corner of my mind wonders what type of man will emerge to fill out the shell that rests in my place on the mattress now that I've entered my own personal apocalypse.

Hours later, a fitful sleep descends upon me, gnawing at my bones with nightmares for teeth.

Chapter 11

Chloe

My eyes open wide when I hear the door swing inward. I never quite feel safe outside of Harville, but the sight of Jackson pushing the door shut relaxes me.

It isn't The Fangs, nor is it some random stranger coming to harm me.

The sound isn't Jenny, breaking through a window to gnaw on our flesh while we sleep. After all, we're in her territory now. We'll have to keep our eyes peeled for her. The mountain lion tends to leave me alone after our last two interactions. The beast got a little too close, and though I took a few scratches, a couple of them rather deep, Jenny lost a toe the first time and the tip of her tail on the second rough encounter.

Now, she mostly skirts around me, giving me a wide berth. Still, it never hurts to be cautious. Recklessness is almost never rewarded these days.

"Your turn, sis," Jackson says with a yawn, glad to pass the torch. Second watch is always rough, and he's ready to go back to sleep.

Stretching, I accept the fate of the early morning, merely glad I got to sleep straight through the night. I throw my legs over the edge of the bed, and as I climb out, Jackson crawls right in to take my place.

From the nightstand, I grab my hoodie and a small journal I found last night and make my way downstairs. I pass the room Grant occupies with the lightest step I can manage, hoping not to wake him.

At Christian's door, I don't try quite so hard to disguise the sound of my footsteps. I almost hope he'll wake to join me for a bit of time away from Grant and Jackson.

Once downstairs, I grab the cup of tea Jackson left for me, as he usually does when we trade off, and make a quick round through the house. Assured of our safety, I take my tea and the journal and plop down on the porch stairs. I close the screen door but leave the main door open.

Taking a sip, I let the warm tea fend off the mild chill in the air and pull on my hoodie. I prop the journal open on my knees and do what I can to make out the handwriting. After a bit, my eyes adjust to the style and the shape of the letters.

It seems that good ole Terry kept a record of the decline of Sawton, for which I'm thankful. A single flu epidemic wouldn't account for having only three survivors left behind. My curiosity builds, knowing the answers are within my grasp.

The flu that came through decimated them, sure enough. Only a select few escaped the pandemic without contracting it, and the virus claimed the lives of nearly half the population of Sawton, primarily the elderly and the children. Mortality rates under the age of 10 and over the age of 65 were nearly one hundred percent. Between those ages, survival seems to have been a toss-up.

I sip at my tea, calmly turning through page after page of death. Names are listed with ages and causes of death, primarily the virus that swept through town. At least, for a while.

A month in, a new pattern developed. After weeks of burning their children, their parents, and their grandparents, a few committed suicide, sparking an epidemic of a completely different nature.

For two weeks, the flu was the second leading cause of death, increasing the burden on those left behind to feed the fire. It took about a month, but the suicides petered out, dwindling into nothingness. Those remaining carried their scars, as well as they could, trudging on into an uncertain future.

A great many fled, unable to stomach the memories that haunted the streets or the halls of their own homes, apparently hoping a change of scenery would help them find peace through distance. Had that been the only reason to leave, those remaining might have been able to rebuild, but of course, as is the way of life now, it wasn't.

When it rains, it doesn't just pour. It comes in like a hurricane, savaging everything.

During the outbreak, the gardens weren't maintained and resources were stretched tight, causing even more people to run for the hills with everything they could carry. The last departure was three and a half weeks ago. A woman and her teenage son, recognizing that the town was on its last legs, said their goodbyes to the home the boy was raised in and the pyre his father was burned upon and left.

Terry, Ben, and Jack were all that was left.

Now, there are none.

I sigh and close the journal. Setting it down on the porch, I stare out over the ghost town called Sawton. Once a thriving mill town, now it lies still and silent amongst the woodland that once sustained it, waiting for the trees to come in and take back their land. Branches lie cracked and splintered across dilapidated porches and rooves along the street thanks to the storm, adding to the broken aura of the place.

Behind me, old stairs creak and floorboards complain. I glance back and find Christian approaching the door. He looks worried, panicked even, until I call, "Morning, sleepyhead."

Pushing the door open, he offers up half a smile. "Morning."

His eyes are bloodshot and puffy, making me wonder.

Is it allergies? Or has he been crying? Did everything finally hit him?

Without another word, he settles onto the porch behind me, placing one leg on either side of my hips with his feet planted one step down. "Is this okay?" he asks.

His concern quiets the mild, irrational panic beginning to set in. Yesterday, with a man behind me and a knife to my throat, I was taken back over ten years to the last time a man loomed behind me, to Robert-fucking-Myers.

To date, having a man behind me, *this close*, hasn't really gone well for me, but Christian's gentle words and attentive nature go a long way toward calming me. I nod, not quite able to manage words.

He wraps his arms around my shoulders and nuzzles his face into my neck, careful to do so on the uninjured side. My skin tingles and my insides grow warm. I do everything within my power to control my breathing as I enjoy the shockingly pleasant sensation of having him so near.

Something about him is so blatantly, painstakingly different from Jack, from Robert. The stark contrast soothes me. I lean back, settling into his embrace.

Christian takes a deep breath and both our bodies rock with the movement. "You smell good," he murmurs, words muffled by my red hair and the gauze on my neck.

The compliment catches me off guard. I've been on the road, doing only essential washes, for nearly two weeks. I'd honestly been growing worried I was beginning to stink and hadn't noticed merely because I'd grown accustomed to it as it happened.

An old saying about boiling frogs comes to mind, something about using slow and gradual temperature increases to keep them from hopping out of the water. Surely it works similarly with body odor.

Throwing me off once more, Christian lifts his head from my shoulder. Staring out at the ramshackle homes and shattered trees, he asks, "So, is this a better time for you to tell me why you know how to kick ass so well?"

I sigh and reprimand myself.

Of course, he was going to ask again. He's smart and curious about who he's traveling with. It's not like he would have forgotten since asking at dinner. Why wouldn't he ask?

I try to quell any hopes that he's curious about me specifically, attributing his curiosity to his own well-being.

"When I, uh..." I clear my throat and begin again, "When I was 16, there was this guy, Robert Myers." The name feels like filth in my mouth, and I have to force myself not to spit after speaking it aloud.

"He was a few years older than me, five years, I think. He was super popular, good at sports. He played all through high school, set all kinds of records, got some stupid scholarship for the college in Breyerville out of it. Everyone loved him. His parents spoiled the little shit because he was their miracle baby, their 'turns out we're not sterile after all' baby. He was so charismatic, so manipulative…They had no idea what he really was."

Shivers rattle my bones, and Christian's arms slacken about my shoulders to allow for it. When I still, he tightens his hold again.

"He could have had pretty much any girl he wanted," I say, nearly choking on the irony. "They all threw themselves at him."

With a sigh, I switch tracks. "During the investigation, they searched his house. He'd been stalking me for a long time. He had pictures of me all over his room, had my whole schedule figured out with all my classes marked in the calendar on his phone. He even knew my parents' and my brother's schedules, their habits."

A shiver of disgust rocks me. "That's how he planned it."

Going into far more detail than I originally intended, I say, "My parents went to the theater every Friday night. They always did, for as long as I can remember. It was their date-night-thing. They loved movies, even bad ones."

Succumbing to a strange dream-like state, I set the scene. "They left at like…6:00. The movie started just after 7:00. It was all the way in Breyerville. They would have been gone for a few hours, at least, longer if they went for drinks after."

Tears form, pricking the corners of my eyes.

They were so happy...

"He showed up about twenty minutes later, feigning car trouble. He asked to use our phone, saying his was dead."

Chest rising sharply then falling quite abruptly, I say, "I trusted him. He just...had that effect on people. I didn't even think about it. I'd seen him around, I knew who he was. He smiled and laughed and joked about crappy cars and the life of a broke college student."

I shake my head. "When I gave him the phone, he wouldn't let go of my hand. He tried to pull me in, tried to kiss me. I told him, 'no,' and he got mad. He tried harder."

My voice becomes small. "I tried to run..."

Behind me, Christian's spine stiffens. His arms loosen, just enough for his thumbs to caress my biceps. He knows what's coming. I could spare him the details. I could skip over it. I know he's leaving as soon as he's healed. He won't be around long enough to need any more information than this.

But I don't skip.

For some reason, it feels important for him to know me and all I've seen.

"I tried...I got my hand free. I made it a few steps, but...he was too fast." I stammer, "He grabbed me around the waist and slammed me to the ground. I was reaching back over my head, scratching at his face. I reached back and clawed his arms."

A few tears roll down my cheeks and fall squarely onto Christian's arms. His sleeves shine with them for a moment before they soak into the fabric. My throat grows tight, but I force the words out, all the while telling myself it's normal to cry.

With furrowed brows, I say, "He slammed my head down. All I could see was the fucking wood grain. I loved those floors before that. I helped pick the stain, I sanded them, I finished them. My knees hurt for so goddamn long for those *fucking* floors…After that night, I put down carpet."

I shake my head.

"The whole time, when I wasn't panicking and crying and screaming and kicking, when I wasn't dizzy from having my head slammed into that fucking floor, I tried my best to focus on this stupid little nail in the floor. I've got a scar from it, just below my belly button. I just…needed something to think about that wasn't…him."

"Neither of us heard the door open. We heard my mom scream though. She forgot her purse." Throat closing around the next words, I struggle to speak. "He shoved her. Dad came in and tried to fight him. He shot my dad. I didn't see the gun, I didn't know he…"

Words cease, tears taking their place.

A few ragged breaths later, soothed by Christian's gentle voice uttering apologies for things he had no part in, I continue. "He shot my mom, too. She wasn't fighting anymore. She wasn't saying anything. When he shoved her, she hit her head. She had to have been unconscious."

"He shot her anyway."

Eyes closed, I gather myself up.

The hard part is over.

Everything else you have to tell him, and you do *have to tell him, is easier.*

Another deep breath. Eyes unopened. "He fired once more, but he was already moving. He barely got me, just caught my side. He ran, got in his car, his perfectly-functioning nice car, and drove off while I dragged myself to the phone, puking at the sight of my parents."

"They used to be so happy…" I muse.

"The cops found him a week later in Missouri. They hauled his ass back. The trial took so long…The whole time I was sitting in court, I just fidgeted with the stupid scab on my stomach, the one from the nail. I don't know if it would've scarred if I'd left it alone, but I couldn't. I just…kept picking at it. Every shirt I wore ended up with a little bloodstain there."

"It dragged on and on and on. He was too smooth, too good at talking. But there was so much evidence. Finally, he got sentenced to ten years. Ten *fucking* years. He only served *five*. He got out, did some community service in Breyerville. He stayed there, as far as I know."

"I was in counseling longer than he was in jail, and I'm still a fucking mess over it eleven years later."

Hands balling into useless fists, I get around to answering the question. "After my side healed up, I vowed I would never, NEVER go through that, again. I took self-defense classes. Jackson took them with me. It didn't feel like enough though, so I moved on to Jiu-Jitsu. Jackson did that, too. He stopped me when I started considering Krav Maga, told me it was enough. He said I was strong enough…for…"

Tears fall freely as I recall the concern in his face. "For anything." He was warning me, telling me that it was becoming an obsession.

My voice softens, dropping near to a whisper as I say, "I don't know what I would've done without him, without my counselor. They held me together when all my pieces wanted to fall out and run as far away as they could."

Christian's hold tightens around my shoulder, and he plants a tender kiss on my scalp, just behind my ear. Leaning into him, I wrap my hands around his arms and drop my face on them.

We sit that way for a long while, each sad in our own way, and watch the sun lift itself from the grasp of the trees on the horizon.

Chapter 12

Karen

"Mom, come on..." Tate drawls, nudging me gently.

I stir and glance at him. "Hi there, sweetie," I say.

A smile spreads over my face, but my heart is pained. I see how careful he is not to touch any spots he knows are bruised. I pull him into my arms for a hug, wishing that act could somehow shield him from the horrors of the world.

The sun shines bright outside, filling the room with light.

How long did I sleep? It must be noon.

I laugh at the archaic notion of time. I haven't seen a functioning clock in over a year, but old habits die hard.

"Why'd you sleep so long?" Tate groans, squashed against me.

He's anxious to eat, anxious to learn. I can practically feel his little muscles itching to get up and move. But an edge of concern outlines his tone.

"I was just really tired, honey," I say, refusing to say that I didn't get home until the horizon was pink with the first rays of dawn. No need to worry him with what I had to do last night. "We can get up now, though."

Tate leaps from the bed, concern for my bruises forgotten in his excitement.

I laugh, glad for his exuberance. It means that not all of his childish spirit has withered. I shuffle out of bed, wrapping a blanket around my shoulders, and meander into the kitchen.

Tate already has his plastic step stool pulled over to the cabinet with the door hanging open, a true sign of his hunger. "Wow, Mommy!" he exclaims, eyes wide. "You got so much food!"

My eyes rove over the contents of our pitiful pantry, hating that this is what he calls an abundance of food. By current standards though, it is. I brought in quite a haul this time. Four cans of fruits and vegetables, a bag of barbecue chips, half a box of chocolate cereal, a bag of turkey jerky, a twelve-pack of water bottles, and a full box of granola. Not bad for a night's work, nowadays. I even had to use a few bags to get it all home.

For Tate's sake, I don't dwell on the work I did, choosing instead to revel in the sweetness of his appreciation. All I say is, "We still have to be careful with it, okay?"

Nodding, he looks at me, all wonder, and asks, "What can I have?"

Knowing his propensity for sweets, I suggest the chocolate cereal. We can't eat all of it, obviously, but it will make him happy just the same.

He grabs the box, jumps from his step stool, and launches across the open apartment, barely touching the floor at all until he reaches the "couch."

It isn't as nice as our old one, which we burned last winter for warmth. The metal frame of our dead neighbor's guest room futon is an eyesore, to say the least, but the cushion is still intact if a little worn down from Christian sleeping on it.

A twinge of sadness creeps into my heart for our lost little family.

Maybe Christian was unconscious when death finally took him…

Tate bounces onto the futon, and I wince for him. It has to hurt to land on the bars, barely softened by an old mattress. It would hurt me in a million different ways, but he's young. His body is still relatively unscathed by this life.

I dig out a bottle of water and shut the cabinet. Following Tate, I make a much less energetic trek to the couch and settle in for breakfast. Or rather, lunch. After lifting myself off the couch enough to pull the blanket from beneath me, I drape it across our laps.

Tate tells me about fantastical dreams of dinosaurs and robots, speaking louder and louder as his enthusiasm builds. His words almost drown out the sound of a fight in the street outside our building.

I smile, pulling a handful of crispy chocolate rice from the box and dumping it into my mouth.

Barely eating, Tate gestures wildly with his hands as he describes a gigantic raptor that was so big it fought off three "mean T-rex dinosaurs" at one time. It is, after all, imperative to the story to specify whether or not a T-rex is mean.

Outside, voices rise steadily, competing for my attention, but they can't quite pull my ears away from the little boy busily explaining that, "The raptor was big because of science stuff. The scientist people wanted me to help them train it to fight the mean dinosaurs because I'm the best raptor trainer ever since this other guy that was a little bit better got squished by a ginormous stegosaurus on accident."

I giggle inwardly, loving the vivid nature of his imagination.

Maybe, just maybe, he hasn't been broken yet.

But life isn't quite done with us.

Not by a long shot.

In the street, the shouting comes to an abrupt halt as a bullet erupts into the air. Our eyes shoot to the window, though the murder scene is three floors beneath us. Thankfully. Anguished screams fly up to our ears, taking the place of the anger that boiled from those same throats seconds before.

I turn away first.

Tate stares at the window for several moments, all joy gone from his face. Eventually, he reaches into the cereal box, pulling out a tiny handful. Settling in beneath my arm, he becomes thoughtful.

My hand drifts through his locks, the hair he wants long like his uncle's. Appetite dramatically lessened, I don't reach for more cereal just yet.

"Mommy," Tate begins, unsure. "Do you think Daddy went to heaven?"

My eyes close, and my heart nearly stops.

Tate doesn't notice that my hand stills in his hair, and if he does, he makes no mention of it. Instead, he says, "I know Uncle Christian did…But did Daddy? He *used to* be nice, didn't he? Is that good enough for God?"

"I…um…I don't know," I stammer, blindsided by the turn our morning is taking.

Tate nestles in closer and grabs more food. For a few moments, we eat in silence. I stare out the window at the broken skyline beyond. Smoke rises to the heavens a few blocks away, the remnants of whatever fire was glowing brighter than the sunrise as I hurried home this morning. A few scattered pillars of smoke punctuate the buildings, rising from the homes lucky enough to possess a fireplace.

Mouth dry, I uncap the water bottle and take a swig. I hand it to Tate, knowing full well that little crumbs of cereal will adorn the rim of the bottle when he hands it back. He chugs a fourth of the bottle, mouth apparently transformed into a desert by talking and crisp rice.

Another bite and he looks up at me, the excitement having found its way back into his eyes. "OH! I forgot. Do you want to hear the rest of my dream?"

My lips lift into a smile, but it doesn't reach my eyes, not yet. "Of course."

He goes on rather animatedly about how he trained the big raptor, but my mind wanders.

Is it good enough? Is Jesse in heaven?

Shame warms my face when I realize a portion of me hopes that he isn't.

Chapter 13

Christian

Packed into the front of the UTV, fondly referred to as Deadweight by my companions, I find I don't mind having Grant's and Jackson's elbows digging into my sides.

Of course, that's primarily because it means Chloe is nestled on my lap. My arms are tight around her waist, and her fingers trace small patterns on the skin of my hands. Warmth flows through me at her touch.

My mind drifts briefly to our conversation about her past and the name I *know* I recognize. Robert Myers. I know it from somewhere, but I can't place it. Somehow, for reasons aside from what Chloe told me, it makes me angry.

As if I would need more reasons to hate a man like that.

For some reason, I think it has something to do with Karen.

Maybe she talked about the trial?

My eyes fall shut, and the old days flicker through my mind. I see Karen and Jesse, smiling and happy, holding newborn Tate. Them handing the sleeping baby boy over so I could hold him for the first time.

Tears threaten to spill over, but I force them back. I can't think about Karen right now. Not her, not Tate, not Jesse. I sigh, burying my face in Chloe's hair.

Here, as close to other people as I can possibly *reasonably* hope to be, they are my life raft, the only thing keeping me afloat amidst churning, rolling seas. I have to keep it together in front of them.

Chloe wouldn't look down on me, I don't think. Grant would, without a doubt. Jackson…

I sigh. The man is a coin toss. He's hard to read.

Loss of traction is a risk I can ill afford, so I bury my face in Chloe's shoulder and my feelings deep, deep down. I can air them out on my own time, and this…this is most assuredly *not* my own time.

So, I take a deep breath, inhaling the sweet feminine scent of Chloe. I focus on the air rushing past us as we speed along on an old, worn down highway toward a tire factory that Grant worked at before.

I'm not entirely sure what they hope to gain from the place, or where they plan to put it for that matter, but it isn't for me to worry about just yet. Essentially, I'm just along for the ride, bumpy as the cracked and pocked roads may make it.

***

A monstrous cement building sprawls out across acres, grinning at us behind chain-link wrapped parking lots. A few abandoned cars lie, faded and peeling, waiting for long-lost owners to come back to claim them. A couple of loose shopping bags roll by, skipping over the safety glass of broken windows like modern-day tumbleweeds.

Jackson navigates the crumbling pavement up to the fence and disembarks from the UTV. Unfastening a few small, metal clips, he pulls a section of chain-link aside, gaining entrance to still more busted pavement.

Grant jumps out to fasten the fence behind us and hops back in. We bounce along to the racket of our cargo rattling together, all the way up to a set of turnstiles and even more chain-link separating us from the entrance. As with the last fence, a small section has been cut.

Clearly, they've done this *before.*

We clamor out of the UTV and Grant opens up the fence. Chloe digs out two hand-crank powered flashlights and hands one to Grant.

Jackson turns to me and says, "Will you go with him? I want to talk to Chloe about something."

Groaning internally at the prospect of quality time with Grant, I answer, "Sure."

Because, really, what else can I say? I take the proffered flashlight from Chloe and ignore Grant's rolling eyes, winding the crank a few times. With a mild sigh, I follow after him, wandering past gaping doors into a dark hallway.

Ahead, I see the beam of Grant's flashlight click on. Behind, I hear Chloe ask her brother, "You sure about that?"

Jackson's answer is drowned out by Grant shouting, "Keep up. I'm not coming to find you if you get lost."

His words echo back, lending me some idea of the scale of the hall we walk through. I crank the flashlight a few more times and click it on just as we leave the hall behind, entering the massive factory.

Several stories above our heads, a ceiling full of pipes, tanks, and conveyors looms, waiting for an earthquake or a downpour of rain onto the huge flat roof to bring it down. Across an aisle the size of a highway lies a maze of multilayered conveyors, stacked atop one another. They curve, rise, descend, and weave in every possible direction.

Grant walks past it without a second thought, but my eyes, and my flashlight, linger as my feet carry me forward.

Someone thought all of this up…

I'm careful to keep my fascination to myself. The inner workings of things, the manner in which they're put together…these things never cease to amaze me.

A portion of the ceiling some 200 yards back has caved in, littering the scene with debris and backlighting the plants taking root in the thin soil which has blown in atop the conveyors. Already nature is reclaiming this place, this testament to human innovation.

A bird chirps somewhere far off, happy to have found such vast shelter. Yet, aside from the twittering of an excited bird, silence abounds, eerie in a place I assume would have been deafening if it were running.

"Keep your eyes open for a bike," Grant commands, voice like a roar in this still place. "Grab it if you see one."

"There are bikes, here?" Surprise is evident in my tone.

"Yeah," Grant says, somewhat less condescendingly than expected. "Supervisors rode them. Set-up techs, electricians, and mechanics used them to get their tools from one machine to another."

"Huh," I reply. I'd never thought about that aspect of a place like this, simply assuming that people would walk, or use a forklift or something.

We walk on in silence, weaving through giant pallets and carts full of tires, cured and uncured. Megalithic metal beasts loom in darkness, waiting for the return of power which will never come. They almost gleam beneath a thick layer of dust, seemingly hungry to move, to spring to life. Guardrails protect them from the forklifts which now lie useless, and not very happy about it.

After nearly ten minutes of walking through the maze of machinery, surely covering at least a mile, we finally reach a wall. Along our trek, we find only one bike, which is actually a tricycle with a basket between the back wheels, a technicality that didn't seem to matter to the people who once worked here.

In the wall ahead, three doors wait, two of which are bathrooms. Above the far right one, a sign simply reads, "Nurse." Yet another surprise.

"They had a nurse's station in here?!" I exclaim.

Grant glances at me and gestures back at the mess of hazards we just walked through. "Did you not pay attention out there?" Exasperation draws his words out. "Of course, there's a nurse's station. Everything out there," Grant points, "that isn't *bolted to the floor* moves. There are about a million different ways to get hurt out there."

"Cuts, burns, sprains, strains," Grant turns back to the door, tan skin gleaming under the beam of my flashlight, "lost limbs, broken limbs, death. You name it, it could happen out there."

I cast my mind over the machines which reach several stories into the air and spread out larger than the square footage of my old apartment, imagining the terrible potential they hold. "Did anyone ever die out there?"

"Not in *this* plant."

The implication is sobering.

Grant opens the door to the nurse's station, and we enter, meandering to a large metal cabinet. The few remaining contents, several boxes of ace bandages, gauze, and medical tape, are stowed safely in the basket of the bike.

Flashlight beams find boxes of gloves and antiseptic wipes in another cabinet, and we take those, as well. A bit of scrounging turns up a few bottles of rubbing alcohol and office supplies, all of which are taken, filling the basket nearly halfway.

Then, we move on, pulling the door shut on the dark little nurse's station. I turn, half expecting to go back the way we came, but Grant's flashlight bounces off to the left, further into the maze of metal via the widest aisle yet, spanning the equivalent of four lanes of highway traffic.

It even includes a pedestrian lane, protected from forklift traffic by a lengthy system of sturdy rails. With no traffic and with the bike in tow, Grant apparently sees little use in staying in the walkway, simply strolling down the middle of what is, basically, an indoor road.

Occasionally, the wall on our left opens up. When it does, it reveals rooms the size of Olympic stadiums and machines like the playthings of Gods, too large for mere mortals to comprehend, whilst the chasm to our right overflows with such things.

Nearly 100 feet ahead, a collapsed section of roof blocks our path, lending the place a bit of ambient light. A few birds roosting in the nooks and crannies of Grant's former livelihood take flight, shying away from us. Grant leads me between two steel giants and beneath a conveyor to another, smaller aisle.

Eventually, we reach a brick room the size of a small house with a chain-link gate for a door. It contains at least thirty of these "bikes," though these are clearly the ones for mechanics, bringing the realization that the one we found first was for a supervisor.

These new bikes are a great deal more customized. Their rims, their handlebars, their frames, the height, and the length are all different from one bike to the next. Grant approaches one with a black wooden cabinet settled on the back axle. On top of the cabinet rests a vivid blue toolbox and the seat from an office chair in place of a bike seat.

After stuffing the basket, the cabinet, and the toolbox full of tools and various types of tape and wire, Grant turns to me.

"Before we go back, there's something I need to say to you." He takes a deep breath.

My heart rate soars. This man has had it out for me since we met. Anything Grant needs to steady himself for is not going to go well for me. My stomach sours with the anticipation of whatever attack may follow. I stand, patient but certainly on edge.

"Leave Chloe alone." Grant's jaw sets, firm and unforgiving.

"Really?" I ask. A few seconds of silence pass and I say, "Are you serious? You're jealous and now you're going to start shit over it? She's a grown woman. She can make up her own mind about me. She's already made her mind up about you, clearly. You just haven't accepted it."

"She's been through more than enough already, without you fucking things up, and she's too good for the likes of some inconsiderate asshole like you, anyway," Grant snaps.

"Excuse me?" I try desperately to keep my anger in check, but it surges through my veins. I have to hear this out, much as it boils my blood to do so. "You don't know *shit* about me." Despite my best efforts, my voice leaves the controlled range of a normal conversation, though I manage to keep it below a shout as I say, "How the fuck can you sit there and call me an inconsiderate asshole?"

"Maybe because you are one?" Grant's expression is smug. It tugs on my nerves, testing my patience.

I pull in a long breath, willing myself to be calm. "How do you figure?"

"Oh, gee, I don't know…" Grant leaves the mechanic's bike behind, taking a few steps toward me. "Maybe because you're stringing her along? Or maybe because you're working your way up to fucking her, just in time to leave. Or, and this one's my favorite, maybe it's because you're running off to save some other girl, who, by the way, I'm pretty sure you're just going to fuck, too."

He takes another step toward me, almost within arm's reach, and his voice drops to a sinister whisper. "Maybe, just maybe, it's because you're using Chloe to forget about your dead brother."

Practically spitting, Grant says, "Why don't you just fucking pick a reason, *dick-wad*."

Hands balling up into fists, words hissing out through gritted teeth, I say, "Fuck. Off."

"Witty comeback," Grant sneers, turning his back, exceedingly confident in his safety. "Don't worry, jackass. I'm done. I can't handle another zinger like that." Sarcasm drips from his words as he grabs the mechanic's bike and begins making his way out of the plant.

Trying desperately to keep my rage from bleeding out, I close my eyes for as long as I can risk. I grab the other bike, gripping the handles white-knuckle tight, and follow along at a distance. I can't afford to get lost in this place, but every second, I hate having to rely on such an asshole.

Chloe knows I have to leave. If she wants to get involved with me, if she takes that chance, that's her decision.

Right?

She could tell me no. She could tell me to back off. And I would. I would leave her be.

I know I shouldn't let Grant's jealous words get to me, but parts of them ring true. I *am* hiding from my feelings about Jesse. I *am* running off to save another girl. But for the reasons Grant listed?

No. Karen is my sister. Not by blood, sure, but my sister, nonetheless.

And if I make it out alive, I'd like to come back. Maybe then whatever I have with Chloe won't have to end.

The walk out of the plant drags on long enough for me to go from fuming at Grant to imagining scraping out some kind of life with Chloe from this terrible world. Karen and Tate could live nearby, safe and healthy. Maybe even happy.

I know it's far too early for daydreams of that nature, despite the pull I feel toward her, but what the hell? I probably won't see the end of another month, anyway.

Why not think of pleasant things while I can?

Chapter 14

Chloe

"You sure about that?" I ask, skeptical. My hands are on my hips as I stare at the two beams of light drifting into the darkness of the factory.

"Well, since neither one wants you mad at them, and since that's exactly what would happen if one came back without the other..." Jackson drawls, "Yeah. I'm sure."

I turn to face him and find him sitting in Deadweight. He pats the seat and reminds me that they're going to be a while. The place is huge.

How Grant doesn't get lost in there is a mystery to me.

Climbing into the seat, I pull my hood up. Not that it's particularly cold, but it provides a bit more cushion as I lean my head back against the headrest. I stall, momentarily, checking the little white handkerchief tied to my belt loop to see if it's attracted any ticks along our travels. None. It's still early in the year.

Turning my head slightly, I crack, saying, "So, what is it?"

"I don't know if you're going to like this," Jackson says, staring out across the parking lot.

"Has that ever stopped you before?" I laugh to cover the nervousness budding within my stomach.

"I guess not," Jackson says, chuckling. The tension eases, just a smidge. Even when serious, he naturally diffuses stress. It's a gift.

He looks at me, bright eyes suddenly shrewd and analytical. "What are you doing?" he asks.

"What do you mean?"

I have a feeling he means with Christian but I want to stall. I'm afraid of his disapproval. I genuinely like Christian and thought Jackson did, too. If I'm being honest with myself though, I'm afraid of his approval, as well.

One less reason to drag my feet.

"You know what I mean," he says and jerks his head at the hallway that swallowed Christian mere moments ago. "He likes you. Even with everything that's going on, that much is obvious. So, what are you doing?"

I shake my head and stare into the blackness. The wintry sun makes it all the more impenetrable, concealing an entire world, a whole life.

"I don't know," I say quietly, realizing that that's possibly the most honest answer I can give. "I don't know what *to* do," I add in a whisper.

"Quit getting in your way, that's what."

I look at my brother, the man who walked me through the most horrendous part of my life. His face is serious but gentle.

Green eyes kind but firm, he speaks out of love. "You need to let go, have a little fun. All you do is take care of people and worry. All the dirty jobs that no one wants to do, you do. You push yourself, all the time. Whether it's hunting when you're all crampy or stitching yourself up in the field so no one else has to bother with it, you're always worried about everyone else. You don't do enough stuff just for you."

Attempting to throw him off my scent, I say, "You're one to talk."

"That's fair," he allows. "And if we'd found a beautiful, single woman out in that field, this would be a *very* different conversation."

He smiles, and I laugh.

"We *did* find a handsome, single man, though," he says. "Now, that's not *my* cup of tea, but it is *your* thing."

We sit quietly for a moment as I process his words. Gradually, the smile falls from my face, slipping through my fingers and landing well beyond my grasp. My eyes drift over to the dark hallway again.

"But…" I begin, still hesitant, "he's leaving."

I don't say that I'm just going to get hurt. But my tone implies it.

"Maybe he'll come back," Jackson supplies, thinking it helpful.

I shake my head, eyes on the black abyss of the plant. "People don't come back, Jackson. Once they're gone, they're gone."

"We'll just see about that," he says conspiratorially, as if he knows something I don't. "After all, we leave Harville all the time, and we come back, don't we?"

The edges of my lips pull back in a pursed smile, the physical interpretation of, "I guess." I breathe in deeply.

Jackson pats my leg and says, "Get out of your way, sis."

Climbing out of Deadweight, he adds, "Let's get some food out. Grant and I have to eat our Wheaties. We have one *hell* of a bike ride ahead of us." Then, with a smile, "You and Christian can have the ole girl, here."

He pats Deadweight's hood affectionately. "Have to give the easy job to the invalids--I mean, the wounded."

***

Christian and Grant emerge from the black hole, looking none too pleased. They seem to have found a good amount of stuff, but all positivity has been left behind in the plant as a forfeit for the tools and medical supplies.

I frown but say nothing, digging out our canteens. I can imagine what kind of fight they may have had and barely keep my eyes from rolling at how overprotective Grant is being. Overprotective. Clingy. Jealous. Knowing him, the delivery of whatever he said was probably overwhelmingly rude.

We sit on the concrete between the turnstiles and the entrance, eating our food while simmering in a kettle of angst. Grant stays relatively silent, and Christian seems lost in thought. Jackson does his best to ease the tension, but to little avail, a true testament to the depth of their anger. He nudges me, nodding in Christian's direction.

I pretend I don't see, all the while debating on what I should do.

Chapter 15

Christian

I watch the wind swirling Chloe's hair about her face, beautiful red strands glimmering in the sunlight. Her smile is easy and free. I once thought there couldn't be moments like this anymore, but now, she reaches for my hand, sending tingles up and down my spine.

She drives the UTV, cruising at a steady eight miles per hour, watching as Grant and Jackson pedal along ahead of us. She giggles a bit when they hit a pothole, and all the random stuff in their bikes bounces and crashes together. The guys struggle a bit on the hills, pedaling through the tremendous weight.

After a mile, Jackson waves Chloe ahead. He points to a rather large blob moving through the field to our left. I squint, unable to make out much detail amidst the tall, dry grass.

"Yep," she yells, "I'm on it." She pulls up alongside them, making sure to position us between them and the blob.

"What is it?" I wonder aloud. The shape slinks closer and closer to the road, allowing its true form to come into focus. "Is that a fucking cougar?" I ask, incredulous. My nerves wind tightly, twisting my stomach into knots.

"Yeah, that's Jenny," comes Chloe's reply.

"What? You named it?"

Why do they have such a propensity for naming things? First, the UTV and now, a cougar?

And why did Jackson wave Chloe up to get between them and that thing? Sure, Deadweight offers more protection than a bike, but still...

"Yeah," she says, as though naming gigantic man-eating beasts were a common thing, something to be expected.

Then, surprising me yet again, she slows to a stop and climbs out of the UTV.

I stare after her, openmouthed.

Is she kidding?

She has to be. Why else would she not be moving away from a massive predator? Is this some cruel joke with someone in a very convincing catsuit prowling through a goddamn field?

"What are you doing?" I whisper, words awed to a hush. A very worried hush.

But Chloe doesn't answer. She pulls a hatchet from the bed of the UTV and a dagger from a sheath on her thigh and squares up.

"You're not going to fight that fucking thing, are you?"

"Hopefully not. Jenny and I have an understanding."

"An understanding?" I gape. From the bikes, Jackson and Grant shush me, murmuring that she can handle this and telling me not to move. The whole thing makes me wonder, yet again, at the sanity of these people.

Chloe stands up straight, hands gripping the weapons tightly. Her eyes never leave the cougar.

For her part, "Jenny" watches Chloe with far more wariness than I expected. Her nostrils flare, sizing up her opponent. She slows her gait. She apparently doesn't like what she finds blowing toward her on the wind. The animal stops in her tracks 20 yards out and shifts her posture, leaning away from Chloe.

This close, I notice Jenny's tail comes to a very abrupt end about six inches shy of where it should be, completely eliminating the customary black tip, and a toe on one paw is missing entirely.

Jenny is looking rough...

I hope that might help Chloe out if it comes to a fight, at least long enough for me to grab the bow from the back. My heart gallops wildly in my chest. Everything about what's happening reeks of recklessness.

The cougar's ears twitch, and her golden eyes narrow. For several unbearable minutes, we sit in a silent stalemate. Chloe's fingers clench the handles of the hatchet and the dagger tightly, turning her already pale knuckles completely white. At long last, Jenny takes a step back. Her eyes never leave Chloe, but she begins backing away. Realization falls over me like soft rain, tiny droplets of understanding landing upon me.

Jenny is afraid of Chloe.

A massive beast of prey is afraid of this little 5'7" woman.

Jaw open, I say nothing. None of us move until Jenny becomes a tiny blob in the dry grass, and Chloe's fists unclench and her shoulders relax. Sheathing her dagger, she turns and drops the hatchet into Deadweight's bed.

"Thank God," Jackson whispers, air whooshing out of him.

Only then do I dare to speak. "What the fuck just happened?"

Apparently, the expression on my face is of an entertaining variety of perplexity, for when Chloe finally looks at me, her eyes glitter with suppressed laughter. Only a small, alluring smile slips through her control to grace her lips.

"I told you, Jenny and I have an understanding."

I laugh, greeting insanity with insanity. "What 'understanding' could you have with a wild animal? How would you even negotiate a deal with her?"

Becoming somewhat more serious as she climbs back into Deadweight, with Jackson and Grant pulling away slowly, she says, "Well, the understanding is that if she leaves me alone, I won't cut off pieces of her."

I swallow a hard lump.

This is a matter of survival, after all. Kill or be killed. Eat or be eaten. I recall the cougar's tail, her missing toe, and blink several times at the impossibility. Chloe is a formidable fighter. I've seen that with my own eyes.

But she's not very big. And that cougar, Jenny, certainly is.

"I don't want to kill her," Chloe goes on. "She keeps the coyote population pretty well under control. I'm afraid I may have to if she comes at me, again, though. Next time, I have a feeling one of us won't walk away."

Creeping along behind the bikes, all traces of mirth gone from her features, she says, "As for the negotiations, they weren't exactly fun. I managed to avoid getting bitten both times. Somehow. But her claws…Well, they hurt like hell."

I listen, riveted to the spot, as she continues.

"My left leg is pretty scarred up. I had to stitch it in the field. Almost didn't make it back that night. Scared the shit out of Jackson when I dragged my bloody ass up the road, limping like crazy. My pants were shredded. The calf I'd been out looking for had shown up an hour before, didn't have a scratch on it."

She laughs at the irony.

I laugh at the insanity.

"The other time, my pack took the brunt of the attack. My stuff went everywhere, but I only got a small cut on my lower back. Basically," she says, glancing briefly at me, "I got lucky as hell. I'd heard her, at the last second and I just, instinctively, stepped to the side before spinning around. Jenny flew past me, one massive paw catching my pack. It spun me all the way around to see where she landed, where I *would have* landed. Like I said, I didn't want to kill her, but I had to do something. Her tail was right there. My hatchet was within reach."

She shakes her head. "Somehow, it made Jenny either afraid of me or at least earned me a bit of her respect. So now, *for now*, she doesn't test me. She sees me and goes on about her day. I just don't know how long that'll last."

"You're amazing," I find myself saying, despite myself, despite any reservations I may have had about hurting her.

She smiles at me and my bewilderment, emerald eyes sparkling and soft red mane fluttering in the wind. A surge of affection rushes through me.

She takes my hand once more, and I realize the implications of my slip.

Jesus fucking Christ…

I am *an asshole…*

Chapter 16

Chloe

We crest a hill, and Harville practically leaps up on the horizon like an overexcited puppy greeting its owner after a long absence. Solar panels sparkle on every roof, especially the community center. It glitters like a disco ball.

I take a deep breath, immensely glad to be home. Well, almost home. Jackson and Grant have slowed considerably. The next mile will test them, I know, but they refused to let the injured among us do the heavy lifting.

And by 'they,' I mostly mean Jackson. Grant would have happily switched with Christian when he offered up his seat in Deadweight on a water break, but Jackson and I wouldn't hear of it. I offered as well, but even my minor injuries insured my spot as the driver.

After coasting down the hill, we stop for another water break, though Jackson, Grant, and I are all itching to just get home already. Christian waits patiently, still unaware of the haven that awaits us.

Once our thirst is sated, at least partially, we press on toward home, thankful for the pavement, despite its many imperfections. The curve of the highway extends our trek by a bit, but going through the overgrown fields with the bikes so heavily laden would be an absolute nightmare.

Finally pulling into Harville just before dinner time, I'm thankful for another successful trip out. My hand is wrapped tightly in Christian's, and a great feeling of calm envelops me. I pull in a great gust of air, loving the way it feels to stretch my lungs to their full potential.

We turn right down Main Street and ride on to the community center to unload our haul. The building, complete with several offices, a bathroom, a kitchenette, a large meeting room, and even a gymnasium, has been used to serve nearly every community need since the collapse.

The water office is still used as such, though the primary occupation switched from maintaining the town water pipes and tank to the conversion of every house to well water and then the maintenance of such things. The office once used as the treasury now serves as Trent's office, housing all his tech gear and every book we can find on electronics.

The gym is used for social events, town meetings, and school for the children. Holden Vincent runs our health center in the meeting room with the attached kitchen and bathroom. He was a registered nurse before and has been an absolute godsend.

As we roll into the parking lot, we're greeted by the smiling faces of Holden's parents, Aiko and Johnathan Vincent. Aiko's long, silky black hair is pulled back in an artful bun with traditional Japanese hairpins holding it together. A few strands hang loose about her face, suggesting that perhaps she worked in her garden, today.

Nearly a foot taller than her, Johnathan still holds the same posture he held when he was an officer in the marines, all those years ago. His face is creased and wrinkled, but his zest for life is not.

Smiling widely, he calls out, voice deep and booming, "I'm so glad you're back safe!"

Aiko bows gently, welcoming us, "It's good to see you all, again." Her accent is still present, despite having moved to America well over 30 years prior. She and Johnathan tried the long-distance thing after his time in Japan ended, but they couldn't stand it. He was stationed in Florida at the time, but they later moved to Illinois to become alpaca farmers.

Incidentally, that passion is what led their son to meet his wife, Calista. The whole Vincent family went to a workshop to learn new methods of spinning wool, and Calista happened to be teaching.

Now, with a tender hand on his wife's back, Johnathan Vincent helps her into their UTV. As he climbs in behind the steering wheel, he says, "Come by and see us, sometime. We'll have tea."

Climbing out of Deadweight, I wave as they drive off. Christian and I grab some boxes while Jackson and Grant take a breather. I lead Christian inside past Calista's gleaming silver bike. The rear basket is filled to the brim with freshly spun yarn. Holden's bike sits next to hers. Previously a mechanic's bike from the plant, now the toolbox is filled with emergency medical supplies.

My own bike sits right where I left it in the corner of the parking lot, in case anyone needed to borrow it while we were gone. Another rescue from the factory, the satin finish on the denim paint sparkles in the sunlight. I smile at the familiar object and pull the door shut behind me.

The place is comfortably warm, chasing the chill from my bones. The fireplace seems to be holding up rather well. It was bricked over in the last set of renovations about five years back, but after we lost electricity and gas, we freed it, returning it to working order.

Through the lobby and into Holden's domain, I find him speaking excitedly with his wife. Though it's only been a couple of weeks, her belly seems much larger than when I last saw her. The poor girl, pregnant with twins, looks like she could snap in half at any moment. It makes me glad for the three-wheeled bikes. Balancing on a normal one might be difficult for her.

Her hair, kept in dreadlocks, is pulled back in a ponytail. Her handmade clothes, once a statement, are very fitting for the world into which we've all been thrust. Her warm caramel skin is smooth as ever, despite the demands of this new era.

Holden offers up a rather stark contrast with exceedingly pale skin and short dark hair that barely brushes the tips of his ears. His mother's genetics shine through in nearly every way, except his height. That, he got from his father, bringing him in just above six feet.

They look up at the sound of our footsteps. Their smiles are wiped away briefly by confusion, then kept at bay by concern as they take in the bandages on my neck and Christian's head. They can't see the ones concealed by our clothing, but if they could, their frowns would only deepen.

Holden glances at his wife and rushes forward, with her hot on his heels. They take the boxes from our arms amidst a chorus of "What happened?" and "Who's the new guy?" Their words crash together as they trade phrases and repeat them over each other.

With my arms free of cargo, I shush them gently, ushering in a calmer atmosphere. After all, we were injured days ago. With steady antibiotics, the infection in Christian's side has disappeared. We're well on our way to healing.

"Well, it's nice to see you, too," I mock. Then, "First things first. This is Christian Jacobs."

"I'm so sorry," the Vincents say in unison. They glance at each other and smile at their own synchronization.

"I'm Calista, and this is my husband, Holden." Her voice is slow and sultry, practically begging for the swirling smoke of incense and the scent of ylang-ylang or patchouli to waft through the air behind her words.

"I'll take these," she says, grabbing the boxes of gauze and gloves from her husband. She uses her belly to balance them between her hands and says, "It's nice to meet you," before walking to the counter of the attached kitchenette.

Extending a hand, Holden greets Christian and, joking about the quality of my patch-up jobs, urges us both to sit so he can look us over.

"I do just fine, thank you very much," I quip, smiling.

Holden only looks at us a little strangely when we remove our outer layers. As soon as Holden sees the additional bandages, he understands, though he does 'tsk' a bit.

I do my best to keep my eyes above Christian's shoulders as we're seen to.

Meanwhile, nearly everyone in the building turns out to carry our plunder in from Deadweight. Calista closes the health center door most of the way to allow some privacy, but Jackson and Grant can still be heard every time the outer door opens, talking and occasionally laughing with friends.

The snap of rubber gloves centers my attention on Holden's hands as they go to work. While he removes the gauze and medical tape from Christian, I undo my own wrappings. Sarcastic remarks about not having shaved off some of Christian's beautiful hair to better care for his injuries are met with equally sardonic retorts about the multitude of razors in our possession, at the time.

After a brief inspection, Holden compliments me on a job well done. I thank him genuinely, surprised. I never think much of my work with a needle given how little training I've had, though my snappy witticisms imply otherwise.

Holden cleans and rewraps us, making us somewhat less mummy-esque in doing so than I did. Finally, with naught to keep his hands busy and no more cuts or scuffs to draw his eyes, he looks at me with bad news writ plainly in his eyes. Attempting to brace myself, I listen to the normality of Calista unpacking boxes in the kitchenette.

"What is it?" I ask, unwilling to wait him out.

"It's…" his face softens as if to cushion the blow his words will deliver. "It's Mrs. Ableman…she passed while you were away."

Blinking several times, I try to process the news. Never quite satisfied to leave it at that, I ask, "How did it happen?" I have to know.

Holden doesn't blink, doesn't find my curiosity odd or misplaced, as so many others often do. "She was asleep. I couldn't bring myself to do an autopsy," he says, "but I'm pretty sure it was her heart."

I shiver at the thought of him cutting poor Mrs. Ableman open but nod at his conclusion. Greta

Ableman's high blood pressure was the least of her heart problems. She never slowed down to accommodate her heart, even when her blood pressure soared. She didn't always remember her medicine.

This death makes sense. The only surprising thing about it is that she made it so long.

And yet, despite the logical progression leading to this point, it hits me hard. My jaw clenches to hold back tears. Mrs. Ableman was my neighbor for as long as I can remember. I watched the woman's grandkids grow up. They were at the sweet, old woman's house every weekend…before.

Back when the trial was at its worst, if Jackson was at work, I knew I could find a comforting shoulder to cry on in my neighbor's outdated living room. Stubborn as an ox when it came to caring for herself, Greta Ableman never hesitated to help others.

My stomach tightens, and my heart shrivels hiding from the pain of my own thoughts of the woman forming in the past tense so soon.

I can't cry here. Not in front of Holden. Not in front of Calista. Christian…

If I'm honest with myself, I'm not entirely sure whether it would be ok to cry in front of him, or not. But the debate is short-lived.

He seems to sense the ache building within me, to feel the prickly itch budding at the corners of my eyes as they promise rain. He leaves his perch on the table, the closest thing we have to a proper exam room set up. The shirt he'd been about to put on lies forgotten on the table. In seconds, he gathers me up in his bare arms, pressing me to his chest.

I'd been about to put on my long-sleeved shirt, but now it hangs loose, the hem clutched in a tight fist between my chest and Christian's. I vaguely wonder if this is some sort of trade, offered up by God or whoever is out there.

I lose someone who helped me through the past, but I get him?

For a week? Two?

In the spirit of trades, I resolve to let myself feel the loss, just for a second. Feel it all at once, but only once. A voice in the back of my mind tells me it won't work that way, but I try, regardless.

I open myself to the chasm of grief and immediately feel it reaching up for me. My heart plummets, instantly giving itself over to pain.

And why shouldn't it?

Like an old friend dropping in for a visit, grief makes itself at home in my heart, weighing me down. The rest of my body revolts against the agony, reaching up to the light, and I feel my back threaten to break under the strain.

Beneath me, at the imaginary bottom of a bottomless pit, like an oasis in the desert shimmering in the distance, I can almost see Mrs. Ableman. My mom. My dad.

But I know, no matter how long I might fall, I'll never reach them.

Not without death.

Arms tighten around my waist, catching me just before I fall completely to pieces. Barely back to reality, I wrap my arms around Christian's torso. Burying my face in his chest, I let out one, single sob, prompting him to tighten his hold even further. One hand leaves my lower back, and his fingers thread into my hair.

Okay.

You felt it, now put it away. You're done, now.

I lie to myself so easily, making it seem so simple to move on.

I focus on the world around me, honing in on the sensation of being held. Strong arms cradle me protectively. My head rests upon the pillow of a muscled chest.

Christian's skin is warm, and the scent of him fills my lungs with something akin to fresh sawdust and the sweetness of a summer evening spent lying beneath the stars. His lean stomach expands with his chest as he takes a deep breath, nose buried in my hair.

Gradually, I remember the rest of our surroundings, feel the chill of the late winter air rushing at us as someone makes another trip out to Deadweight. Recalling one hand from its place on Christian's back, I wipe away a tear or two, assuring myself that there's no need to count them.

Even just one is enough to incriminate me as being weak.

A deep breath brings my counselor's words rushing back. Feeling sad is not weak. Grief doesn't make me weak. It's a sign of loving someone now lost. It means I still have the capacity to love.

But the words don't quite sink in.

I pull back to look at Christian. "Thank you," I mumble, dropping my gaze, unable to look into his oceanic eyes any longer. I stare at the shirt still clutched within my hand.

Glancing over, I find Holden staring, face the embodiment of "Um…" with his brows up and his mouth agape.

Chapter 17

Karen

Tate's golden laughter warms my heart as I chase him through our dingy apartment, playing dinosaurs. I do my best impression of a raptor's call, loving the fresh burst of laughter from the next room mixed with a squeal of excitement. Tate insisted I be the carnivore this time, and he would be the nice dinosaur.

A stegosaurus, to be exact.

A smile brightens my face, and I crouch down, imitating a raptor's walk, purely for his benefit. Not that this is the best time I've had in over two years. Not that I enjoy playing like this.

Who am I kidding? Yes, I do.

Giddy with the momentary repression of the world around me, I burst from Tate's room with all his toys littering the floor behind me, spared thanks to the noxious fumes they would emit if burned for warmth.

Thank you, plastic.

Crouch-running to the living room, I make another raptor call, laughing when Tate says, "Moo," the sound he insists the stegosaurus would make.

I run at him, and he turns, slamming his little hip into my leg.

"Spiky tail!" he shouts, victorious.

Genuinely staggered, I take a step to regain my footing before turning to pretend-bite his ribs, wrapping my lips over my teeth so it doesn't hurt him.

"Om nom nom," I say, giggling.

Tate laughs, dropping to his knees when I tickle him. Beautiful, carefree laughter fills the air around us for a few precious moments.

When we calm ourselves, Tate says, "I wish I could see a dinosaur."

"I don't," I say. "They're scary…"

Something in my tone prompts a strange little smirk from Tate. "Mom, you know dinosaurs aren't real anymore, right? They all died *at least* a hundred years before you were born."

"At least," I answer, nodding.

How old does he think I am?

But my eyes land upon a folded piece of paper on the floor, slipped under the front door from the hall. Unnoticed until now, that little note stops my heart. Nothing good can come of it, I'm sure.

Beside me on the floor, Tate goes on, unperturbed. "Besides, Mom, you're never scared. Why would dinosaurs scare you?"

Attention momentarily diverted from the ill-meaning paper, I glance at my son. His rumpled shirt clings to him, now a touch too small. Shaggy hair covers his eyes. Brushing it back, I say, "I get scared, sometimes."

"Really?" Tate asks, tilting his head in disbelief.

"Mm-hm. I just don't let it stop me," I say.

At least, I try not to…

Heart plummeting as I speak, knowing that someone taking the time to find paper to deliver a secret message can only bring bad things, I say, "It's ok to be scared. Life is hard sometimes. Being scared doesn't mean anything bad, as long as you still do what you need to do."

"Is it okay to be sad, too? And mad?" Little eyes stare out, holding in far more sights than a four-year-old should have to contain. His fingers fiddle with the hem of my shirt as he speaks, tugging at a loose string.

I nod, hating the world my baby boy must contend with. "Those are okay, too. Just so long as you don't let your feelings make you do bad things."

My mind goes to Jesse, then seeks out images of Billy and The Wolf. I suppress a shudder, knowing Tate would ask why I shivered. He isn't old enough for that explanation.

Nodding, Tate considers a few things. Apparently having reached a level of peace that I wish I could find, he brightens considerably. "Can we play more, now?"

My eyes fall upon the note, still waiting by the door, practically tapping its little paper fingers in impatience. "How about you play in your room, for a while? I've got to check something real quick before we eat."

"Ok," he says, springing to his feet. He launches himself down the hall, happy that he doesn't have to do any chores.

Only when he's tucked away in his room and I can hear the crash of even more toys being pulled from their chests do I rise from the floor. Hauling my tiny frame over to the door, I repeat to myself the lessons I just extolled to Tate.

It's ok to be afraid. It's ok to worry.

That's normal.

Stooping to pick up the folded paper, my stomach fills with dread. A key falls out, and I pick that up, as well.

The paper practically shivers with negative energy, a thing I never believed in before. Maybe it's my own reticence to deal with anything new or to expand the circus of horrors that my life has become. Maybe it's my trembling fingers. Maybe it's the concoction of worry and doubt in my own coping mechanisms curdling within me.

Either way, I unfold the old insurance statement to peer at the handwritten letter on its back. I recognize the chicken-scratch writing as belonging to my neighbor, Lyla. The young woman was a nurse for about five years back before the world tore itself to pieces. She'd been so free, so kind.

But the past couple of years aged her about 20 years and completely broke her spirit.

Turning the key over in my hands, I begin reading.

Karen...

I just...can't do this anymore.

The word "can't" is etched in with such force that the paper nearly tore as it was written. It draws my attention to the rest of the words and their raised edges on the back of the page, like an ill-informed attempt at Braille.

I'm so tired of being used...I can't go back there, again. I can't perform any more abortions. And it's only going to get worse. The Wolf is doling out the last box of condoms now, and I just...can't do it. I'm not strong enough to keep going.

I gathered as much as I could stand, for you and Tate. Ration it, please, so you don't have to be there as much.

Ice forms lumps in my chest, making it difficult for my heart to beat. I recall Lyla's sudden shift in personality a few days ago, maybe a week, I'm not sure. Time is such a strange, elusive beast, now.

Lyla actually smiled, an expression I hadn't seen on her face since before. Granted, the smile was weak, half-resigned. But it was backed by a measure of determination, the likes of which hadn't graced that girl's spine in years.

Hindsight paints it the color of a decision made.

"I should have seen it…" I whisper, recalling all my training on such things when I was becoming a teacher, when I was signing my understanding of mandated reporting.

The rest of the writing blurs before my eyes, and I look away from it, blinking back tears. Staring down the hall, I steady my voice, and call out, "Stay in your room, Tate, ok? I'll be right back. Don't open the door for anyone."

Gathering my keys, I leave Lyla's suicide note in the cabinet next to a few bottles of water and am surprised by Tate's arms throwing themselves around my legs. A light smile graces my lips, despite the situation. Though the pain never leaves, he covers it up, if only for a moment.

Turning, I kneel and hug him.

"I love you, mommy."

"I love you, too, sweetie. I'll try not to be gone too long."

Truthfully, I have no idea how long I'll be gone. I merely hope I'm not too late.

"Ok," I say, pushing myself into motion. I pull back and kiss Tate on the forehead. His hair sticks to my lips when I pull back. "Now, you play in your room. I'll be back, soon."

He nods and scurries away.

Keys in hand, I hurry out the door. My mind fills with a million repetitions of, "I should have seen it," and, "Why didn't I make an effort to bring her around more? To include her?"

Jesse preoccupied Christian and me, unfortunately. Otherwise, who knows, maybe Christian would have hit it off with her. He could have helped her, too.

Maybe with another person to carry the food and another pair of arms to take turns cradling Tate as we walked, maybe we could have gotten away. As it were, we couldn't afford to trust her with the knowledge of our escape. We didn't even try, in case she might sell us out to The Wolf for a few days' peace.

Yet, she dragged herself through countless levels of hell.

For us.

For me.

For Tate.

My stomach drops, and my heart clenches.

The lock slams into place with a reassuring "thunk," and I plod carefully down the dim hall. A bit of light trickles in through doors open to abandoned, looted apartments and through the stairwells on either end of the hall, but it's nowhere near adequate.

Ahead, past a pile of broken toasters and coffee pots and scraps of musty cloth, on the left of the hall, Lyla's door waits. Darkness seems to emanate from it, sucking the light from the hall. The air around it is still and foreboding.

I swallow hard, forcing myself to unlock the door. Even that sound, small as it is, feels hollow. I know it must be my imagination painting the scene a million shades of despair, but that doesn't change the shrill, haunting shriek let out by sagging hinges when I push the door inward.

As if to spare me the trouble of hunting through her apartment and stumbling upon her body, Lyla arranged all the food she gathered in the barren floor of her living room. Pushing the door shut, I lock it, all the while fearing the weights about to drop on me. Every footfall pulls one down, plummeting into my stomach and filling me with dread.

But I push forward.

One empty room after another, I search. A kitchen with all its cabinets intact, save the doors. Was she not strong enough to break them apart to burn when last year's winter hit hardest? A barren guest bedroom, an empty bathroom. A dining room table with two legs and no chairs.

Light peeks around the edges of the curtains and falls out beneath them. My footsteps are loud in the otherwise silent apartment as they fall on ceramic tile, made to look like hardwood. My hands trail the marble countertop as I pass through the kitchen once more, headed for the hall on the other side of the living room.

Meanwhile, my mind spirals with the possibilities of what I'll find.

"Lyla?" I call out.

My heart pounds against my eardrums, so loudly that I question the silence that answers me. Did I miss Lyla's voice? Was it covered by the hammering in my chest?

Hand upon the door to the master bedroom, I hesitate.

"Lyla? Are you in there?"

No answer.

I turn the knob. Locked.

She's in there. She didn't want me to see her.

Mouth dry, I try to block the metallic scent of blood filling my nose, hoping I'm not too late. Try as I might, I can't hold back the panic bubbling up within me. Jiggling the handle, I try to force my way through, becoming more and more frantic with every passing second.

"Lyla!" I shout, jerking the door back and forth with all my might. It rattles uselessly in its frame.

One fist pounding against it, I call again, "Lyla! Honey, please, open the door!"

No answer.

Not a single sound beyond the door.

Only my shambling, sprinting heart and the sounds of my fists and feet slamming into the wooden door, over and over amidst a cacophony of, "Lyla, don't do this!"

Tears fall, and something inside me snaps. I haul one foot up and kick the door right next to the knob with every ounce of strength I have left. It flies back, slamming into the wall in a flurry of splinters. Wood trim falls to the floor around me as I rush through.

The master bedroom, though dark, looks untouched by the ravages of the apocalypse. The bed still has a perfect, carved wooden headboard and beautiful dark purple and grey bedding. The nightstand is intact, and several books rest upon it. Reading glasses perch atop them. Plush carpet wraps around my feet as my eyes search frantically for my neighbor.

No luck.

I open one door and find a massive closet, now mostly empty. Shaking my head, nearly running to the only other door in the room, I open it. The master bathroom lies beyond, quiet and foreboding.

The marble floor plays host to a walk-in shower and a beautiful vanity. Another door, open, leads to a toilet. Off to the left, though, beneath a massive window, lies a claw-foot tub, and there I find Lyla.

Dressed in a flowing brown skirt and a short-sleeved, olive tunic, Lyla reclines in the empty tub. Blood has cascaded from under her left arm, up near the armpit, staining her pretty clothes and the pristine porcelain the color of death.

I race forward and drop to my knees beside the tub. Leaning forward, I cradle Lyla's head in my hands.

"Lyla?" I beg. "Are you still here? Please, Lyla, answer me."

But the poor girl's head lolls in my hands. Dark circles mar the skin beneath her baby blues, nearly disguising the yellow tint of a healing black eye. Open eyes stare into the heavens, wishing they'd had a better run. Her pale skin nearly matches her porcelain coffin, drawing my eyes to all the bruises which discolor her poor broken body.

Blood now merely trickles from the gash on her arm. Still, I try desperately to rouse her.

"Lyla, please, answer me. Please, I'm so sorry! I should have seen. I'm sorry."

Cradling Lyla's head to my chest, I weep. "I'm sorry. I'm so sorry. I let you down. I should've helped you, but I…I just couldn't see it. I didn't see you."

A huge sob forces itself from my body, and I hug the girl I should have banded together with. Flaxen hair tangles around my fingers. Limp arms flop off Lyla's torso landing with a thud and a clank as they rattle her knife against the porcelain.

"And all you did was see us. You didn't have to do this. You didn't have to do this just to feed us. Oh God, Lyla. I'm so sorry."

But Lyla can't hear me, now.

Trapped within this mortal world, my cries fall on deaf ears. My fingers probe Lyla's neck, searching frantically for a pulse. They find nothing. Fresh waves of agony wash over me, dragging me into the undertow.

I sit there much longer than I could have ever intended to be away from Tate, hugging my long-dead neighbor over the lip of the clawfoot tub. Eventually, a feeling of numbness descends on me, and I notice the cramping in my legs.

So I sit, reclining against the tub and staring at a bathroom that would have made me jealous before. Now, it will be forever burned into my memory, haunting me with a scene I could've prevented.

"Why didn't I talk to her? Why didn't I try? I could have helped her…" I whisper, shaking my head.

The light from the window begins to fade, becoming amber, and then gray. After hours spent agonizing on the hard marble, brows carving deep lines in my forehead, I stand. Leaning over my neighbor, I lower Lyla's eyelids.

At the door, I look back at Lyla's tiny frame, even smaller now that death has stolen her spirit away. My heart sinks further, retreating to the farthest corners of my being. It cowers in the soles of my feet, getting stepped on as I retreat from the blood which streaks the tub and the vacant eyes, once so vibrant. I close my eyes, though I know the sight will plague me for the rest of my days.

With a sigh, I say, "Thank you." Then, "I'm sorry."

I pull the door shut and fight off the urge to cry, again. In the living room, I begin the long process of transporting food from Lyla's apartment to my own. It's enough to last nearly two weeks if I'm really careful.

"What did she have to do to get so much?" I wonder with a shudder.

Chapter 18
Christian

Everyone available assembles in the gym of Harville's community center to greet their newly returned friends. And to gawk at the man who's dumb enough to go back to Breyerville. Of course, that's the phrasing I overhear Grant use in conversation with the nurse's wife, Calista. She rolls her eyes but says nothing.

Just when I begin to wonder if anyone likes this man, a brunette in shorts cut to skank-length and a skin-tight tank top throws her arms around Grant. Her coat hangs open, and Grant's arms slide around her waist. She glares openly at Chloe, which makes no sense.

She apparently hasn't noticed the chill outside. Or Grant's overwhelmingly repellant nature, for that matter. My eyes widen briefly as they roll.

Everyone mills about for a while, introducing themselves, though I know I'll never remember all their names. Eventually, we all find seats amidst the bleachers, and Chloe and Jackson stand before us to explain what happened. Thankfully, they don't call me up to stand with them. Public speaking isn't exactly my strong suit.

Opinions appear to be mixed as to me staying with them, even for such a short time. Some say it's only right to help.

Others cry out, "What if he leads the Fangs back here as a trade to get the girl back? Our resources and our lives for their lives?"

While I can see where their concern comes from, the thought of such betrayal hadn't even crossed my mind. Not that anyone suspicious enough to worry over that would believe me if I said as much. So, I stay silent.

"Not likely," Jackson says. "They couldn't make it this far, not now."

The same man, somewhere to my left and blocked from view by the faces of about ten other people, says, "How can you be so sure? We don't know what resources they have."

"If they could make it here, they would have done it a long time ago," Jackson reassures them.

The same man, buoyed by the paranoid whisperings of a few other people in the crowd, carries on, lobbying his cause. But he pushes Chloe just past the edge of her patience for the day.

"The Fangs who came for them," she gestures at me, "were on foot."

After a pause for emphasis, she goes on, "They traveled thirty miles from Breyerville, *on foot*. With the express intention of coming back with more people than they left with. If they had a vehicle, of any sort, that could make it *here*, one that could carry them more than twice the distance, they would have driven it to catch them."

Just to bring the point home, Jackson adds, "Their mobility ran out as soon as the gas did. Any fuel left now, unless they used a lot of stabilizers, is garbage. And something tells me, they didn't set up any electric UTV's with solar panels. Probably didn't even have any in the city, to begin with, let alone have someone willing to do the tech work just so they could destroy the lives of even more people."

The sense of their words and all further arguments are lost on me, though.

Thirty miles? That's all? Two and a half days of walking, and we only made it thirty miles from that hell hole?

I know we had to stop often to accommodate Tate. He's just a boy. He can't quite take a long journey without breaks, and we couldn't very well carry him the whole way.

And, sure, we wound through an abandoned part of town, walking in somewhat of a serpentine fashion to keep buildings between us and the walled-off part of Breyerville in case the Fangs were using scopes or binoculars to find us.

But thirty miles?

Maybe we got our directions mixed up?

Jesse and I always used to navigate fairly well when we hunted, but...maybe fear clouded our judgment?

I remember feeling lost a couple of times, having caught myself worrying over Tate watching his parents fight, worrying over Karen having to deal with even more abuse at the hands of the one person in the world who swore never to do such things. Worrying over what Jesse was becoming...

Did I lose track so badly, though? Did we double back at some point?

I should've paid more attention. I should've pushed harder or carried Tate more.

I stare blankly at the gym floor. The wood planks disappear, replaced by the memory of overgrown vegetation choking the roads, the green light filtering through leaves as I cut away at the vines of honeysuckle that never quite withered away this winter.

I remember the reluctance of giving Jesse a turn with the machete for fear that he may get angry again. I recall the ache in my arms and my back as I swung, over and over, at the limbs of saplings which sprang up through cracks in the pavement. When we could, we slipped under the branches, slid between trees and abandoned cars, just to save time on chopping our way through.

Thirty miles, though?

We had to have made up time when we escaped to the fields around the city. Prairie grass is so much easier to walk through than tangled vines and crumpled buildings. We pushed on through waist-high grass, trying our best not to think about the rattlesnakes that were surely slithering all about us or the ticks that no doubt tasted our blood.

We moved in a straight line, then. Southeast. I thought we were headed toward Sawton.

Not that it would've done us any good to get there...

All the while the temperature was dropping, and then the blizzard hit. I run a hand over my face, careful not to shove my fingers into my hair. No need to dislodge the stitches, again.

Slowly, I lift my head, and my eyes drift upward, finding their way to Chloe's gaze. She smiles softly, even though she's known pain today. She does it for my benefit.

By now, they're on to discussing the various things they've brought home from their trip. I completely missed their verdict on what to do with me.

Her words wash over me, rolling right off my shoulders. None of it really sinks in. Something about a new pump and some PVC pipe to fix someone's well. More knitting needles. Enough stuff for Trent to assemble another solar panel. The pieces he needs to fix someone's deep freeze.

A multitude of tools and wire and wax and fabric and new clothes and medical supplies…

All of it resonates with a life I thought was gone, and it seems so out of place in the world I know now. As such, it has no influence on my thoughts, does nothing to pull me out of the loop of, "We only made it thirty miles?"

Hours of angry silence and minutes which felt like hours filled with shouting that I was sure would, at any moment, draw the Fangs down upon us. Countless missteps because the foliage was too thick to see the molehills and snake holes we walked over. Aching muscles due to the heavy packs and the weight of a four-year-old who wasn't ready for such a harsh life.

The struggle of rationing food and water with a child and a man who was quickly moving beyond the reach of reason. The pain of watching Karen give up her food and water for her son, for her husband, only to be shafted by that same man when we found a puddle of water we could boil over a fire.

And it was all for nothing.

My view of Chloe splinters as my lashes draw together, then goes black when my eyes finally close. She's replaced by the sight of Jesse, lying face up in the snow, a single rivulet of blood running from his forehead to his temple, only to drip onto the otherwise unblemished snow. The still air rang with the crack of the pistol, then ripped open once more as a shot flew over my head, missing only because I ducked immediately after the first.

Unable, or unwilling, to relive it again, I open my eyes.

Perfect green gems lay upon me, filled with concern. Can I lay this burden upon her? Can I do as Grant accused me, and use her to forget my pain for a while?

Is that all this is?

My gut says there's more to it, that I would've been drawn to her even if Jesse were alive and we were all together. But does that make it right to trouble her with my baggage, knowing I can't stay?

If I die in Breyerville, if I'm robbed of the chance to return, will I regret paining her? Or will the regret of never kissing her be harder to bear?

Could I be okay with Chloe being the last woman I kiss? The last woman I hold close or make love to?

My eyes narrow, scrutinizing the prospect even as I watch her deftly answer questions about her own injuries and the downfall of Sawton. Her eyes soften further as she tells them what she read in a journal of deaths and departures.

A faint voice in the back of my head says yes. She could be my last. Of course, the short span of time I expect to live may have some effect on that. But then again, maybe not.

I can't deny that something about her calls to me on a cellular level.

But…

Could I ever justify such selfishness?

***

While Chloe showers and Jackson starts dinner, I carry in boxes of candle making supplies and park Deadweight in the detached garage, right between a blacked-out, luxury sport sedan and a gnarly looking motorcycle.

Pulling the door down after myself, I survey the truck parked in front of the garage, blocking the sedan in. Well, the remnants of a truck, anyway.

Dust coats its shiny blue paint, but it's obvious that it was fairly new when everything went to shit. It sits there, with multiple pieces pulled off to be used for various purposes around the farm now that gas and diesel are a thing of the past, utilitarian even in its death.

Out back, I see the hood has been used to patch a leak in the roof of a chicken coop. Two rims have been stacked and fashioned into a fire pit on the back patio, leaving the front of the truck on blocks. The tires are nowhere to be seen, having been pressed off the rims, but I'm sure they've been put to use somewhere.

The bed of the truck rests atop a couple of 6-inch by 6-inch wooden beams amidst a cow pasture. A tarp lines it, holding water in for the cows to drink. Zip ties fasten the metal rings of the tarp to holes drilled in the side of the truck bed.

On approaching the remnants of the truck, I find the interior of the extended cab stripped bare. The seats are missing, likely being used elsewhere, and in their place, lie more planters than I would have thought could fit in a truck. Healthy plants fill them, loving the ingenious greenhouse. Ripe tomatoes and peppers decorate their limbs, soaking in the sunlight from the windows and the sunroof.

Jackson appears on the wraparound porch and calls out, "Open her up. Rear passenger door, please."

I oblige, opening the door, and wonder how they reach the plants in the middle. The mystery is solved quickly, though. As soon as Jackson arrives beside me, the farmer grabs a metal frame concealed by the leaves of the plants and slides half of the planters in the back outward.

With a mild gasp, I say, "That's brilliant…"

"Thanks," Jackson beams. "The frame's from another truck. That one's on the other side of the garage. Can you go get some oregano out of it?"

Laughing incredulously, I say, "Sure."

***

Chloe finishes up her shower, emerging in well-worn flannel pajamas. Her hair is nearly burgundy, darkened by the water. I look up from the green onions I was cutting to smile at her.

Walking up behind me, she reaches around me and grabs a bit of shredded cheese from a bowl on the counter. The scent of berries wafts up to greet me as she gets close.

Her hand rests on the small of my back as she asks me to go out and pick any vegetables and fruits that are ripe, saying she wants dinner to be a surprise. Jackson hands me a plastic tote labeled U. S. Postal Service and nudges me out of the kitchen.

***

"Time to eat!" Chloe yells out the door.

I toss a few more peppers into the tote and heft the thing up to the house, still surprised that the gray siding and burgundy shutters are in such good shape. I adjust the tote in my arms. It probably weighs a good 15 pounds, far more fresh produce than I've seen since the collapse.

Climbing the stairs, my nose sets to work trying to pick out the scent of whatever they've made. Propping the tote on a small table by the door, no doubt placed there for this exact purpose, I pull open the screen, then the big door painted the same dark red as the shutters.

The mouthwatering aroma of pizza slams into me, and I exclaim with all the exuberance of a child, "Are you fucking kidding me? Pizza? We're having pizza?!"

I haven't had that since…before. Long before.

I scarf down piece after piece of freshly baked bacon and hamburger pizza covered with melty cheese with green onions on half of it. Again, they shock me, following the pizza with warm and gooey chocolate chip cookies and ice cold milk in an evening of delicacies that I'd resigned myself to forgetting. A huge smile plasters itself across my face, and I find myself lost in the simple pleasure of a great meal set to the soundtrack of good-humored conversation.

I find my gaze drawn more and more to the glittering gems of Chloe's eyes, sparkling with smiles and laughter. Despite myself, I wish I could stay with her longer, as guilty as that makes me feel.

At the end of the meal, Jackson suggests that I shower while he and Chloe clean up the dining room and kitchen. Stomach stuffed beyond reason for the first time in years, my eyelids begin to droop. I put up enough of an argument to be polite, but truthfully, I'm glad for the chance to clean up. Finally.

"Oh," Chloe says as I push away from the big farm table. "I don't know if it works in Breyerville, I doubt it, but we have hot water."

At this point, I don't understand why I'm still shocked, but nonetheless find myself asking, "Seriously?"

Chloe nods, and Jackson says, "I laid out some of my old night clothes for you. I think they'll fit."

"Thank you," I say and measure my steps all the way down the hall, careful not to let eagerness rush my pace. The lush carpeting practically wraps around my feet, seeming to slow my progress, but I know it's all in my head.

Shutting the door behind me, thankful for the three candles burning bright on the counter behind the sink, I push aside the door on the shower/bathtub combo and turn on the hot water.

After only a second or two, it warms, nearly scalding my outstretched fingers. Instantly, chills run through my body, and tension leaks out of my shoulders.

I strip down as fast as I can manage and unwrap my head, my side. Suddenly, I don't care so much if it's best to keep my stitches dry. I want that hot water all over me. Adding just enough cold so as not to melt the flesh from my bones, I climb in and slide the door into place.

Steam billows around me, and I step beneath the jet. Water cascades over me, hitting squarely on my shoulders before falling over my chest and back. Knots untie themselves within my muscles, erasing so much pent up tension that the corners of my eyes prick with the promise of tears. I tilt my head back, relishing the feel of near-burning water running through my hair.

Aloud, though no one can hear, I say, "Dear God, I've missed this."

Chapter 19

Chloe

Night falls with me staring out the window of my living room. Mrs. Ableman's house lies dark and dormant. The impression that, at any moment, the woman will light a candle and hobble past a window gnaws at me.

On arriving home, I found myself looking for a friendly wave through a window, a smile from the porch. The knowledge that those things will never again come to pass forms a lump in my throat. We'll have to help finish cleaning out her house in the days to come, distributing her belongings to those who need them.

Pulling the heavy, burgundy drapes closed, I turn from the window with a sigh. Thick carpet cradles my feet as I walk down the hall to my bedroom in near darkness, passing by the bathroom where Christian now showers. The sound of the water splashing off his naked body warms my skin far more than the heat from the fireplace I leave behind.

A handful of candles light my room, providing ambient light and keeping the strain off the solar panels which have much more important duties, such as maintaining the pump for the well, the fridge, and the deep freeze. And currently, the high-efficiency water heater, allowing Christian the first steamy shower he's likely had in a while.

I redirect my thoughts once more, choosing to ignore the imagery flooding my mind and the shiver of pleasure sweeping through me. I grab a sketch pad and some pencils from my desk. Curling up on my bed without bothering to pull back my dark gray comforter, soft flannel pajamas caressing my skin, I doodle for a while.

I fill a page with various gesture drawings, warming up, then flick to the next page. The thick, textured paper is soft in my hands. Calista comes to mind, beautiful in the glow of her pregnancy. I do my best to replicate my friend's delicate features. The dreads come naturally, basically sketching themselves for me, but the intricacies of her soft face always elude me, even when I'm not sketching from memory.

I draw her cradling her stomach, already loving the children contained within to such a degree that it boggles the mind. A light smile touches her warm eyes, barely lifting the corners of her mouth. Several scarves adorn her neck, though Calista never actually wears any. She just *feels* like the type to wear a million scarves to go with her flowy cardigans.

I find myself wishing for some vine charcoal, my preferred medium, to soften the drawing and really drive home the shadows. The elevated contrast always appeals to me, but for now, I'm out.

Maybe next time we're out…

I lean over the page, darkening the shadow at the hollow of Calista's collarbone.

"That's really good," a deep voice whispers from the doorway beside me.

I look up, startled, to find Christian. I didn't hear the water shut off, and the carpet dulled the approaching footsteps.

Surprise turns to a smile, and I whisper, "Thank you."

My hushed tone makes no sense to me. I don't need to be quiet. Jackson isn't asleep. I can hear him bustling about his room and I know he has yet to shower.

"May I come in?" Christian asks, only venturing through the doorway when I nod. He takes the seat at my desk, sitting sideways in the chair to face me, not quite bold enough to assume it's okay to sit on my bed.

I set my sketchbook aside and turn the pencil in my hands, waiting for him to speak. For a moment, he sits with one arm draped over the back of the chair, craning his neck to look out the window.

Finally, he speaks, though he doesn't look back at me yet. "Earlier, when everyone was in the gym, I…uh…I got stuck, thinking about how we only made it 30 miles…" His voice catches, and his eyes close. His hair, still damp from the shower, hangs loosely around his face, sending quivering shadows over his skin in the candlelight.

Giving his head a little shake, he looks down at his hand. "I didn't hear the verdict. Am I staying until I heal or leaving now…or getting a ride back…or…" Looking up at me, he waits, letting his words hang, unfinished. He seems to want to ask if they intend to kill him or feed him to Jenny. Or enslave him. Really anything goes, nowadays.

"Nothing's changed there," I assure him. Then, lightening my tone to try lifting his spirits, "We'll be putting you to work, though. You have to earn your keep, one way or another."

He nods and purses his lips thoughtfully. "Good. I'm tired of being a leech." One corner of his mouth lifts, an attempt to return my humor, but it's short-lived.

In the next breath, his eyes fall to his hand, resting upon his lap. "I know the odds are…" he falters, searching for the words. "The odds are slim, but…if I make it out of Breyerville with Karen and Tate…would it be alright to bring them here?"

"Of course." Smiling, I add, "I look forward to meeting them." I say it confidently, trying to convince him that he'll make it out, even if I'm not one hundred percent certain of it, myself.

His eyes find me, shining gray, changed by the dim light. "Thank you," he says.

My skin warms beneath his gaze, and my lips spread into a smile. For a minute, we just gaze at each other. Far from feeling awkward, I begin hoping he might come to sit with me on the bed.

I see him shift in his chair, leaning forward with his elbows on his knees. Propping his head on one hand, he starts to say something but thinks better of it. His mouth opens, for just a second, then closes again. He shakes his head, almost imperceptibly, and looks down.

But he doesn't get up. He neither approaches me nor leaves the room, even though it's well past midnight.

Is he too afraid of shattering the sweet tension building between us? Or is this merely awkward for him?

Needing something to say, and something to busy my hands with, I reach for my sketch pad again and say, "This is…silly." I look down at the paper. "And maybe it's poorly timed, but…do you mind if I draw you?"

"Not at all," he whispers, somewhat more huskily than I expected.

My heart shivers and my insides feel heavy.

I flip to a fresh page and set to work. I hold my pencil out and line it up even with the edges of his face, capturing the angles of his strong jaw. I fill in the softness of the shadows caressing his neck and linger over the lines of his mouth.

In the past, in various figure drawing classes, I had no trouble maintaining a professional outlook, even when the model was nude. I just broke the figure down into shapes, lines, and planes. The body became a composition to capture on paper.

But here, with Christian's eyes smiling at me, a delicious heat builds within me as my pencil moves over the luxurious paper.

A certain level of intimacy takes shape between us as I trace the shape of the hand holding his head up. My pencil moves across the waves of his hair as my fingers wish to do, transcribing them in minute detail on the page.

I've always had the gift of drawing, honed by years of practice, so it only takes me half an hour. But by the end of it, Christian's eyes have softened dramatically. He gazes at me with millions of delicate emotions undulating in the blue-gray pools of his irises. My heart stutters when I look up at him.

Setting the pencil down on my nightstand, I ask, "Do you want to see it?" My voice comes out low, sultry. It surprises me, but he doesn't seem phased.

Christian nods, very slowly, and I throw my feet off the bed. Nervous, I don't walk over to him. Instead, I move to the foot of my bed, putting him within arms' reach, and hand him the sketchbook. Our fingers brush as he takes the pages in hand, and electricity shoots up my arm.

"Damn," he says when he sees my drawing. "This is…unbelievable." He looks up at me briefly. Then, looking closer at the page, he says, "So, this is how you see me?"

Somehow, I feel like I've exposed something about myself, about how I feel about him, by doing this drawing. Does he understand what even I can't quite figure out?

He smiles at me and stands up. Taking a couple of steps, he hands my sketchbook back to me. Our fingers brush again, and Christian lets his hand linger. Again, he starts to say something but stops himself short.

After a deep breath, he says, "Goodnight. Sweet dreams."

"Goodnight," I answer.

Christian leaves the room, hand trailing the edge of the pad rather than letting go all at once, as though releasing it so abruptly might hurt. He glances back at me from the shadows of the hall.

Somehow, the absence in his wake leaves me feeling rejected. I watch the dark hallway long after he's disappeared to sleep on the couch.

What did I expect?

God…What was I hoping for?

***

I tape fresh gauze over my arm and neck, which are healing rather nicely. The rising sun sends amber light slanting through my bedroom windows, begging me to come out and play. A few roosters crow in the distance, and out in the barn, the bull stirs.

I wonder briefly if Christian will be awake, yet. Is he accustomed to waking with the sun? Farm life is certainly a different life than he's been living in Breyerville.

I survey my work, and when satisfied that the tape will hold up through the day, I don a few more layers. My mind doesn't shift topics, though, revolving around Christian.

No longer seriously injured, he can tend his own wounds, much to my disappointment. It's an aspect of closeness lost. Not to mention the way the days of healing tug at the rope of the advancing deadline, pulling it ever closer.

Not that I want him hurt.

I just…don't want to say goodbye.

Guilt swirls through me like smoke, clouding my mind. His sister-in-law and his nephew are suffering. It's right for him to go to them. If he were willing to forsake them, he'd be a different person, one I might not like so much.

Sighing, I shuffle out of my room, ready for a long day of hard work. Time to play catch up. Sure, Jackson had his friends, Melissa and Bradley, look in on our cattle, chickens, and greenhouses during our outing, but they have their own gardens and animals to care for. Adding another farm to their responsibilities for a couple of weeks is a large undertaking.

Two baritone voices rumble toward me from the kitchen, punctuated by the clinking of dishes and the scrape of a skillet being pulled off the burner. I smile. I pull my bedroom door shut, and the sound alerts the guys that I'm awake.

"About time!" Jackson calls out with a laugh.

My smile broadens as I move through the hall, lined with all the family photos I once took down out of guilt. Beautiful new frames hang on sage walls, holding the smiling faces of my parents. My hand trails the white wainscoting.

The smell of eggs and bacon reaches my nose, and my smile deepens. My heart warms as I think of Christian's reaction to this food, recalling the joy that blossomed on his face when we shared pizza and cookies last night.

Chapter 20
Christian

Climbing the porch stairs, I try my damnedest to get as much of the mud off my boots as possible before going in. I know the mudroom on the back of the house has no carpeting, the only room in the house about which this can be said, but I still don't want to sully it. Despite the apocalypse, Chloe and Jackson keep a clean house.

I pull open the door, painted burgundy to match the one at the front of the house, and step in onto a black welcome mat resting atop gray and white faux-marble tile. A beautiful wooden room divider greets me, nestled in next to a mahogany cabinet that conceals a laundry hamper. To my right, a small cabinet sits, waiting to hide muddy shoes from view.

I bypass the shoe cabinet, making my way to the ingenious seating. Once a wide dresser with three sets of drawers, the wooden masterpiece now seats two comfortably, allowing for storage in the center.

Before sitting, I take a moment to admire it, wishing I could be making things, again. The outer drawers have been removed, and the dresser itself has been shaved down. The outer walls have been left in place, and the base has been shored up to accommodate a person's weight, with a cushion waiting to cradle whoever may be lucky enough to sit atop it.

Clearly, innovation has been the way of things around this farm for a long time, certainly not just since the collapse.

No wonder they've gotten by so well. They've been making things work since day one, never actually taking advantage of the infrastructure the way people in the city did.

Settling in on dark grey cushions, with burgundy and olive accent pillows cradling my arms, I marvel at the clean pale grey walls and white crown molding. I tug my boots off without bothering to untie them, then meander to the shoe cabinet. Kneeling, I stash them safely out of sight. The inside of the cabinet is a far cry from the outside, with dirt and dried up leaves crunched in the bottom. For some reason, this makes me smile.

The door opens beside me, and I stand abruptly, trying to get out of the way. I just end up even more in the way though, and Chloe very nearly barrels into me. Little pieces of mud fall from her hair and clothes as she skids to a halt.

"Ope," we both mumble, "Sorry."

With my hands on Chloe's waist and all the breath rushing out of me, my words come out a bit garbled, coating the traditional southern Illinois version of, "Excuse me," with a much deeper southern accent.

Chloe's dirt-caked face splits into a smile. Leaves decorate her hair, and her clothing appears as though it will never come clean.

"Why do you sound like you're from a swamp?" she teases me, placing muddy hands on my shoulders.

"Why do you *look* like you're from a swamp?" I jest, earning a laugh.

Pulling a hand from her waist, I wipe a chunk of mud from her cheek and a smear of dirt from her lips. My hand freezes, resting upon her face, and some irresistible gravity pulls me closer.

Her eyes dart to my lips, then back to meet my gaze. Her lids hang heavy over those beautiful emeralds, and I swallow nervously, trying not to think about how long it's been since I kissed anyone. Our lips brush, delicate and seductive.

Chloe's hand knots in my hair, pulling me closer, and my skin burns at her touch. Mouths part and tongues dance as they try desperately to melt together. A delectable warmth pools in my stomach, urging me to tighten my grip around her, to press myself to her and push her back to the wall. My veins boil, begging for more as our kiss continues.

The chance for more is torn from my grasp. Chloe pulls back, just far enough for a few atoms of air to fit between our lips. Gazing up at me, she smiles and brushes her nose against mine. Sparks fly between us, arcing back and forth between our lips, calling out for us to join again.

I watch her eyes close. I feel her chest rise with a deep breath, pressing her breasts against me and sending a shiver through me. When her eyes open, she whispers, voice deep and husky, "We should probably change clothes."

"Probably," I answer, voice catching. Then, as she extricates herself from my arms, I add, "Swamp monster."

She laughs and rolls her eyes. Kicking off her shoes, she slides them into the cabinet. She hangs her jacket on a hook on the wall, and I do the same with my own. From the top drawer in the center of the little dresser-couch, she retrieves some leggings and a tank top.

"Jackson's clothes are in the bottom drawer," she says and slips behind the room divider in the corner. "Pick through and find some that'll fit you, at least well enough to get by until you shower."

I pull the drawer open, thankful that I must face away from her to do so. Otherwise, my eyes might have been drawn to the hinges of the divider, straining to see. Aching for a distraction, I ask, "So, what happened, anyway? Why are you so muddy?"

I'd thought I was dirty, but she puts me to shame.

"Some stupid cow pulled me into a mud puddle," she says with acid dripping from her words. "Same damn cow that, well, you remember the calf I said I was looking for when Jenny showed up and attacked me? Yeah, that one."

I laugh at the animosity she feels for this animal as I settle on a pair of jeans and a black v-neck shirt.

"She's been nothing but trouble since she was born," Chloe says, chuckling at the silliness of her own temper. "She might have to be the next one on the butcher block." Mirth fills her words, lifting the mood.

She steps out from behind the screen as I rise, and her clothes cling tightly to her curves.

I still myself with a breath. Picking a couple of leaves from her hair, I say, "Much better." Despite myself, I let my lips find hers, again.

Releasing her, loving the blush that creeps over her skin, I take my turn behind the screen. "I'll go start dinner. It's early, but it'll be okay," Chloe says, tossing her dirty clothes into the hamper.

The door to the rest of the house opens and closes by the time I even get the clean shirt over my head. I pull it down, careful not to rub the neck of it over the stitched-up part of my head. My side stretches, but it's merely uncomfortable, now. No lightning bolts of pain as stitches threaten to rip themselves free of my flesh.

Perhaps it should, though. There should be some sort of penance for what I just did.

Twice? I had to kiss her twice? Talk about leading her on. Once would have been bad enough.

As much as I try to berate myself, the guilt I feel can't outweigh the exhilaration. My heart soars, light as a feather and more carefree than it's been since everything went to shit. Something about her, about this place, just feels right. I hate myself for thinking that maybe I'm supposed to be here, maybe I should stay.

I know I can't, but this little farm calls to me. *She* calls to me.

"I just have to survive the Fangs," I say aloud, rolling my eyes at the impossibility of such a thing.

***

After yet another meal I had no hopes of tasting ever again, homemade chicken noodle soup with vegetables I picked this afternoon, I begin work on the crib I agreed to make for Holden and Calista Vincent. Jackson leads me past a pile of dark wood, taken from alongside the railroads, to the woodshop. A small stack of treated lumber waits, harvested from the many abandoned construction sites throughout the countryside. The rough wood stares up at me, waiting to be shaped.

Thankfully, Chloe stays inside, busily making candles. After the mudroom, I need some room to think. I need distance.

Part of me cries out to just enjoy myself. Chloe obviously doesn't mind that I'm leaving soon. She isn't shying away. If I thought for a second that this was normal behavior for her, throwing herself at any random guy, the situation would be drastically different. I'd have no reason to worry about how she'll feel when I leave because there'd be some other guy to take my place.

Though, that would make me want very little to do with her, solving the problem by eliminating it, altogether.

I can tell it isn't like that, though. Grant is living proof.

For a moment, as I take stock of the tools at my disposal, I toy with the idea of convincing myself that she's trying to manipulate me into staying. Being angry at her would solve my problem.

But I know she understands the pull of family. She's felt the agony of loss. She wouldn't try to stop me.

Sighing, I set down the candles Jackson sent out with me. It isn't the safest idea, working out here past dark, sawing by candlelight. But it's nice to have the option. I begin designing the crib on a piece of paper left on a workbench, finally settling on a simple design.

When I get an acceptable sketch, I set to work measuring and cutting all my boards, glad to finally be working with my hands, again. The base of the crib comes easily. By the time I move on to the rails, I've found my groove, settling into the flow of physical labor. Muscle memory kicks in, surprising me. I was worried my body would have forgotten it all, by now.

All I need now is some music, but that would be far too much to ask even here, a point which is driven home by the need for candles as the winter sun dips toward the horizon. Luckily, by that point, the crib is mostly done.

Taking a step back, sipping water from a cold glass that Jackson snuck out to me, my mind drifts across time and space to the last crib I built, the only other one I've ever built. Karen and Jesse told me they were expecting, and I bought the lumber for it that night. There were still six months left in the pregnancy, but I was too excited to wait.

It would have been finished in a matter of days, regardless of the intricate carving I did on it, had I not also been working on my house, at the time. I swallow down the bitterness that creeps up my throat like bile.

"Filthy fuckin' bastard," I grumble, then take another sip to try to wash the taste down.

I didn't know I could hate someone quite so much as I hated The Wolf when he stole my goddamn house. Granted, that was long before Billy caught sight of Karen, and they forced her into the disgusting brothel The Wolf was running. Out of *my* house.

A carefully controlled sigh hisses out between clenched teeth, and I run a hand over the smooth wooden rails of the crib. I do my best to fend off the memories that bubble up within me, but I can't help it. My eyes close, and I feel myself transported to Jesse and Karen's condo.

They'd just brought Tate home from the hospital, and Jesse promised me the honor of being the first to lay Tate down in the crib I made. I remember cradling the tiny baby in my arms, one thumb lost in the mane of hair the boy had from day one. Tate always wanted to keep it long, too, because that's how I wear mine.

Another sigh, this one almost accompanied by tears.

I open my eyes and stare at the woodshop around me. It isn't mine. It certainly isn't the place I built a crib for Tate. So many things have changed since that day, and now, I don't even know if Tate's alive.

My mind swirls with all the possible scenarios, in which the Fangs tire of having a child cramping their so-called "style." My brain conjures a million different deaths, billions of different tragedies that could befall Tate and Karen.

My knees buckle, and my hand slips from the rail of the crib. I fall to the floor, a huddled mess, cradling my head in my hands. The weight of grief is staggering, far more than I can endure.

I should have pushed harder. We should've gotten farther.

Pulling my legs out from under me, I scoot back, leaning against a wall. My dirty, dusty hand wipes at my face, leaving bits of sawdust in its wake, but I don't care. I stopped noticing that stuff years ago.

The flickering of the candles draws my attention, holding my eyes. I don't pull my gaze free. Rather, I let it rest there on the burning wicks. They scorch all thoughts of my past, of the coming days and the terror of finding them already lost.

The light of the candles brings me the peace of a clear mind, and for many minutes, nearly an hour, I sit there, unmoving, barely blinking. Only when Chloe comes out, clad in flannel pajamas and rubber boots with a fleece blanket thrown around her shoulders, do I return to the world.

I push myself up from the ground and snuff all but one of the candles. I let her lead me back to the house and thank her for everything before saying goodnight at the door to the bathroom.

I don't let myself watch after her as she disappears down the hall and into her room. Instead, I throw myself into the shower, thankful yet again for the magnificent steam.

Chapter 21

Chloe

My hand trails along the fence on the way to the barn. My breath comes out in clouds in the late winter air, slipping away behind me. Mist hangs heavy in the fields, serene in the gray light, waiting for the sun to sparkle upon it.

My rubber boots clomp through the dirt, finally dried out from the storm a few days ago, alerting the cows and chickens to their oncoming meal. Feathers rustle in the coop. Hooves stamp at the ground, and the bull snorts, ever restless to be freed from the barn.

Behind me, Christian opens the woodshop, eager to get his hands dirty, once more. I smile and redirect my gaze. It wouldn't do to be caught staring. The door to the barn opens, and Jackson releases the bull into the pasture. I freed my newly made candles from their molds as he went on to begin milking, and now I wonder how far he made it through the chore.

Glancing up at the clouded early morning sky, I wonder at the disparity in the distribution of hardship. Christian and so many others have had it unbelievably rough since the collapse, but here, life has gone on with very little change. The Amish towns nearby have seen even less change and given the distance from any major cities, very little trouble from outsiders.

By and large, none of it makes any sense. Not that life made any sense before, either.

I give a derisive snort, briefly casting my mind over the world. My hand finds the latch on the door of the barn. Regardless of what happens, no matter how hard things may get, life goes on. Chores have to be done.

My momentary lapse into the wonders of karma, God, fate, or whatever may be out there now over, I stroll into the barn. Seven cows, three of which are nearly ready to calve, wait in the free pen. Jackson already has one cow milked and released with the bull, with another in his stall.

I grab my stool and bucket, place them in my stall, and meander over to my least favorite cow of all. Trish. The one that pulled me into the mud. The one that got me attacked by Jenny. The one that always makes milking as difficult as possible, despite how much the other cows look forward to it.

The one that I can't cook yet, because she can still calve, thereby producing milk.

"May as well get it over with," I sigh, leading the beast out of the pen.

The familiar scent of straw and manure fills my nose as I settle onto my stool. Time to get to work.

***

After a long morning of chores and a nice meal in our cozy house, I help load the beautiful crib Christian made onto Deadweight's trailer, nestling a crate of milk jugs underneath it. I insist that Jackson stay behind, promising that, injured as we may be, we've healed enough to unload the crib without his help.

Christian says little as we ride slowly across Harville, dodging potholes and cracks in the road. His eyes are bloodshot, again. Yet again, I wonder if having him work on a crib was a bad idea given the absence of his nephew.

176

He insisted though, happy to build something, happy to contribute after all we've given him. Hoping to offer him some sort of support, I take his hand.

As if shaken from a trance, he looks at me and sighs. His fingers tighten around mine, but he looks away, staring at the passing houses and the people bustling about.

The yards, though not as nice as they once were, are kept below mid-calf. The houses are kept up within reason, though a few windows here and there have been boarded up after storms last spring decided tree limbs should be the newest residents of those houses. All in all, Harville has fared relatively well.

On the coldest of nights, those without fireplaces or wood-burning stoves stay over with friends and neighbors. Holden cares for all our injuries. Jackson and I go out searching for the equipment and medicine he needs.

We've only buried a few select people, Mrs. Ableman included. Pain slices through me at the thought of her.

Sawton comes to mind, with all the horrors they faced. Stories of The Wolf and all his doings follow close on their heels. The few run-ins we've had with his Fangs scream into focus. Ambushes in the suburbs of Breyerville where Jackson and I barely made it out alive. Being tracked by them when we happened upon the same small store, only to be saved by the fortuitous arrival of Jenny.

And Christian lived under their thumbs for two and a half years. What must this all look like to him?

People raising kids with ease, knowing perfectly well where their next meal will come from, with the understanding that all they must do to get it is to put in an honest day's labor. Nothing more.

No fear of a pompous gangster deciding he wants what we have. No fear of thugs breaking into our homes to attack us, just because.

Does this all smack of injustice?

Rerouting my thoughts yet again, I glance up ahead and catch sight of Becky, Grant's sort-of girlfriend, climbing the steps at Holden and Calista's house.

Great...This ought to be fun.

I roll my eyes and sigh audibly, catching Christian's attention.

It's no secret around Harville that the woman harbors a great deal of animosity for me, not that it's my fault Grant took such a liking to me. I haven't exactly encouraged him. Regardless of my endless rebuffs of Grant's affections in the past, Becky always treats me as though I were actively trying to steal Grant away, like it's all some sort of competition.

Even now that they're technically together, regardless of my role in getting Grant to give Becky a chance, the woman still feels the need to posture when I come around.

I purse my lips.

Brown hair shining in the late afternoon sun, Becky turns to face us when she hears the whine of the electric motor and the drone of our tires. Her hands fly to her hips, one of which juts out, practically screaming, "Are you kidding me?"

Feeling's mutual.

I roll my eyes but say nothing.

Beside me, Christian appears not to have noticed our impending company, staring out at the blissful little town. He waves to the Thevin family, a little smile curling one side of his lips when both children, Jack and Tara, age eight and five respectively, wave back.

Meanwhile, Becky knocks urgently, perhaps hoping to finish her business with Calista before I get there. After all, the crib makes it painfully obvious that's where I intend to go. No one comes to the door, though.

From around the back of the brick, ranch-style house, Calista appears, hands covered in dirt. Alerted by Deadweight, she waves to us, oblivious to Becky's arrival, a fact which will no doubt weigh against me.

The crib finally registers in Calista's view, and her hands rush to cover her open mouth. "Oh my God…" she says. "Oh, it's so beautiful." Her steps quicken, and she half jogs, half waddles over to look at Christian's work.

A huge smile spreads over my face as Calista's eyes light up. For the first time all day, Christian glows with happiness. Becky's expression remains sour, though she does abandon the front door, gradually picking her way through the grass.

When Calista reaches us, her hand strokes the rails of the crib appreciatively, even as her other hand rests upon her belly. "It's perfect," she says. "Thank you so much, Christian."

I rub Christian's lower back gently. An evil glint creeps into Becky's eyes, but I dismiss it as a product of my own existence.

After a good deal of going on about the quality of Christian's work and the disparity between its craftsmanship and that of the pre-collapse, store-bought crib given to the Vincent family by the Thevins, the item is carried in. Calista isn't allowed to help, for obvious reasons. Becky grudgingly assists at Christian's request, a dynamic I'm not sure what to think of, yet.

Once inside, Calista leads Becky and me through her home to fetch the things she made for us, leaving Christian to fix the rails on the older crib. Becky grabs her yarn and says a quick thank you. Promising produce in trade, she takes her leave, much to my relief.

As soon as she's out of earshot, Calista starts in with a line of questions.

"Is he staying?"

"No."

"Do you like him?"

A grudging, "Yes."

Calista drapes a handmade scarf over her shoulders, mainly to get it out of the way as she digs through a basket full of them. Another drapes over it, then another, as she searches for the one she knitted for me, lending her the aesthetic I always imagine for her.

"Is he coming back after he gets…Who is it? His sister and nephew?" Calista asks.

My mind careens back to the sincere expression on Christian's face when he asked if returning would be amenable to us. "If he makes it out of there," I whisper, words hushed beneath their own weight.

"Are you going with him?"

"I…don't know." No other answer comes to mind. There is no moment of blinding clarity. The entirety of our futures doesn't lay itself out before my eyes.

I know Grant wasn't wrong when he called this a suicide mission, much as I hate to admit it. I wish I could be certain of his return, of the arrival of an actual pre-school teacher and a bouncing little boy.

Harville could use the influx of citizens. I could use the brightness they could offer, the little ray of sunshine that would pierce the clouds of Mrs. Ableman's death.

Pulling me from my reverie, Calista says, "Better make the most of the time you've got, then," and finally unearths my new black scarf from the pile.

Truer words have seldom been spoken, and I contemplate taking them to heart.

With my scarf in hand and Calista close on my heels, I head back into the living room, fully expecting to find Christian. The other crib only needed a single board reattached and the sliding rail back on its track, a couple of fixes I expected him to make quick work of.

And yet, the rich tapestries hanging on the walls surround nothing but empty air. Delicate porcelain sculptures, made by Holden back when he had access to more than just the red clay nearby, adorn every table and shelf largely at Calista's request. But there is no sweet and skillful man here to admire them.

A small, "Hm," of bemused surprise finds its way past my lips, and we wander down the hall to the nursery. The air around us cries out for the scent of incense which used to fill it.

Not quite as surprised as me, Calista makes small talk about the goings-on of Harville as we plod from one lush red area rug to another. I find myself giving half-answers, paying far more attention to the weight sinking steadily in my stomach.

Down a seemingly neverending hallway, two voices reach out from the nursery. Christian. And Becky.

Oh, God...

My heart sinks, and suddenly that glint in Becky's eyes outside makes more sense. My mind runs freely. It drags my heart through the rocky mud behind it as it sprints through a chasm filled with the many ways Becky could exact her revenge for a million imagined slights.

A single word distinguishes itself from the jumbled conversation in the nursery.

"No." Firm and clear, as though it had been said several times already.

"Look," Christian says, "I'm not interested."

My feet rush onward, my head shaking back and forth. The hall fades from my awareness, replaced by concern for what Becky is doing. How far is she willing to push this to "get back" at me?

Rounding the corner, peering through the doorway, I stop in my tracks. Calista nearly barrels into me. Christian stands, eyes like a deer in headlights, holding Becky's wrists out as far from his body as he can. Becky leans up against him regardless, turning my vision red with rage.

Our arrival prompts Becky to twist her head around, smiling cruelly at me. Spinning back around, she presses her lips to Christian's. For his part, he squirms away, pushing Becky away almost hard enough for her to trip, though not quite. She does stumble though, egging her temper on.

Through gritted teeth, I say, "Didn't anyone tell you? No means no."

Turning on her heel, Becky stares at me, finally ready to face off. Stomping over, fully prepared to pretend she didn't almost fall on her ass a moment ago, she says, "What? Afraid I'll steal him? You couldn't hold onto Grant, either."

"I didn't want Grant. I've told you that," I hiss. "Not that that matters, now. Back. The fuck. Off. He said no."

Taking a few more steps, Becky gets in close. Far too close. Her breath scratches over my skin. "Don't tell me what to do. I'm not afraid of you."

Slow, careful breaths. I make every effort to calm myself, but my mind is awash with rage.

This bitch...

My hands itch to reach out and throttle something, preferably the woman whose eyes drill into mine with contemptuous hatred.

Don't hurt her. Do not *hurt her.*

Becky's hands come up, and she pushes me. Sort-of. She tries, but her effort is largely a waste.

I've long since adopted a wider stance, keeping my feet shoulder-width apart at all times. I never lock my knees, grounding myself without becoming rigid. Now, I take a single step back, absorbing the minute force.

Meanwhile, Calista takes a very wise step back, moving further down the hall. Her hands go to her stomach, and her jaw falls open just a bit, surprised at the hostility that's been brewing beneath her nose.

Don't hurt her. Don't hurt her. Don't do it.

I grit my teeth and lift my chin. My shoulders, always pulled back with good posture, shift further as my chest rises with yet another attempt to steady my temper.

"Everyone looks at you like you're some big, bad fighter chick," Becky says, quite eloquently, in my very sarcastic opinion. "I know what you really are, deep down. You're nothing but a coward, walking around here, all talk. But you aren't shit."

Heart pounding behind my ears, vision blurring and teeth grinding into each other, I dip my head, glaring at Becky. My jaw clenches tightly, and my head screams at me to breathe. One long, shuddering breath jerks and jolts through me and my hands make tight fists.

Still eerily quiet, I stare.

Maybe just hurt her a little bit.

My eyes narrow, and I see a hint of something, maybe hesitation, in Becky's eyes. But it doesn't last long.

A tiny, ruthless smile lifts one corner of her mouth. "Maybe…" she says, voice lowering and head tipping just slightly to the side. She's going for the jugular. "If you'd been able to defend yourself before, maybe your parents would be alive. Maybe you could have fought him off."

Calista gasps.

Self-control begs to take its leave, promising satisfaction will follow in its wake, but still, I hold firm. My hands shake. My jaw aches from the pressure of my teeth trying to grind their way through each other. My body pleads with me for some sort of release.

All I allow myself is this, "Fuck. You." I spit the words, low and guttural.

In an act of stupidity of the purest variety, Becky slaps me, harsh and sharp. Pain blossoms across my cheek, spreading through my head in a second, but years of training taught me to ignore it, even as my eyes water.

Deliberately avoiding anything that might permanently injure Becky, I grab the woman's wrist, and sidestep, positioning myself behind her. Lifting up, I bend her arm up past the center of her back and force her to lean forward.

The threat of dislocation becomes a real possibility if I lift just a bit too high. Becky drops to her knees, apparently hoping to avoid some pain, but it does her no favors. The sudden jerk with all her weight falling into it pops her shoulder from its socket.

A small cry escapes Becky, far quieter than expected. Fat tears fall to the hardwood floor beneath her, and I drop her arm. It falls limply to her side, and Becky slumps onto her haunches, grasping at it with her good arm.

Cradling her arm to her chest, doing everything she can to ease the agony, she whimpers, "What did you do to me? You bitch!" Even now, her anger holds fast.

"Less than you deserved," I snarl, adrenaline shivering through me. I ache for release. Nostrils flaring, I count my breaths.

From the hall, Calista says, tone deliberately even, "Get up. We'll go to Holden. He'll pop it back in."

Clamoring up from her perch on the floor, making every effort not to swing or sway her arm, Becky says pointedly, ever the victim and always starving for attention, "At least *some* people are decent."

"Some," Calista says. A smug little smirk creeps onto Becky's face in the instant before Calista says, "Too bad you aren't on that list, dear."

Christian comes up behind me, placing a gentle hand on the small of my back. Still on high alert, I spin quickly to face a threat only to find that none exists. He reaches up, tenderly lifting my chin to peer at my cheek. I wince, but only slightly.

Concern furrows his brows, purses his lips. His magnificent blue eyes pierce mine. To the tune of Calista and Becky's footsteps, he whispers, "Thank you." With a small laugh of derision, he adds, "And...Sorry." A small shake of his head.

"Don't be." I drop my eyes, unable to hold his gaze much longer for fear that the adrenaline may make me do something rash.

"Come on," he jerks his head in the direction of the front door. "We should probably go, too. Get you checked out."

"I'm fine," I assure him. "We should go to make sure she doesn't twist this whole thing around." I roll my eyes and lead Christian out of the house.

We walk about fifteen feet behind Calista and Becky, hoping not to aggravate the situation. Christian whispers, "What will happen to her? Will she...be punished?"

He shivers, and I wonder how something like this would have been dealt with in Breyerville. Would The Wolf and his Fangs have taken it upon themselves to break Becky's spirit? Or would they have killed her?

Or would they perhaps have trained her and given her a gun, inducting her immediately?

"I don't know," I simply say. "We don't have police or a jail. That was definitely sexual harassment, at the very least. And she struck me first...but..." I trail off, thinking. My feet kick at the dirt, sending little whirls of debris up ahead of us as we walk.

After a moment, I go on, "Until now, everything here was pretty calm. The world outside was enough of a common enemy to keep people in check."

Sighing, I add, "Apparently not anymore."

Chapter 22

Christian

Night descends quickly. The stars hide from view, pulling blankets of clouds over their heads to shield themselves from the boogeymen of deep space. I help light candles throughout the house and throw an extra log in the hearth, hoping for a brighter flame.

A knock at the door sends panic freefalling through me. That is, until I recall the relative safety of my location. None of The Wolf's Fangs will have found their way so far. Much to my surprise, Calista, Holden, and a couple of Jackson's friends have ventured through the inky streets, finding their way to the Tucker threshold.

"Oh yeah," Chloe chirps excitedly from her corner spot on the couch. "It *is* Friday, isn't it?"

The notion strikes me as odd. I haven't thought of days of the week in over a year. I gave up on applying any concept of order to the world long ago. In Breyerville, it seemed almost laughable. Here, perhaps it's more sensible.

Everyone shuffles through the door, and I'm introduced to Melissa and Bradley McEnroy, the couple who watched over the Tucker farm while Chloe and Jackson were out. Then, we meander to the basement. It's one of two parts of the house I have yet to visit, with the other being whatever lies upstairs. Though, that part of the house seems to be avoided altogether.

The stairwell bottoms out in a large open room, filled to the brim with shelves of dried goods. Canisters of flour and sugar, sacks of rice and noodles, and jar upon jar of spices adorn the rows of metal racks, as valuable in Breyerville as gold used to be. Two deep freezes sit in a corner, beneath even more shelves full of jars of jams, fruits, and vegetables. I have no doubt that they're packed with delicacies, as well.

For a moment, it all catches me off guard, and I halt, frozen. Only when Chloe starts walking back toward me do I realize that the rest of the group has disappeared through a door in the back of the room.

Catching my breath, I speak in a hush. "Sorry."

I don't mean to be so awestruck, but this is more food than I've seen in one place since before. I doubt even the warehouse-style bulk store The Wolf guards could boast of more food than the people of Harville have at their disposal.

Not anymore, at least. Not even if you add the food from the paltry gardens in the Breyerville city park.

It's no wonder the people here are doing so well. They have the knowledge and the means to sustain themselves. Hunger hasn't twisted their morals.

Picking my jaw up from its resting place on the floor, I bring myself back to the present, right as Chloe wraps her hand around mine. Her grip is warm and tender, yet strong, an apt representation of the woman as a whole.

The light in her sparkling green eyes outshines that of the candle in her hands, putting it to shame in its meager attempts to brighten my world. Her brilliant red hair drinks in the light and the loose waves undulate between intense shine and deep shadows.

Beautiful as she is, I know that within her chest, there beats the heart of a warrior. Her soul is old as time, whether reincarnated a million times over or merely aged by the life she's been thrust into, I can't tell.

She's seen pain, and I may very well cause her more. Though I know I should slip my fingers from hers to spare her, I don't.

Instead, I let her lead me to the back room of the basement, mesmerized by her beauty and my inconceivable surroundings. Vaguely, I'm aware that, were it anyone else, I'd question this scenario, worrying over what fate truly awaits me in the next room.

But I trust her.

The realization strikes hard. Karen and Tate's safety, their lives, their sanity rest with me. Yet I'm willing to put not only my own life in Chloe's hands but theirs, as well, by extension.

Feet working automatically, I shuffle into the small back room. My eyes land upon the chairs, first. The seats from the trucks which have been converted to greenhouses outside. They're arranged around an old card table, each seat resting upon a small wooden frame.

Words, half-formed and barely acknowledged, float through my head like unnoticed leaves on a lazy river.

Guess that's where those seats went.

Everyone else already sits around the table. A light blue bench seat waits for us, a thing I suspect may have been engineered by Jackson. He deals cards for a game of poker with his lips curling into a devilish grin.

Letting go of my hand, Chloe takes her seat and pats the worn fabric of the truck's back seat, urging me to get comfortable. Despite my better judgment, my face quirks into a smile.

May as well.

The knowledge that humanity has a real chance somewhere in the world buoys my spirits. In Breyerville, I'd never thought about places like this, at least not while lending credence to the possibility of their existence. I just assumed that everyone lost their damn minds when the world ended.

Apparently, not so much here. It gives me a little hope, even if not for my own situation.

The Midwest, much of the south, and some of the west are comprised mostly of small farm towns and people who know how to eke a living from the land. Up in the mountains, all the people who have cabins for hunting, they might be okay.

Until now, I'd been so preoccupied with the mess that became of Karen and Jesse, with the shitty world that Tate would inherit, and the odds of his surviving long enough to inherit said world…The idea of people maintaining some semblance of normalcy seemed nothing but a pipedream.

Now though, as the rules are agreed upon, bargaining chips are doled out equally, and I glance down at my cards to find the makings of a royal flush, things start to look up. I'm handed a bottle of homebrew, cinnamon-honey Mead.

As I sweep hand after hand with a bit of alcohol warming my blood, I start myself into believing I may be successful in Breyerville. After all, things I thought were impossible are clearly not. Friends are gathered around me, laughing and enjoying a Friday night, as though they hadn't a care in the world. Everyone but Calista enjoys the Mead, comfortable that our surroundings are safe enough to drink.

And, by all accounts, they are.

***

Amidst the warmth of alcohol and candlelight, the last hand draws to a close. Lady Luck left my side halfway through the night, taking up her position next to Bradley, apparently her usual spot. Now, I'm merely lucky they don't play for anything other than sport.

I hand over my useless cards and take a sip from my third bottle of Mead. The sweetness of the honey has begun to build up in the back of my throat, no longer cut appropriately by the cinnamon, and the need to pace myself isn't simply out of fear of an apocalypse-induced lowered tolerance. The cloying, pricking honey has become overbearing.

Not that I can say that aloud.

It's a drink freely given in the interest of a good evening. Insulting their ability to make it would be rude. Luckily, when Bradley begins to hand another to his wife, Melissa declines for exactly that reason. After a brief conversation about honing in the recipe, Melissa shifts the tectonic plates beneath my chair in a jarring subject change.

"So, I've been meaning to ask," she begins, sweetly, innocently. "How'd you get out of Breyerville, anyway? Isn't there a big wall? How are you getting back in?"

Her tan cheeks are flushed from the liquor, and wild auburn curls hang frantically about her face. But her warm brown eyes shine intelligently, waiting for the answer to a puzzle she's clearly been fiddling with for a while.

Taking a moment to collect my thoughts, I find myself thankful I didn't drink more, lest I get too emotional. In my mind, the dank musty tunnels of the water treatment plant close in over my mind, trapping me within them. In my mind's eye, cramped corridors inch by, redolent with the stench of fear and lit only by our torches.

We needed to move faster. We needed out of there. We had to be as far away as possible by sunrise.

Poor Tate grew more and more restless with every step. Up hours later than normal, he was tired and cranky. His tiny limbs ached to lie down, and his lids begged to fall shut. After a while, we shifted our packs around, redistributing the weight amongst ourselves so I could carry him. The boy fell asleep in my arms almost instantly, shaggy hair whispering over my cheek.

I carried my nephew, thankful for the quiet sounds of Tate's breathing to tie me to the real world. For the most part, it kept my mind from conjuring enemies in the shadows and hearing voices in the rustling of rat feet on discarded papers.

Even when my arms began to ache and my back cried out under the weight of my pack, I was thankful to be holding Tate. It kept the boy in the front of the line, just a bit further from the Fangs, and kept him out of Jesse's grasp. Angry bruises still sprawled across Karen's face, and I had no intention of seeing them on Tate's, as well.

Old pipes creaked in the distance, groaning with disuse and clearly very unhappy that no electric pumps forced water through them. Their complaints echoed through the place, reverberating through damp, grey halls. Every now and then, our lights illuminated a shock of vibrant graffiti, spattered with mold.

Rats scurried through the darkness, curious about the invaders tromping through their home. One ran over

Karen's foot, and she barely muffled her scream. Still, one dark moldy hall after another, we pushed forward with our hearts beating in our throats, making it hard to breathe.

Even now, my blood near to boils as I recall the whisper-shouting as Jesse grew increasingly frustrated. Every wrong turn, each misremembered hallway was a thorn in the man's side, sticking and clawing at him with every unnecessary step.

It had been over five years, though. I don't know how much Jesse could have reasonably expected from me. That was my mistake, though. I was trying to apply logic. Anger cares naught for the 90-degree angles and straight lines of reason. Fury detests the very thought of it.

So we fought, repeatedly, as we crept through lonesome halls.

Abandoned when the power grid faltered and the generators ran out of fuel to burn, The Wolf closed the place up. Guards always stand outside the front doors, and aside from teenagers itching to prove to each other that they have the guts to sneak in through a side door, Breyerville residents are typically too intimidated to go near the place.

But I was on the crew Jesse sent in for the expansion a few years back. For weeks, I worked there, pouring concrete or running electrical lines, anything they needed, basically. But by the time came to escape Breyerville, it had been a long time since I'd been there. My memory of the layout wasn't perfect.

We were desperate though, and out of options. We had to try. It worked well enough, too.

Despite our imaginations' many attempts to convince us otherwise, no Fangs waited around the many corners to assail us. Karen's knowledge of the reservoir led us beyond the sight of the guards posted out front, and she circumvented the doors used by local ruffians to get us in.

Now, in the basement of Chloe's house, I do my best to simplify my tale, recounting only the important parts.

It's not like they'll be coming with me, anyway. They don't need to know the layout. They don't need to know how many halls we had to wander down, or how many times Jesse nearly screamed at me.

Bradley leans forward. Shadows mold themselves around his crooked nose and fill in the dimple in his chin. "Is that how you're getting back in, then? You're just going to wander through the water treatment plant until you find your way through?" Mild skepticism rings in his tone. "What if there are guards at the door? What if there are Fangs in there? If they figured out how you got out?"

As if I hadn't thought about those very problems a million times over. I've been away from Breyerville just over a week, and my mind has done little but circle the problem of getting Tate and Karen to safety.

How much worse have things gotten since I left? Have they posted more guards at the plant? Have they figured it out?

I've only had one distraction this whole time. I glance over at Chloe, then drop my gaze to the table.

"I have to try," is all I can say. "There are weak spots in the wall, but they guard those. They're too obvious. And they do patrols, anyway. Shitty as the Fangs are, they're organized enough to keep people in."

Wouldn't want their victims to escape, after all.

I wipe my hand over the lower half of my face, hoping it will have a sobering effect or perhaps show me an easier way to get to Karen and Tate. No luck. Beside me, Chloe shifts a bit closer and wraps her fingers around mine.

My lips lift into a small slip of a smile, but it doesn't touch my eyes. Why would it?

The easiness of the night, the pleasant evening has evaporated. In its place, the responsibilities and hardships of my life have crashed down upon my shoulders, heavier now after their absence. The guilt of enjoying myself, of having forgotten my worries even if only for a few hours now weighs me down, as well.

For their sake, I put on a brave face. "The water treatment plant is my best bet." I nod and take a drink of my Mead, not caring about the sweetness.

Across the table, Calista yawns, sparking an epidemic that sweeps through us all in turn. Bradley glances down at his wrist, drawing my eyes to the man's watch, yet another relic of days gone by.

"It's pretty late," he says and squeezes Melissa's knee under the table. "Shall we?"

She nods her assent.

Goodbyes are said, and we rise from our chairs. We clear the table, gathering bottles and carrying them upstairs. As we tromp and stomp our way up the stairs, lit only by the candles we carry, Holden invites Chloe and me to come by the community center the following afternoon to have our stitches removed.

Another set of goodbyes in the kitchen is followed by a conversation about a need for help with a fence at the McEnroy farm the next morning. Promises of aid are followed by more goodbyes, and then, another conversation.

In true Midwest fashion, it takes about four times of saying goodbye before Calista, Holden, Melissa, and Bradley actually make their way down the street, a strange custom I've never fully wrapped my head around. I imagine they'll repeat it, saying goodnight several times over when the two couples part from each other somewhere in town, and I chuckle.

***

Emboldened by the lack of man-made light and the moon's absence, the stars throw off the yolk of their cloudy blanket. They sparkle beautifully beyond the kitchen window, relishing the collapse and the freedom to shine that it has allowed them.

The click of a door and soft footsteps sound behind me, prompting me to turn my back on the heavens, just as they turned their back on humanity just over two years ago.

Chloe's sweet voice whispers, "Come with me," and her hand reaches out. She leaves it in the air, offer extended, awaiting my response.

I consider begging off and going to bed. Really, I do.

But remnants of Mead linger within me, warming my blood and lifting my hand up to take hers. A peculiar glow seems to emanate from her. The small bit of me that's still rational suspects it's only the light of the hearth in the living room, newly stoked by Jackson before he turned in for the night.

Just as I should do.

Only a bit unstable, I follow Chloe's swaying hips to the mudroom. We put on jackets, and she sashays to the door, glancing at me over her shoulder. The meadows of her eyes beg seductively for me to let my spirit run through them. I oblige, following, hypnotized, through the door.

The chilly air bites into my flesh but doesn't completely break the spell. Her hand finds mine once more, sending jolts of electricity through me and countering the cold night air.

Some silly notion forms in my mind that perhaps I hear a choir, harkening this fortuitous event. Or maybe that's just a lucky combination of owls and wolves, a different, more primitive chorus. Either way, as she leads me down the stairs and out under the brazen stars, something in me answers the call.

Settling onto a blanket spread in the plush grass, tugging another blanket up over us, I feel myself warm as Chloe nestles up against me. I barely contain a delicate shiver of pleasure as she slides her hand up to rest upon my chest. Her head fits perfectly on my shoulder, a sign from the Gods, mayhap, and her hair sends waves of exotic fruits up to greet my nose.

With my heart firmly lodged in my throat, I try to calm its frantic pace, but it resists, hammering my windpipe in staccato bursts. Air gets harder and harder to come by.

It's just been a while...

Still, I deny that Chloe herself is the cause of the sensations coursing through me and boiling my blood. After all, if it's merely the primitive call of a woman pressed to me, maybe it will be easier to resist the temptation of tipping her chin upward and the magnetism of my lips aching to join with hers.

I can quell physical urges easily, but deep down, I know that isn't the only thing at work here. My heart and body join forces, taking up arms against their common enemy, my self-control.

Words husky, Chloe asks, "What's on your mind?"

As if she doesn't know, already.

If she were to throw her leg over my lap, as I wish she would, she would know exactly what I'm thinking. Yet, her legs rest, one atop the other, nestled gently against me.

Clearing my throat, telling myself to come up with something, anything, that isn't dirty or incoherent, I scramble for words. All things considered, I'm not overly disappointed when I hear myself say, "I haven't actually looked at the stars since the world ended. I didn't have time, and it never felt safe enough to just lay around, staring at the sky…I didn't realize how much I missed it. It's…nice."

I look down to find Chloe gazing at me with millions of stars reflecting in her eyes. She smiles, and the air I was breathing just seconds ago vanishes. I gasp, ever so slightly. She sees my parted lips as an invitation, one I desperately wanted to extend but couldn't bring myself to put forth.

Her lips find mine, gentle in their uncertainty but buzzing with electric promises. She pulls away, cutting off the kiss I was about to give her, and stares into my eyes. Her confidence wavers with every second, and a smattering of hurt splays across her eyes as I look up at her.

Before she can doubt herself further, before my self-control can reassert itself over the alcohol still slinking through my veins, my hand is on the back of her neck, pulling her to me. Our lips meld, hot enough to melt steel. Her hands, one on my chest and one on my face, sear my flesh. Hungry mouths race to devour one another.

I grasp her buttock, crushing her against me, as I roll onto my side to meet her. She grapples with my jacket in a desperate attempt to get closer. Pushing her onto her back, I rear up and nearly tear the jacket asunder in an attempt to feel her hands on my arms, my chest.

Positioning myself between her legs, I cover her with my body, letting my lips wander to her neck. With one hand clutching at my hair, Chloe pulls me tighter against her, calling forth a guttural moan.

Inhibitions have a funny way of creeping up at the worst of times though, and reluctant mutterings of, "I can't do this," reverberate through my mind.

She'll hurt even more if we go through with this and I don't make it back, which is pretty likely.

After all, the Fangs found us once. Why wouldn't they do it again?

Pulling back, hating the cold air that rushes into the space between us, I rest my head upon her shoulder, trying desperately to clear my head. Careful, controlled breaths try their damnedest to slow the beating of my heart. Frustrated discomfort pools within me, but I tell myself it's for the best.

Beneath me, Chloe shifts, and I let her thumb lift my chin so she might gaze into my eyes. "Is everything okay?" she asks, all sweetness and concern.

I nod, imperceptibly, but say, "I...I can't...do this."

Chapter 23

Chloe

A chill settles over me as Christian sits back on his haunches. The blanket goes with him, and frigid winter air rushes over me, a shock to my flushed skin and heated blood.

Confusion settles over me, and all I can utter is, "What?"

Disappointment wars with relief in the depths of my stomach. Thwarted desire curdles, leaving frustration in its wake. I wanted this, nervous as I may have been.

"It just...wouldn't be right," Christian says by way of an inadequate explanation.

He pushes himself up to his feet, uttering apologies all the while. He starts toward the house, hand running over his face.

"Look," I say, scrambling to my feet. "If you're worried about pregnancy, I've got a condom."

Christian stops in his tracks, turning to face me. The expression in his brilliant blue eyes, barely visible by the light of the stars, tells me that I guessed wrong. I can't fathom something worse in this world than an unplanned birth with no anesthesia and no partner to care for the child if I die in the process, though.

At least, nothing that relates directly to *this*.

"It's not that," he says, voice an odd mixture of gruff concern.

"Then, what?"

"Just, if I don't make it back..." He leaves it hanging. The air thickens with the words he won't say.

"Don't you think I've thought about that?" I ask. An inkling of frustration trickles into my heart.

"I don't want to hurt you," Christian answers. "I can't just make this harder on you without even thinking about it. One of us has to think clearly about this."

One of us has to think clearly?

Is he fucking kidding?

Indignation burns hot on my cheeks. "You're protecting me, right now? That's what this is? Do you have any idea how hard this was for me? To put myself out there like this?"

Sensing I'm not done, or perhaps merely stunned by the anger in my voice, Christian doesn't speak.

"After everything that happened before, I didn't date for years, couldn't stand the idea of letting a man touch me. When I did date, I only did *this*," I gesture to the blanket on the ground behind me, "once. One time. Then, there was the fucking apocalypse, and I gave up on finding someone."

My tone softens despite my anger. "Then, there was you. I wanted this, so bad, and I thought you did, too. But I wouldn't let myself do anything about it. I thought about it, *so much*, and finally, *finally*, I decided to go for it. I knew I'd regret it if I didn't."

"But now, you apparently have cold feet. Which," I throw my hands up in resignation, letting them fall and smack into my legs, "I guess is fine. I just wish you hadn't led me on this whole time."

Shaking my head, I add, "Pick a signal and stick to it, Christian."

He winces, just a bit, and I wonder if he's realizing that he's hurt me more by holding back than the pain he would have otherwise left in his wake.

"I'm an adult. You don't need to protect me. I can decide what risks to take for myself," I say. I walk away, leaving him in the grass staring after me.

If he said he just didn't want to, if he said he didn't like me...

That would've been different. But this?

Implying I can't take care of myself? Insinuating that my mind isn't strong enough to overcome physical drives and make a proper decision?

I fume all the way to the bathroom. Slamming the door shut, I turn to the mirror. The decided lack of steam rising from my ears surprises me.

Red hair tousled and eyes wild, I discard the image of myself cut off in the throes of desire, closing my eyes to fight it off. I take a deep breath as I turn on the shower, reminding myself that wanting sex, *desiring* sex, doesn't make me an animal. It doesn't weaken my mind or turn me savage.

Shame blooms, burning its way across my cheeks, down my neck. It spreads until my entire body is on fire with it.

The words of my counselor come back, telling me not to be ashamed of desire. It's normal. It's natural.

I stare at the drain, watching the water rush down from the back of the tub where the showerhead is pointed, racing down to oblivion.

"This is normal," I tell myself, over and over, but I feel my heart retreating from the pain.

A cold front sweeps through me, chilling me to the marrow. Stepping up to the mirror again, I peer deep into my own eyes. Striations of green with streaks of amber emanating from the pupil stare out, cold and unyielding.

Steam billows around me, and I want to shrink from my own gaze. I hold steady, forcing my perspective to shift.

The eyes looking at me are not those of a mindless beast. They are the eyes of a smart, caring woman who merely wanted to enjoy herself with someone she cares for.

Nothing more. Nothing less.

I am not some unthinking creature of lust.

I am not *Robert Myers.*

Before my eyes, I see my mental state shifting in my face. My features seem to transform from hard-angled and beastlike to soft and considerate. Humanity creeps back into my eyes. Sighing, I turn toward the shower, no longer quite as ashamed.

Never one to miss an opportunity to inflict pain, my mind refuses to let go of the agony. Instead, it supplies it with a new source, my reaction to Christian's refusal. Guilt wells within me and regret over my outburst weighs me down.

I should have stayed out there. I should have talked to him about this. But I'm not sure I can be that vulnerable with him, yet.

Clothes fall to the floor, and I step into the water's welcoming embrace, thankful as always that we prioritized the water heater when we hooked up the solar panels. Maybe, just maybe, the hot liquid can pry guilt's cold fingers off my heart.

"Not likely," I scoff.

Yet, I try to ease my pain.

"I'm not weak. I will not be made a victim by my desires. My emotions will not rule me. They *will not* leave me helpless." I speak the words aloud, pronouncing every syllable carefully, but the water masks the sound. No one outside the bathroom could hope to hear my little pep talk.

I close my eyes and lean my head against the wall of the shower, letting the water run over my back, hating what Christian must think of me. My hands rest atop my head, threaded through my hair.

"He didn't mean any of this…"

Through gritted teeth, I spit, "I'm just fucked up. That isn't *his* fault." My hands release my hair, abandoning my skull for the wall and making tight fists upon it.

"Goddamn it…" Head shaking, I don't see where the tears land. Somewhere. It doesn't matter. "Why is this still *so hard*?"

STOP! NO!

"Deep breaths…Just. Breathe."

I count each beat of my heart, giving my mind something solid to focus on.

One.

Two.

Three.

Four.

Five.

Maybe then my thoughts will stop spiraling.

"I'm not fucked up. I'm not."

Inhale.

Exhale.

Blistering hot water pummels my shoulder blades, beating the knots into submission.

"I'm hurt. That's all."

Inhale.

Exhale.

"I'm healing."

Unclenching shaking hands, I repeat it. "I'm healing. I have to be patient. Just…"

Inhale.

"Breathe."

Exhale.

***

The morning passes too quickly, yet crawls at a snail's pace. Terrified that I might see a loss of respect in Christian's eyes, worried he may pity me, I get up before he and Jackson even consider rising. I drank considerably less than either of them last night and wake easily at 6:00.

I eat a quick breakfast of buttered bread with milk, unwilling to cook anything for fear of waking them. Silently, I head out to the barn, knowing I'll be milking alone, today. It's best to get an early start. After all, Jackson and Christian will be at Melissa and Bradley's fixing that fence when they get up.

Delicate fronds of frost decorate the windows and make the grass crunch beneath my feet. My breath steams out in great clouds in the grey air, and I rub my arms for a bit of added warmth. My gloves catch on my wool hoodie, sliding strangely from side to side over my hands.

I make a mental note to check the greenhouses, missing the days of semi-reliable weather forecasts. Had I known it would frost, I would've taken the plants indoors.

No help for it, now.

I go to the pen in the barn, and my least favorite cow is right at the gate, trying to muscle her way past another to get out. Groaning, I tell her to wait her turn, chiding myself for wasting my breath.

Of course, as soon as the gate is open, Trish tries pushing her way out. Thankfully, the other stops her, eager to be milked. I point a finger at the troublemaker and say, "You're the next one in the freezer, I swear."

When I sit to begin milking, an odd crinkle sounds from the front pocket of my jeans. The wrapper of the condom. I forgot to put it back in my room and didn't think about it when I put the same jeans on this morning.

I fish it out of my pocket and stare at it for a moment. It expires May 20, two months from now. Briefly, I consider throwing the thing away so I don't have to think about it but decide against the pointless waste.

I'll just give it to Melissa and Bradley.

I shove it deep into my pocket and as far from my mind as I can manage. Rerouting my thoughts, I focus on the date. March 20th. The first official day of spring. We'll be planting, soon. I organize the garden in my mind, looking forward to the feel of the soil in my hands and the warm sun on my skin.

Lost in my reverie for nearly an hour, I don't notice the sound of approaching footsteps until they venture into the barn. My head jerks up, and my hands still on an udder. Jackson and Christian walk my way, sleep still tugging heavily on their eyelids.

"Good morning," I say. I quickly go back to work, dipping my eyes away from them, letting them fall to the steam wafting up from the bucket of warm milk and the straw beneath it. I keep my eyes trained on my hands, tugging skillfully at the cow's udder.

My periphery tells me Christian's gaze rarely lifts from the floor. Just as well. I'm not quite ready to face him, yet. If ever.

I feel my old reclusive tendencies creeping up within me. Poisonous vines twist around my vocal cords, stopping me from speaking.

"You should've woke us up," Jackson says. "We would've helped."

"You needed to sleep off the Mead," I feign a chuckle, forcing my tone to lighten. "Can't have you hammering nails with a headache."

It's solid logic, and I know it. Hard to argue with that. I suspect Jackson may see through my tone, but at least this way he might not ask about it for the time being.

"I guess," he says. "Still, though."

I toss him a look, my best attempt at, "Please. I've got this," and rise, ready to release this cow into the pasture. Halfway done.

Jackson rolls his eyes, and says, "You're too independent for your own good."

Don't I know it...

Turning, Jackson slaps Christian on the shoulder and, sticking his tongue out at me, says, "Let's go get the eggs brought in before we leave."

***

With morning chores out of the way, I meander over to see Calista with the basket of my bike filled with candles. I need to deliver them, but that isn't the real reason for my visit. It's merely an excuse. I need company. I don't want to sink back into isolation.

For years, I lived nearly alone, only interacting with Jackson and my counselor, Mary. When things get stressful, I always feel myself going back there. Solitude pulls at my feet like quicksand, dragging me into the mire.

I hated it then, and I hate it, now. Back then, the warning signs were masked by fear and worry that no one would want someone so broken. Now that I've been trained against it, I see it happening.

So, hands shaking, candles cradled against my chest, I knock on Calista's door, determined to pull myself free from the muck of anxiety. It won't go away, I know. It will always be there, tucked away in a dark spot concealed in the forest of my mind, but I've learned to cope much more efficiently than I once did.

Antidepressants aren't an option anymore with the majority having been looted from pharmacies for recreational use long ago. I just have to rely on the coping mechanisms Mary taught me. That, and sheer force of will.

Calista opens the door, and her cardigan flows with the gentle breeze. Warm eyes like melted chocolate soften further when she takes in my expression.

"What happened?" Calista asks, stepping aside to allow me to pass.

"I fucked up," I say.

I enter and slip my shoes off in the entryway. Moving to the dining room, my feet relax into the plush red area rug, and I set the candles down on the table.

Calista has bundles of yarn strewn about the mahogany surface, organized by color and ready for knitting. I watch my friend gather her knitting needles and pull up a chair. She sits farther back from the table than ever before with the twins in her belly growing steadily.

"Want to talk about it?" Calista asks.

Light cascades through the bay window behind her and sparkles on the knitting needles. Taking the seat across from her, I sit and watch my friend's nimble fingers work.

"Not yet," I say with a sigh. "I just need some company, for now." It feels like an admission of weakness. Rationally, I know Calista would never judge me for this, but my heart still fears a smirk, a cruel look.

Or worse…a cruel thought and a fake smile.

"Okay," Calista says. Smiling compassionately, she adds, "Me, too, actually. I've been psyching myself out all morning worrying about the babies." Her hands stop moving, and one rubs her stomach protectively.

My brows furrow, asking silently for Calista to go on. To remind me that the drama between Christian and I isn't all that big of a deal, after all.

"I'm just scared they'll come too early." Reluctantly, she pulls her hand from her stomach and resumes her work, needles clicking together madly. "Holden says I'm healthy, and that the babies are healthy, as far as he can tell. He says there's no reason for me not to go to full term."

"Then, what's got you worried?"

"I…I don't know. Nothing, I guess. Just overthinking." She barely lifts her eyes, and when she does, it's only to stare at the ceiling, wiping away tears.

"Sorry," Calista says. "I just always thought…my mom would be here to tell me to stop worrying. I thought she'd be here for my babies."

Tears stream down her face in earnest causing my eyes to prick with sympathy. Pushing back from the table, I round it and sit next to my friend. Pulling her into my arms, I do what little I can to comfort her.

Calista shoves away her knitting work and leans into my embrace. "I miss her," she sobs. "I'm supposed to have my mom here. She's supposed to walk me through all this pregnancy stuff. She's my mom and she isn't here…"

I remember the day we heard about the bombing of St. Louis. Calista's mom was there for an appointment with her heart doctor, despite Calista's attempts to get her to reschedule.

She had a weird feeling about it.

Funny how accurate those can be sometimes.

But it had taken nearly a month and a half to get that appointment. The next available one was two months out. She had two weeks' worth of medication left and had to have a check-up before more could be prescribed. So, Joanna went.

Then, the bombs dropped.

Calista was a wreck. Barely talked, barely left her house for nearly two months. Everyone in town pitched in to pick up the slack with their farm, shearing alpacas and planting their garden.

Now, just like then, Calista weeps openly in my arms, body shaking and breath catching in desperate hiccups. "She should *be* here," Calista intones, heart breaking, all over again.

With no other recourse in sight, I rub my friend's back as calmly and reassuringly as I can. The pain of losing my own parents by fate's cruel hands rather than those of nature creeps back up inside me, but I've had far longer to process the ache.

Impossible as it seemed at the time, life went on. I adjusted to their absence, and in time, so will Calista. Knowing that those words won't help, having heard all the lame things people say in unsuccessful attempts at comfort, I stay quiet, opting to let her cry it out, a release I doubt she's had.

Holden undoubtedly wants to help, but men tend to seek ways to fix the problem in place of merely venting. As this can't be fixed, that method is woefully unhelpful. I'm sure the poor guy feels helpless because of it. Of course, the stress and hormones of pregnancy don't exactly make any of this easier for either of them.

After nearly fifteen minutes, Calista's sobs ease, and an even, sturdy pace reasserts itself over her lungs. Under her breath, she reassures herself, "It's just part of God's plan."

Her words dig at me, but Calista doesn't notice the slight stiffening of my posture.

She extricates herself from my arms, thanking me profusely and leaving me with a dilemma. At long last, the openness of the window at my back bothers me enough that I venture back to my original seat, craving the comfort of a wall at my back.

Within moments, I find myself venting to Calista about the mess with Christian, though mildly less agitated about it now that I've been given some perspective.

By the end of it, Calista speaks aloud the conclusion I was dreading. "Just talk to him. You guys need to sort this out or you're just going to be bitter about it after he leaves."

Her words echo Mary, my counselor. "Face it now, or face it always," she said one day. The words ring true, even now, in a completely different context. Nevertheless, knowing the necessity of digging my way out doesn't lessen the strain of wielding the shovel.

"I was afraid you'd say that," I say, fiddling with the end of some red yarn.

The natural fiber shines almost orange in the sunlight streaming through the window. Unable to lift my eyes, I study its strands, trying to hide from the confrontation I know I must instigate.

Sighing, I force myself to set it down gently, all while forcefully shoving my hermit-like tendencies away. How tempting it is to build myself a little hovel near the quicksand of my depression and social anxiety…How it calls to me, promising a life free of the let-downs and stress of other people.

But I know it also shields me from the happiness of companionship, the freedom of laughing with a friend…the embrace of a loved one. All the best parts of life are kept so far from that place, and I know the minor comforts of total solitude are too high a cost to pay.

A fortifying breath gives strength to my legs, raising me from my chair. That same breath exits my body on a, "Thank you," uttered sincerely, and carries me to the front door of my friend's home, a friend I wouldn't have if I moored myself to the quicksand.

With shaking hands and a stomach full of butterflies, knees practically knocking together with each step, I push myself home. That's where Christian and Jackson should be by now. I hope they will be…and hope they won't.

Just get it over with, while you've still got the nerve.

Yet I hope for the relief of finding them absent. Not that I'd be able to relax. I'd just sit there, drowning in a slimy black pool of dread, conveniently located next door to the quicksand.

The nip in the air, fended off by my scarf and hoodie, goes unnoticed, as does the warmth of the sun on my face. The colors of the grass, trees, and spring's earliest daffodils all bleed together, lost on my unfocused eyes.

All I see are the blurred shapes of my feet, one step after another, against the gray backdrop of old, crumbling pavement.

Muscle memory takes over, dragging me home while my mind ruminates on the million different ways my upcoming conversation with Christian can explode in my face. Birds chirp overhead. But all I hear are the ways Christian can reject me, yet again, and thoughts of my own un-worth.

Before I know it, the massive windows in the peak of the second story, the master suite, loom over me, dark ever since my parents' deaths. A weary eye searches for Deadweight, hoping and not hoping to see her. The UTV's absence sparks a fierce undercurrent of anxiety, raging beneath a peaceful surface wave of relief.

The lull of, "I've done what I can, for now. I can hide away for a bit," pulls me through the burgundy front door, down the hall, and into my bedroom.

Given the circumstances, I allow myself a rare treat, the comfort of music. Shaky fingers plug the stereo in and press play on the CD. I don't bother trying the radio, knowing the static will come too close to an auditory representation of my nerves, only serving to stir them into a deeper frenzy.

Falling onto my bed with my favorite band crashing around me, I wait.

Chapter 24

Christian

Sweat beads on my forehead, despite the chilly morning. If I were anywhere else, without a warm hearth with hot chocolate and warm stew to chase winter's last hoorah from my bones, the sweat could well spell my doom.

Here, though, it merely calms my mind. The exertion, the work I'm finally able to do with my hands, and the feeling of usefulness combine into a potent tonic, soothing my soul.

Bradley, Jackson, and I work well together, and Bradley keeps the conversation light, for which I'm grateful. The two farmers lament the lack of power tools, having long since relinquished them to the list of luxuries they can't afford to waste batteries or electricity on.

I don't mind it so much as my companions seem to. Rather, I enjoy the pull of my muscles as I cut up the offending branch with a hand saw and pull it off the fence, bit by bit. Likewise, each swing of the hammer takes me just a bit closer to clarity, in a way no nail gun ever could. In my own home, in my woodshop, power tools were nearly always a last resort.

By the time we finish our work, my spirits have lifted. I no longer feel ashamed of myself. Though still stressed over everything with Chloe, my mind is clearer.

The removal of my stitches and my imminent return to Breyerville loom large on the horizon, but I accept my fate. This is just the way of it.

I'll try to smooth things out with Chloe before I leave. Then, I may or may not die quickly.

My death is almost guaranteed, at least in my mind, but I know I'll do what I can to save Karen and Tate. That's good enough for me.

I'm not sure what awaits me in the afterlife if anything, but I hope it's better than the short life I'll leave behind. Staring out across the field, I lean upon the newly repaired fence.

I'll miss this place and these people, though.

Bradley and Melissa show their thanks with a warm meal and pleasantries about how good it's been having me around. Their goodbye is shorter than the customary Midwest farewell, as it only happens twice.

Climbing into the UTV, I let my eyes roam over this peaceful place. The rolling pastures and the lines of fences, the gentle breeze swishing through the grass. It all stirs something deep in my soul, begging me not to leave.

From the driver's seat, Jackson asks, "So, what happened with Chloe?"

Uh oh.

The hairs on the back of my neck stand, fearing the conversation to come.

This isn't something I expected. I can't just say, "Well, we almost had sex."

To her brother.

Awkwardness lands in the seat between us, flopping around like a dying fish, and I struggle for words.

With a single sideways glance, Jackson says, "Come on. You guys were a mess this morning.

Obviously, something happened. Maybe I can help. I know her pretty well."

For a minute, we cruise along, creeping at just above a snail's pace. When I appear unsure what to say, Jackson starts talking.

"Sorry if I seem…overly involved. I just want her to be happy. She's my baby sister. And she's had such a shitty life…" He stares ahead, mind clearly elsewhere. "I couldn't protect her when it happened. I was on some stupid, shitty date, with a girl I wasn't even sure I liked…"

His voice becomes unsteady, and he pulls off to the side of the road, staring into a field overgrown with prairie grass. Several minutes pass in silence before he finally continues. "I just…I tried to take care of her, after. I don't know how well I did, but…I tried."

"You're too hard on yourself," I say. "She doesn't blame you for not being there. Chloe loves you. She knows how much you've done for her."

The lump in my throat makes it hard to speak, and the one in Jackson's is almost visible behind his Adam's apple. Head leaning against the headrest, he holds his gaze upon the field, reluctant to look at me.

The pressures of being the big brother and the need to care for the younger sibling pull at my heartstrings in a desperate reminder of my own helpless life. Of course, it's different. Chloe's still around, stronger than ever and pushing forward. Jackson helped her rebuild herself. He pulled her through when she didn't think herself strong enough to go on.

But Jesse…
I failed him.

In the end, I couldn't help him. I couldn't stop him from giving in to the monstrous rage within him.

I couldn't stop the bullet that put him down like an unwanted animal.

Perhaps, on the ride to Breyerville or when I pick my way through the water treatment plant, I'll be able to find some peace with that, too.

I swallow hard.

Better not hold my breath.

I can't fix what happened, nor can I change it.

Turning from the overwhelming waves of anguish which surge toward me, I force my mind to the things I can mend. This fledgling relationship with Chloe, short-lived as it will be.

"We…um…" I clear my throat, not quite believing that I'm attempting to say these things to Chloe's brother. "We…almost…"

Jackson nods his understanding, sparing me the unbelievable awkwardness of saying more.

"I just…couldn't."

Too late, I realize the other possible interpretations of my words and hasten to clear it up. "I didn't want her to hurt more in the long run. One of us had to think it through, and—"

"Did you say that to her? That last bit?" Jackson cuts me off.

"Yeah…"

"Jesus *fuck*, man," Jackson chuckles.

My eyebrows raise, unsure what to make of his reaction.

"How'd *that* go over?" Morbid laughter spills from Chloe's very odd brother.

It's infectious. Self-deprecating mirth lifts my lips as I say, "Not well."

With a quick slap on my knee, Jackson backs the UTV away from the field and begins driving again. "She's a big girl, okay? She knows what she's doing," he chuckles. Sobering up considerably, he adds, "Just don't act like sex or emotion make her weak. That's kind-of a…*thing*…for her. She can explain that more, if she wants to, just don't say *that*, again."

I nod, still unsure of the man beside me, and watch the grass beside the road as we speed along. My eyes are knocked out of focus by the fast-moving stalks and pebbles nearest the road, only restored when I lift my gaze to the tree line dotting the horizon. I find myself wishing for the quickly appearing and disappearing lines of the planted fields of old.

***

The moment I step into the house, a wondrous sound greets me. Music. How long has it been since I heard music? The answer eludes me.

Dark, grungy folk music reaches out from Chloe's room, calling me to her. A low, feminine voice beckons seductively over slow, heavy drum beats and haunting violin. Background vocals bring to mind the howls of a siren, luring sailors into the mist.

I never would have listened to something like this before, but now, having heard no music at all for a couple of years, having been submerged in a veritable hell, I couldn't think of a better reintroduction. I always stuck to alternative rock, but this darker stuff seems more appropriate for this new world.

Plush carpet cradles my feet as I walk toward Chloe's room. The music grows louder on approach, relaxing me with every step despite the terrible potential of the upcoming conversation.

Leaning against Chloe's doorframe, I find her sitting on her bed, reclining against the headboard. Her knees are drawn up nearly to her chest, and her sketchpad rests on her lap, open to a blank page. She holds a pencil rather loosely and stares into nothingness.

"Can I come in?" I ask sheepishly.

Startled, Chloe turns quickly to look at me. She takes a deep breath before nodding, leaving the impression that she's been dreading this.

That bodes well.

Chloe throws her feet off the bed and crosses to her stereo. Turning the volume down, she gestures for me to sit on her bed. Waiting for her to speak, I sit, uncertain.

Chloe shuts the door, and her hands press into it for a moment before she turns to face me. Footsteps border on reluctant as she pulls herself to the bed. When she sits next to me, her hands shake in her lap.

Baby steps.

I reach over and wrap my hand around hers. Her fingers tremble against mine, but at long last, she looks me in the eye.

"I'm sorry," Chloe begins. "I didn't handle yesterday…very well."

"No, Chloe, you don't need to apologize. You're fine."

She shakes her head and drops her eyes to the floor. Another deep breath raises her chest. "It just…hurt, I guess."

I watch her shoulders lift in a painful shrug.

"I *am* capable of thinking these things through," she says. "I'm not some animal. I know there are risks. Believe me, I weighed it out for days on end. I thought about this."

Sighing, she continues, "You can't protect everyone, *all the time*. I know it's sorta your thing, but you can't do it constantly. Protecting Karen and Tate from Jesse…Yeah, that made sense. I saw him when we found you. He was a big guy."

Her casual use of the past tense makes me flinch and holds my lips still.

"Protecting them from The Wolf and his Fangs. Makes sense." Her hand lies limp in mine, and the other trembles freely on her lap. Pausing, she steadies it by clenching it upon her knee.

Finally, Chloe looks back up at me. "Protecting me from a decision that *I made*? Can't be done." She shakes her head. "I chose it. No matter what, there are consequences for me. I knew that, and I chose to accept those consequences. That's not something you can protect me from."

I try desperately not to get lost analyzing my entire life, but I really do spend most of my time worrying about protecting everyone around me. I just never considered doing otherwise. Growing up, I wanted to protect Jesse from the world around us, from our parents…from his own self-destructive tendencies.

Releasing Chloe's hand, I rise and pace for a moment, finally settling by the window. One hand runs over my face, smudging my features around, and the other comes to rest on my hip.

How many times have I messed things up, thinking I knew best?

I work through my life, straining to see what I thought was a good character trait as a flaw.

How many people were driven away by my need to save them from everything? How many times did perpetual victims flock to me, thinking their life would be easier with a rescuer on hand?

How much extra stress did I bring on myself?

My head spins as memories flood me, showing me all the times I let myself be taken advantage of.

Sure, in this case, it was ushered forward by Grant, the slimy bastard, but looking back...It isn't the only time I've stepped on my own toes trying to help someone.

Staring out, I listen as Chloe continues, putting an end to my internal monologue.

"If..." She sighs, hesitating. "If you didn't want to because your mind was elsewhere...If you don't want to do that with *me*, that's one thing. That's fine. Hell, it's understandable."

Pain coats her words, and I turn to find her on her feet. "If it's me you have a problem with, say so. If you were just...*protecting* me..." she shakes her head, determined. "Don't."

In a few steps, I cross the room, only to pause in front of her. Suddenly, every action needs to be thought out, repeatedly. I want to wipe the worry and doubt off her face, but is it for the sake of being the savior? Or something else?

My heart aches to see her so pained, and my arms itch to wrap around her. I know that when I leave she'll hurt, to some degree. But she's made it infinitely clear that I shouldn't worry over that.

So, I loosen my control over my arms, letting them reach out. They fold themselves around Chloe's waist, pulling her to me.

A great gust of air rushes from her, and she leans against me.

Knots of tension fall slack, and I relax against her, letting the quiet music lull me further. My head dips, resting atop hers, and the scent of her gorgeous red hair fills me. I breathe deep, and warmth spreads through me.

Closing my eyes, I whisper, "Of course, I wanted to."

Within me, the depth of my feelings for Chloe rises into my consciousness, and I wonder how I could have fallen so far, so fast. A million different answers flit through my mind. Nightingale syndrome, the intensity of the situation and the emotions of it all being attributed to her, the relief of finding good people, the need for companionship after so long spent purely in the company of family…

But none of those explanations stick around long. I know they're all wrong. As I draw back and lift her chin, the vibrant green of her eyes overwhelms me, and I know.

It's her.

Nothing else explains it. No one else could have pulled me in so fast.

My heart flails wildly in my chest, nervous and all a-twitter. Eyes fluttering slightly, I lean in, testing the waters.

She doesn't flinch. Rather, she lifts her head, breathing rapidly, and tentatively brushes her lips against mine.

The air around us swelters, pulsing with the beguiling music. Gravity builds between us, and all at once, our mouths crash together. Frantic hands pull at clothing and tangle in hair. Eyes beg, and lips land hotly upon exposed skin.

Feet shuffle to the bed.

Chapter 25

Chloe

Basking in the afterglow of our love, I relish the feel of Christian's fingers tracing indecipherable patterns on my back. I scoot in closer, pressing against his side, and wrap an arm around his waist. With one leg thrown over his lap, I nearly lay on top of him, and I'm surprised by my own openness.

Perhaps it comes down to the slow, gentle treatment he just afforded me, determined not to rush. His patience and restraint certainly won him a great many points in my book, whether it was done for my comfort or his own preference.

Caressing my thigh, Christian speaks after several silent moments of breath-catching. "How did you guys set this place up so well?" His voice is dreamy and low with the threat of a nap.

"Well," I begin, "we were lucky everything started in spring. Those of us who didn't have a garden planted or in the works traded with the Amish people down the road for seeds. They helped, so much."

My hand splays across Christian's chest, threading through a tiny patch of hair.

"We got some more things planted, and we hunted and foraged in the meantime. The first winter was still rough, though." A long sigh escapes me as I remember digging graves in rock hard dirt.

"We lost people. We didn't put back enough for everyone. The ones who survived lost all their fast food weight and their beer bellies," I say, laughing humorlessly. "We even lost a few to the Amish. They converted, thinking God took everything to show us how terribly we'd been living."

Christian chuckles, and his chest quakes beneath my head.

"What is it?" I ask.

"Just…people attributing things to God when they have no idea what's going on. All that 'God works in mysterious ways' crap." Sighing, he quiets his laughter.

"I hate that saying," I say, studying my hand closely. "I *hate* that, and I hate when people say that God never gives you more than you can handle. Because it's bullshit. People commit suicide all the time because they *can't* handle what they've been given."

Fully ranting now, I go on. "I hate when people say the shit you go through makes you a better person. *No.* That gives credit to the assholes who hurt other people. I am who I am because *I* struggled onward, because Jackson helped me, because my counselor helped me, because I pulled myself through it. *Not* because of that fucking asshole. *He* did *not* shape me. *I* did."

Teeth gritted, I say, "The whole 'better for it' line of bullshit implies I should be thankful for that bastard, that I should be thankful that God *tested* me."

Inhaling pure anger, I say, "Fuck that."

I shake my head and add, "Needless to say, me and God aren't on good terms. At least, not the Christian, father-figure, all-seeing, all-powerful God."

Craning his neck to look into my eyes, Christian asks, "That version of God, specifically?"

"That version, *especially.*"

I try my best to keep acid from dripping off my words as I explain. "Let's put it in human terms, here. If a human father *watched* as his daughter was raped and did *nothing* to stop it, even though he could, just because he thought she'd be better off for it if she didn't kill herself…that man would go to prison. The other criminals would probably kill him. But because it's God," I pause, partly for breath and partly for emphasis, "I'm supposed to worship him. No."

"Huh," Christian says. "I never really looked at it quite like that." A small nod of understanding moves him beneath me. "Who was it…? Einstein? I don't know. Someone said he thought God made us, then just let us be, unable to intervene. Somehow, that's more comforting than a father that just stands by, ignoring us."

I nod slowly, realizing everything I've just said. Here, deep in the Bible Belt, the words I just uttered are sacrilege. To say such things so openly before the collapse would certainly have been considered blasphemy by all my neighbors, my friends.

"I've never said any of that to anyone before," I whisper.

Not even Jackson.

His faith was shaken when I was raped and our parents were killed, but it never completely crumbled. I never understood it.

Though Jackson never questioned it, he didn't understand why I fell so far from the church, why I didn't look to the heavens for comfort. He didn't push, but he didn't get it, either.

Yet, impossibly, Christian does.

Having opened up more easily than I expected, I wonder at the amount of progress I've made. I actively sought out company to fight off my depression. I've become more confident than I ever thought I'd manage. I allowed myself to be vulnerable with Christian. Hell, for the second time in my life, I willingly had sex.

All of these things were once unimaginably difficult for me, near impossible.

My chest fills with a gust of pride and tears prick at the corners of my eyes as I look back on just how far I've come.

There's so far yet to go, but maybe…maybe I'll get there.

Christian yawns softly, and my body answers with a yawn of my own. Heart and mind soothed by the rhythmic breaths raising and lowering Christian's chest, I drift into a peaceful slumber.

***

I do my best not to drag my feet as Christian and I walk hand in hand to the community center. Time to get our stitches out. Which means that Christian will have to go. I sigh, but the smile never leaves my face. No matter what, I know I would rather have known him than never to have met him, at all.

On entering the medical portion of the community center, we find Calista and Holden, the former hurriedly shoving her arms into the sleeves of her jacket and the latter rushing to button his fly. I contain a smirk at the turn the afternoon took for several of Harville's residents.

With freshly washed hands, Holden begins with the stitches on Christian's scalp. "Now, I may snip a few hairs, in the process," he warns, assembling his tools.

"Oh no," Christian jests. "You mean my hair might be uneven? How will I cope?" He shakes his head, and I smile at him.

"It's ok," Calista says, tone intentionally patronizing. "My hair grows faster on one side than it does on the other. It's always uneven."

Glancing at his wife quite flirtatiously, Holden quips, "Your *face* is uneven."

"Gee thanks," she says with a laugh. "I'd rather it be my hair. I can *fix* that."

Wrapping his arms around her waist, Holden says, "I'm kidding. You're beautiful."

Under any other circumstances, the kiss they share might have made my cheeks warm with embarrassment. Today, it merely brings a smile to my face and sends my eyes darting toward Christian.

He smiles back warmly, and my insides melt. A little voice in the back of my mind warns me of our impending goodbye, but my heart shoves it away, determined not to have this moment ruined.

"This isn't the end," my silly little heart insists.

***

After receiving a clean bill of health, we gather Jackson and, unfortunately, Grant. Venturing so close to Breyerville without filling Deadweight to the brim with manpower would be stupid, and Grant can handle himself pretty well when called upon to do so.

My heart spasms as we load a few guns into the bed and pack our pockets with extra magazines.

"It can't be put off any longer," I remind myself, muttering under my breath as I load a couple of boxes of ammo into the bed alongside the rifles. My .45 is strapped to my thigh, and its weight comforts me.

A glance at Christian, at his magnificent eyes and that shaggy hair, almost makes me want to ask about eating first to ensure it's good and dark when we arrive. To spend just a little more time with him.

I think he almost asks, but he holds the words in.

The thought of his sister-in-law and his nephew going through hell stills my tongue.

If he can be strong, if he can go back, I have no right to stall him.

We pack some food to eat on the way, then pile in with the sun sagging in the sky. Gray air surrounds us as we pull onto the road.

Christian asks, "How far is it?"

I squeeze his hand, resting squarely upon my knee.

Beside me, Jackson answers, "About an hour," and turns onto the main highway.

Christian nods and falls silent.

Grasslands dotted with patches of trees whir past.

An hour. Such a short span of time.

Just an hour to decide.

I squeeze Christian's hand and take a deep breath.

Chapter 26

Karen

One granola bar each. One bottle of water each. A can of green beans to split. Certainly not bad for a late lunch. A veritable feast awaits in the single cabinet with still more stashed in the fridge. And the dishwasher. And the stove.

Lyla really put herself to work before she…

I cut off the thought, unable to dwell on it for long. I say a silent thanks to the sweet woman and take another bite, savoring the little chocolate chips in the granola. Tate loves it even more than I do, especially thankful for the sweets, and scarfs it down in just a few bites.

Sighing, I smile. It does my heart good to see him enjoy himself. It's nothing compared to the dinners we shared before, but we've been eating a far cry better recently. Another silent thanks to Lyla floats through my mind.

I've been saying a lot of those, lately.

Reaching out, I smooth the shaggy curls out of Tate's eyes. He smiles and grabs another green bean from the can. The juice drips off it, splashing onto the floor on the way to his mouth. Popping it onto his tongue, he does a little "I have yummy food" dance, shimmying on his little bitty butt.

I giggle, rather freely. I cast my mind over the stockpile of food and relish the length of time I can be free of the brothel. An easy breath enters and exits my body, soft and quiet. Weight falls off my shoulders.

We eat, mostly in silence, and afterward, Tate only puts up a mild protest when asked to help clean up. Not that it takes long. We just gather up the trash and toss it into our metal trash can. It's nearly full, so I make a mental note to take it out to burn tomorrow.

A brutal fist pounds upon the door, jarring me from my otherwise serene evening. Eyes wide like a deer in headlights, I look up at the door, vibrating in its frame. Panic-stricken, Tate looks at me, uncertain of his next move.

I whisper, "Go to your room. Lock your door and don't come out unless I say so."

Nodding, Tate runs for his little sanctuary. I wait until I hear his lock click before saying, "Who is it?" I manage to keep my voice from cracking, though only just.

"Who the FUCK do you *think* it is?" A hand slams against the door for emphasis and my blood runs cold.

The Wolf.

I swallow, trying to force a lump down. It doesn't work, doesn't even come close.

"Open your fucking door."

Billy.

I shudder, eyes fluttering with the disgust that courses through me.

Why are they here?

My hesitation is not met with patience or forgiveness.

One of the angry men pounds his fist against the door again, over and over. "OPEN THE GODDAMN DOOR, KAREN!" Anger distorts the voice, and I can't tell which man it is.

Glancing at Tate's room, I reassure myself that it's locked and force myself to the front door. My hand pauses on the handle, and I take a few deep breaths.

The door handle jerks in my hand, rattled from the other side, and the door shakes madly.

The Wolf shouts, "FUCKING MOVE IT!"

I throw back the deadbolt and turn the lock. Within seconds, the knob turns, and they push the door open so violently that it knocks me back several steps. I stumble into the metal arm of the futon and nearly go over it onto the worn cushion.

Voice low and dripping menace, The Wolf stalks into the room. Towering over my tiny frame, he snarls, "Where've you been, bitch?'

Likely an attractive man if his face wasn't constantly twisted by malice, his dark eyes lean toward malevolent rather than smoldering. Long lashes serve as a dark outline, adding to the effect instead of mediating it. A few jagged scars claw their way down from his hairline, shredding their way down to his right cheekbone. He said they were from a car crash, back before he revealed his true colors.

No one believes that anymore.

In one swift movement, he shoves me, forcing me over the arm of the futon. I fall back, heart in my throat, and land hard upon the seat. Metal bars beat into my poor back, still struggling to heal from the last time I was at the brothel.

I wince, but I keep my lips firmly shut, holding in a cry.

"It's only been a few days..." I sob. "I was rationing our food, but we're out, now." It's a bald-faced lie that I desperately hope they won't see through. "I'll be there tonight, I promise."

I roll to my side, meaning to get up from the futon. Lying there feels so much more vulnerable than standing, not that I can do much either way.

Utterly defeated, it doesn't even surprise me when Billy rushes forward and drags me into the floor. "Damn right, you'll be there. You're coming with us, now. Fucking move! Get your ass up." He leers at me cruelly, and I know I'm in for it.

Tonight will be unbearable.

I swallow back my fear. Careful not to yelp or cry out in any way, hoping not to scare Tate any more than he likely already is, I rise to my feet.

I turn toward Billy but don't look him in the eye. I don't look at the scarred sections of his arm where he picked ceaselessly when he used Meth before. I don't look at the new scratches from whatever drugs he uses, now. I simply stare at the floor, waiting for him to move toward the door so I can follow behind.

But he doesn't move.

"Where's that little brat of yours?" The Wolf asks, practically spitting the words.

My eyes shoot upward, spearing him for even daring to mention Tate. My lips seal themselves shut, lest I say something I'll pay for later.

"I said. Where. Is. He. Or are you too stupid to speak?" The Wolf tips his head to the side and adds, "You really are a fucking idiot, aren't you?"

Grateful that he's moved back to insulting me, I drop my gaze, showing submission. My heart panics, afraid that he'll come back around, afraid that he'll use

Tate to hurt me. This man's veins run black. No deed is too dark.

Mouth dry, I swallow audibly.

Recognizing the moods of his master, Billy moves aside just in time to avoid being shoved out of the way, and The Wolf bears down upon me. His hand winds its way into my long, black hair, using it to jerk my head back. Forcing eye contact, close enough that his spit lands on my face, he shouts, "WHERE THE FUCK IS HE!?"

His black eyes bore into me, and I worry that his infernal soul may infect me. Still, I say nothing, my only defiance.

So The Wolf drags me, nearly ripping my hair out by the root, over to the only closed door in the apartment. Tate's room. He knows where Tate is. There are only so many places to hide here.

I grab at my hair, trying desperately to lessen the tension on it. I strain my neck, lifting my head up into The Wolf's palm, hoping to ease the pain.

All the while, my mind riots against the horror of The Wolf coming here for Tate.

"NO, LEAVE HIM ALONE!"

I scream and beg, to no avail, promising to come by more often. I barely manage to fight off the images of suffering that The Wolf might inflict upon my poor, baby boy. I spare no energy for fending off the tears, letting them flow freely down my cheeks.

At Tate's door, The Wolf slams my head into its frame. My vision blurs and my head threatens to split open. I inhale sharply, barely containing a whimper. Behind us, Billy laughs at my pain. His vocal cords rasp, low and creaking.

"Please, don't hurt Tate. Oh, God, please, don't hurt him," I sob.

But I'm not sure where God is, or where He's been for the past couple years, for that matter. The words are a habit, a plea, nothing more.

I'm not sure He'll help me, no matter how much I beg.

Pulling my head up by my hair, lifting so high I have to crane my neck and stand on tiptoes, The Wolf growls in my ear, "Shut the fuck up, bitch."

Then, he speaks through the door. "Time to come out and play, little boy. Time to learn what it means to be a man."

My heart stops, and my chest collapses. Soft whimpering sneaks out beneath the door, mingled with the sounds of tiny feet padding across the floor.

A fresh wave of panic raises my voice a few octaves, and I begTate not to come out. "Stay in there, baby. Mommy's fine. Stay in there, please. Don't come out!"

The Wolf slams my head against the doorframe, harder this time, and I can't stop the cry of pain that leaks out.

"I thought I told you to Shut UP!" the Wolf growls.

The lock turns, and I grapple for the doorknob, desperate to hold the door shut. "NO! Tate, lock the door! Please, baby, lock the door!" I plead, begging the universe, God, and everything good that once existed in the world to keep my baby safe.

But The Wolf yanks hard on my hair.

I cry out again but don't let go of the doorknob. The door shudders with the force.

Releasing my hair, The Wolf opts for a more direct route. He shoves me with all his considerable might.

My hands lose grip.

I stumble back, slamming into the wall.

Before I can regain my footing, before my mind can finish screaming out in agony, Tate opens the door. With tears pouring from my eyes, I lunge for him. I throw myself between him and The Wolf, wrapping my arms around him.

"No, no, no, no, no, no." The word spills over my lips and reverberates through my mind, a prayer and a condemnation, all at once.

The Wolf stands over me, smug and obviously aroused by my agony. I manage not to vomit all over my son, though just barely.

"Honey, I told you to stay in there!" I croon, trying desperately to think of a way to lock him in, again. Every plan is a dead end, though. Heart racing, lungs struggling to find air, I cry before my son.

"I know," he whispers. A few tears linger on his thick eyelashes, and the tracks of their fellows stain his cheeks. "I'm sorry. I was so scared, but…They were hurting you. I had to come out. I had to do the right thing, even though I was scared." He puts one tiny hand to my cheek, and says, "Like you said before."

My blood freezes in my veins. I pull Tate to my chest, pressing his head into my neck.

What have I done?

***

Forced to leave my home with a gun pressed to my spine, I cradle Tate, clutching him tightly as we walk through town. I keep my pace even, afraid that any sudden move may pull a bullet from the thing. At this range, it would go straight through me, into Tate.

On all sides, rubble and garbage line the streets. Brittle wind grates against my nerves, and Tate shivers in my arms, defenseless against the cold in only a t-shirt and his little jeans.

"We'll get through this," I whisper, angling my face so the tears on my cheek don't touch him, don't spoil him, though this night likely will.

His spirit, as yet unbroken, has weathered the storms of the past years surprisingly well. He's made of tough stuff, all Kevlar and carbon fiber.

But everyone has a breaking point.

I hug him tighter, and another sob escapes me. His little arms wrap around me fiercely, tiny muscles strengthened by fear. He presses his head to the side of my neck and his shoulder into my windpipe.

If it were anywhere else, I would welcome the warmth of the fireplace when we cross The Wolf's threshold. But I'd rather be cold. I'd rather Tate shiver, chattering his baby teeth together than be subjected to…God knows what.

Pressing his face into my neck, I whisper, "Close your eyes, baby."

The muzzle of Billy's pistol jabs into my back as we climb the stairs and turn down the hall, catching wide-eyed stares from every girl we pass. To their credit, most of the Fangs stop and stare, suddenly unsure of their heinous acts in the presence of a child.

At the door to the master bedroom, Billy's voice, for once, eases some of the tension pulling my muscles taut. "Set him down so we can go play."

My eyes close, and my breath rushes out. I struggle beneath the crushing weight of a surge of fresh tears.

Oh, thank God…

But The Wolf weighs in, stepping on my soul. "What are you doing? Take him in there."

My heart stops.

"What?" Billy asks. "I'm not doing anything to the kid," he insists. "I'm not *that* fucked up."

"Whether you do or don't…that's your business." The Wolf steps closer to Billy, shrugging. "But he's going in there. Just think of him as a tool. Something to break her."

A sick grin splits The Wolf's face wide open, and he presses his own gun to Billy's temple. "Unless you'd like to miss your turn with her, completely." He pulls back the hammer for emphasis. As if anyone in the world could have mistaken his meaning.

Taking a deep breath, he glances at Tate, only moving his eyes. I wait, frozen, knowing any move I might make would get me killed. Then, who would take care of Tate?

Yeah…

Like I'm doing such a fantastic job of that.

What life would he go on to lead if something happened to me? Would The Wolf take him under his wing?

I barely stop myself from shuddering.

"Let's go," Billy says. "Get in there." His teeth grind together, but he caves beneath The Wolf's piercing gaze, cowering before the might of the gun.

Eyes closing, I lose hope. I did everything in my power to hold onto some scrap of it all this time, but now, it slips from my grasp, deserting me in my darkest time.

With a victorious leer, The Wolf points his gun at me and says, "Move along."

I can't hide my tears from Tate now, nor can I hide the shuddering breaths rattling my body. Billy opens the door, and I move through it reluctantly, feeling myself separate from my body. All the while, my mind casts about, searching for some way to reason with these cavemen. Escape isn't an option, not with guns on all sides ready to blow me, or Tate, to bits.

The door closes, and The Wolf's footsteps disappear down the hall so he can fill himself with one drug or another. Billy whispers, "Put the kid in the closet. Cover his eyes, cover his ears."

Relief floods me, prompting a fresh bout of tears. I nod my understanding, thankful for the limits of this man's depravity. I rush to do his bidding.

Setting Tate down in the barren floor of the closet, I pull a shirt from a hanger over his head. As the plastic hanger falls to the floor, I tie the shirt around Tate's head like a blindfold.

"Stay in here, sweetie," I choke past a sob of relief. "Don't take this off and keep your ears covered."

"What about you, Mommy? I'm scared. And they're so mean! They'll hurt you," his words tumble out in a rush, tripping over themselves as they cascade past his lips.

"I'll be ok as long as you're in here," I say, placing a hand on Tate's cheek. I plant a tender kiss on his forehead, ignoring the stale scent of the shirt wrapped around his little face. "I love you."

Then, I put his hands over his ears.
He whispers, "I love you, too."
I shut the closet door.

Chapter 27
Christian

The miles of cracked, shitty pavement roll on, dulling my senses. I can almost feel the end coming to claim me.

If not for the warmth of Chloe's hand wrapped firmly around mine and the sweetness of our afternoon together, I might have lost myself to panic. For now, she anchors me to the real world, fighting off the dissociation that might otherwise overtake me.

We'll see what happens when she leaves me alone on the side of the road...

When I march off to my death.

Motion sickness sweeps through me. I never used to have this problem. After two years of never moving faster than my own legs could carry me, the speed of the UTV makes me uneasy. It does nothing to ease my dour mood.

When we come to a downed power line, we venture off-road, skirting the wire through overgrown fields. Tall grass reaches into the side by side, running long silken fingers over my pant legs like cloying lovers, calling out for me to leave it all behind for them. Amber rays radiate from a pink and orange horizon, piercing the otherwise gray dusk as we bounce along.

A small part of me wonders if I'll be around when the lightning bugs make their first appearance this year or if I'll be rotting in some gutter in Breyerville. Will I smell the fresh blooms of honeysuckle, reaching to me from a block away?

And if not, what will I find waiting for me on the other side?

Jackson pulls Deadweight back onto the pavement, trekking through several large potholes in the process and jarring me from my reverie. The rifles bounce in their cases in the back, and the boxes of ammo topple over loudly. Apparently, a few of their corners find their way to Grant's legs, for he curses loudly.

Chloe's hand grips mine as the UTV climbs over a buckled section of pavement, and she presses our hands into my leg, using me to steady herself. My heart gives a single cry at the irony of finding her when I did, now that I have no time to truly appreciate her.

For what I fear may be the last time, I look her over. With her wavy red hair pulled back in a ponytail and fluttering behind her, she is the epitome of beauty. As we pick up speed, she closes her eyes momentarily, pulling in a deep breath. Her pale skin lights up with the last rays of a dying day, and I try to burn her image into my mind.

When I die, a thing I'm certain will happen before dawn, I want to be able to close my eyes and see her smiling at me. The delicate fans of her lashes, the magnificent shade of emerald that lights her eyes, the full curve of her lips. I commit it all to memory, my one last deed for her.

I'll die to save Karen and Tate, to protect the family Jesse left behind.

All I can offer Chloe is the promise that I'll never forget her.

My insides twist painfully, one last cry against the coming night and the end it surely holds.

***

244

The waxing moon shines bright on the outskirts of Breyerville, half-illuminating the cracked and crumbling buildings. Charred husks of cars lurk around every corner, windowless and gaping. My mind paints a slew of Fangs huddling behind each one, ready to jump us.

Adrenaline courses through me. It hisses through my veins like a wildcat until my hands shake with it. Chloe tightens her grip on my hand, offering comfort the only way she can. No words can pass her lips, not here. The quiet whir of the side by side's electric motor and the crunch of its tires on twigs and rubble is risky enough.

Every second, I expect Jackson to pull over and kick me out. The Wolf's wall looms in the distance 30 blocks away. 25 blocks. Still, he continues, albeit carefully, keeping us concealed within the shadows of various apartment buildings and banks.

With my heart in my chest, I wait for the moment of goodbye, the moment when I will be, for all intents and purposes, set adrift. With every breath, my hand tightens on the "Oh shit" handle bolted into the roof of the side by side, stretching the skin on my knuckles until they're as white as starlight.

20 blocks from the wall, Jackson turns the wheel, steering us toward the water treatment facility.

Surely, he won't drive me all the way up there...

A feral cat rustles through a pile of garbage down an alley, knocking loose a veritable avalanche of trash. A flock of birds takes flight, leaving behind their perch in a nearby copse of saplings which took root on a crumbling roof. Startled, but instantly relieved, we all let loose a deep sigh.

The proximity of the wall stirs our nerves, though. Chloe pulls her .45 from its holster. Jackson does the same with his own gun. In the back, Grant unsnaps one of the hard cases, pulling out a rifle for himself and handing forward a pistol, complete with a silencer, for me.

It's heavy in my hand, but I don't mind. Less recoil. I breathe easier knowing I have some way to defend myself, now. All my weapons were abandoned at my home when The Wolf stole it. I only had a few, anyway. A .357 revolver, a 9mm with an extended magazine, and a .22 long rifle.

To my knowledge, they're still tucked away in the wall safe I installed when I built the place. I was somewhat clever with it, tucking it in the back of the master closet and covering the door with the same paneling as the walls.

Not that I'll ever get there to retrieve them. A shame, too. They weren't cheap. Looking down at the gun in my hand, I wager that it was expensive, as well.

Deep breaths.

I force my mind to focus. My eyes scan the broken-down remnants of the city I once called home. We pass the park Jesse and I played in as children when we couldn't handle the shouting at home. My primary school sits across the street from it, half knocked in by a homemade bomb in the early days of the apocalypse.

Three blocks over, nestled amidst a row of buildings that barely look worse than they did when I was growing up, lies my childhood home. My parents' bodies may now lie within, though I can't be sure. They wouldn't have been able to fend for themselves, and they weren't around when Jesse and I searched for them two years ago, laboring beneath the weight of guilt for not having done so sooner.

Not long after that, the wall was completed, and no one went beyond it but the Fangs.

On the edge of town, butted against the wall, the water treatment plant looms. Its massive bulk looks out of place, having seen relatively little wear since the fall. Concrete, rebar, and I-beams hold up against fire, gunshots, and wind far better than wooden homes or brick and mortar buildings.

Fifteen blocks shy, with the reservoir's shining surface partly visible beyond the crumbling heaps of abandoned homes, Deadweight eases to a stop.

"We can't drive any further," Jackson says, careful to keep his voice low. Almost certainly, no one is within earshot, but it isn't worth the risk.

I nod. "Thank you," I whisper. I didn't expect them to bring me even this far. The surprising boon is just one more reason to be thankful for having met them.

Turning to Chloe, all my words catch in my throat. For a second, she won't meet my eyes. For half a second, I think it's better that way. She won't see the cowardice spilling across my face, threatening to hold me in my seat, or the way my heart wants to beat its way out of my chest.

When she looks up though, I'm glad for it. I needed one last view of her eyes more than I realized. Hopefully, it will be enough to sustain me to the end.

Eyebrows furrowing, I reach up to touch her face. She leans into my touch, closing her eyes. Her soft skin is warm against my palm, and though I want to, I dare not kiss her. I'm not sure I'd have the strength to pull away.

Taking in a long, shuddering breath, I pull my hand away and step out of the side by side. I tell myself the first step is the hardest, that it'll get easier after that.

But it doesn't.

Survival instincts, hard-wired into my brain by evolution, scream at me to turn tail and run.

One more step. It'll get easier.

One more.

Keep going.

Another one.

Behind me, gravel crunches beneath a boot.

"Chloe, what the fuck are you doing?" Grant hisses.

"I'm going with." Despite its low volume, her voice is clear, unmarred by hesitation.

I fight to maintain control over my heart as it rattles hysterically with relief and dread, simultaneously. "I won't be alone!" it screams, all the while panicking at the thought of Chloe placing herself in harm's way.

Even if she survives, she'll just be thrown in the brothel with Karen. Vision fluttering, I nearly puke at the thought. The moonlit night strobes before my eyes as I blink away the idea of her in the hands of the Fangs, in the hands of The Wolf.

I turn on my heel, determined to talk her out of it. Grant attempts to do so, using all manners of logic. Everything from, "You barely know this guy," to "You're going to get yourself killed, or worse, for nothing."

But she doesn't back down. With her pistol holstered once more, she loads her pockets with all the ammunition she can carry.

"Are you really going in there? For him?" Grant asks.

Jackson remains unwaveringly silent.

She attaches a few knives to her belt, then says, "Partly, yes. Partly because his four-year-old nephew is in there with The Wolf and his Fangs. Partly because his sister-in-law is being handed around like a toy. I can't walk away from that, not if I plan to get a good night's sleep ever again. If you can…" she shakes her head, letting her silence speak volumes.

A slight chuckle parts Jackson's lips, surprising me.

What the hell could this man be laughing about, now?

Giving his sister a knowing look, he nods and says, "I didn't think you'd send him in alone. I just wish you would've said so sooner. Could've come up with a plan or something."

Still firmly planted in the bed of the side by side, Grant says, "Are you fucking kidding me, right now? You knew she was going to pull this shit, and you didn't leave her at home?"

"Oh, shut up and help me hide this thing," Jackson says, teasingly. "We all know you're going to go with us, so you may as well save your breath. You're an asshole, but not *that big* of an asshole."

Incredulous, I don't move. "You guys aren't serious? You're not actually going in there with me, are you?"

Scowling, Grant jumps out of the side by side's bed and begins piling garbage on top of it. He grumbles, "Apparent-fucking-ly," and rolls his eyes.

Chapter 28

Chloe

Cold night air whips loose strands of hair against my face as we sneak toward the water treatment facility. Christian takes the lead. I watch as his gait shifts from nervous to downright edgy, noticing a similar change in my own state of mind.

Beyond the wall, orange light shines, and the crackling of fire can be heard even here.

What could possibly be on fire?

I strain my ears, picking out the splintering of beams as some house or building collapses on itself. No one screams, and somehow, that's worse than if they had.

Moving toward the water treatment plant, the shadow of the massive concrete monstrosity falls upon us long before the building itself embraces us. I find myself thankful for the shelter a mere shadow provides, even if it is just a darker section of the night. The parking lot felt so open, so vulnerable.

Christian opens a heavy metal door, and I mentally shush the cursed thing. Rusty hinges creak loudly in the chilly evening air, shattering the stillness of our entrance. Every muscle in my body tenses, waiting for someone to jump out from the nearest corner and start shooting.

Christian slows his movements, attempting to lessen the burden upon the hinges so they might cease their wailing. It merely draws out their torture, and the hairs on the back of my neck rise in fearful anticipation.

Something must be there, waiting to kill us, hiding in the gaping black maw of the hall beyond the doorway. Surely, this is the end. So much for a daring rescue.

Nerves. It's only your nerves.

My heart doesn't care for my attempts at logic though. It keeps hammering away.

One foot on the stairs, I watch the blackness swallow Christian's silhouette, merging with his shadowy form. The only sounds, my breathing, his footsteps, a distant owl.

No screams curdle my blood. No monstrous roars claw my ears.

No bullets burst through the air.

Another step, then another, and the building wraps its arms around me, concealing my presence from the view of any guards posted on the wall. Of course, the relief is short-lived, for I'm one step closer to entering Breyerville.

Stories of The Wolf and his Fangs reverberate through the walls around me, making them hum with the promise of tragedy. Forced slavery. Torture. Rape. Murder. The list goes on.

And yet, I'm walking toward it all.

For Christian.

For his sister-in-law and her son, so that they might know peace once more. They certainly won't find it within the wall.

A hand wraps itself around mine, and I jump, clamping my teeth closed upon my tongue. A lance of pain stabs me, and the metallic taste of blood follows close on its heels. But it centers me.

Focus. Calm down or you'll get yourself killed.

Not exactly a comforting thought, but it's sobering.

The warmth of Christian's skin leaks into me, loosening stiff fingers. It melts my heart just before it freezes against continuing the mission I set for myself.

"Sorry," he whispers. He's close.

Tugging at my hand, he pulls me a few steps inside the door to let Jackson and Grant file in behind me. The door screams out into the night as we pull it shut, but we must. A wide-open door would draw attention if a Fang's scope were to rake the area.

Safe behind a thick door and thicker walls, our flashlights spear the darkness. Beams of light illuminate circles of graffiti and piles of rubbish dragged about by rats and vandals. Old pipes run along the walls, leaking here and there. The air reeks of must and mildew.

And of death.

The decaying body of a rat lies ahead, not far from Christian's feet. Had he led me any further, we would've trampled the rotting thing.

A paranoid thought wonders if the bones would have been strong enough to pierce the sole of my shoe, infecting me with all manner of diseases. I know better, but my fanciful mind runs away with terror and dread, seeking out the worst possible outcomes for even the most benign scenarios.

"Follow me," Christian whispers. His blue eyes sparkle nervously, perhaps because of the trembling of our flashlights, gripped by hands shaking with cold and anxiety. He turns and walks quietly down the hall.

Taking a deep breath, I follow, ignoring the unsteady beat of my heart. I rub one sweaty palm against my thigh and switch the light between my hands.

Behind me, Jackson steps on the dead rat, apparently having missed the grisly sight. The squash of flesh beneath a heavy boot sends a shiver up my spine.

"Ugh," Jackson says. "Disgusting."

Grant laughs nervously in the near-darkness, glad it wasn't his tread which landed upon such filth. "Maybe watch your step?"

"I never would have thought of that," Jackson quips. "Thanks, so much, for the advice." Laughter bubbles up within him, though. As he wipes the remains of the rat off his boot and onto a pipe, the mirth becomes contagious, finding its way into all of us.

"Yeah, yeah. Laugh it up," he chuckles. Pointing at Grant he adds, "You're walking behind me, though. It'll be on your boots, too."

Grant shakes his head, still giggling. "No, it won't. I watch where I'm stepping."

A fresh wave of stench rolls up to greet us, and I gag. "Oh my god," I say, covering my mouth. "Nope, we have to move."

So we do. For what seems like ages, through one dark hall after another, the smell of rot and decay follows us, but so does the morbid laughter.

Damp walls pulse with microbial life and the scent of it slowly overtakes the rot. Mold inches across the concrete, over the pipes. A small puddle splashes underfoot. Twisting, turning halls lined with pipes pass by in a blur.

When I bump my arm against a valve, I don't jump. Calm has reasserted itself over my demeanor. If this goes awry, I know I'll have died doing something worthwhile. The farm, the cattle, the gardens and greenhouses, all our winter stores will be redistributed to the rest of Harville's residents.

There's a strange sort of peace to be found in that.

No matter what happens tonight, something good will come of my deeds. That's a rare and comforting thing in this new world of sacrifice and compromise. I take a deep breath and reach one hand out, placing it tenderly upon Christian's back.

Placing his own hand upon yet another metal door, he glances at me over his shoulder. "You sure about this? You can still turn back."

A gentle smile lifts my lips, and I nod. "Yeah. I'm sure."

He nods but seems unconvinced, eyes falling out of focus to stare at a point behind me. Pushing the door open, he leads us into an office full of musty furniture and toppled filing cabinets. Plumes of dust and spores rise from the carpet with every step.

A nest of rats scurries from the far corner, rushing out the door, which Grant happily holds open for them. "Good riddance," he mumbles.

The little rodents gallop down the hall, headed straight for their dead compatriot. The scavenging beasts will likely eat their mother, their sister, father, or brother. Cousin. Whatever the dead one was to them. I shudder then redirect my attention.

Flashlight beams fall upon rotting furniture with drawers pulled out and papers spread about. Briefcases lie open on four desks or toppled to the floor beside them, left behind in the rush for home when the grid finally collapsed and panic wrapped its talons around everyone's hearts.

Must and musk mingle, weaving their way through my nostrils. Again, I fight back the urge to gag. The pet store scent of too many animals in too little space threatens to cling to my clothing long after I leave this place.

Thankfully, Christian doesn't linger. He doesn't see a need to loot the office for any valuables. It's likely been cleaned out of any real supplies long ago. Not that we can afford to go into Breyerville over-encumbered. We need to move quickly, lithely. Pockets full of office supplies, rattling as paperclips and safety pins swish together, hardly screams stealth.

The office opens onto a much larger room, full of cubicles, all in varying states of disarray. A large, gaping hole stares down at the city, looking out over what was likely a very nicely manicured lawn, before. Now, the skeletons of trees and bushes crowd together, huddling against the cold winter night.

The jagged edges of glass claw at the night sky, reaching for the moon as if to pull it down. The tops of a few nearby buildings are visible, momentarily disorienting me. At no point during our dark and terrible journey through this place did we climb any stairs. We certainly descend two flights though as we leave the cubicle room, giving the illusion that we're entering a basement.

A few more rooms, then a lobby with a dropbox for water payments.

One door, leading out.

My heart stops, and I hope fervently that we won't be going out the front door. Surely, there would be guards there. But Christian's gait never slows, bee-lining for the front door.

No. There's no way.

My feet refuse to move. Grant and Jackson turn to stone behind me.

Lungs panicking, heart suddenly speeding along like the bullet trains of old, I watch helplessly as Christian turns off his flashlight and tiptoes to the door. But his hand never reaches for the handle. Rather, he leans against the wall beside the door frame, listening intently.

I wonder briefly what he hears, if anything. The door can't possibly allow much sound through, and the thick cement wall almost certainly blocks all sound. A deep breath lifts Christian's chest and he gives a small nod.

Without ever truly taking his eyes off the front door, he backs away, leading us instead to a door on the back right side of the lobby. When Grant closes it softly behind us, relief threatens to sweep my legs out from under me.

"What the fuck was that for?" Grant asks, whispering as forcefully as he dares.

"I was making sure the guards were there and not by the door we need," Christian says, unperturbed by Grant's tone. He flicks his flashlight back on, giving the hand crank a turn for good measure.

Meanwhile, I struggle to gain control of my breathing.

The Fangs were there.

They were RIGHT there.

I swallow hard, forcing my frantic thoughts to slow.

Remember, no matter what happens tonight, someone will benefit from this.

My eyes close, and I take a few cleansing breaths, trying to forget about the scent of mold and stale sweat.

The latter strikes an odd chord within me.

Sweat?

I look around, taking stock of this new room, and find several rows of lockers. Most of them hang open with their contents spilled across the floor, pulled about and partially shredded by rats. The center row has been pushed over, and leans precariously against another set of lockers, ready to fall at any moment.

Careful to give that set of dominoes a wide berth, we pick our way across the dirty floor. On the other side of the room, a row of showers stands watching the room with curtains tattered or missing. Several of the shower heads still drip.

Beyond the wall of showers, we find a row of stalls and urinals, standing off against a wall of sinks. On the far wall, a door awaits, ready to let us into the ground floor of the plant. It opens into a hallway, extending out to our right. Another door promises entry into the women's locker rooms, but we don't take it up on its offer. We bypass that one, choosing instead a door on the left of the hall.

The steel creaks as Christian pulls it across the tile floor, and my head jerks back toward the lobby.

They couldn't have heard that, not through the locker rooms and the lobby and all the concrete. They couldn't have.

Yet my heart races. My mouth goes dry.

No sounds of discovery echo through the chasm of the lobby. No screeching door, no pounding footsteps.

No shouts of, "Who's there?"

Eyes wild with the same nervous tension which pulls my mouth into a deep frown, Christian stares. He whispers, "This way," head nodding toward the door.

We follow, knowing that even if we changed our minds now, it would take us an eternity to find our way out of this place. Large water tanks tower over us, groaning in the darkness. Filters and pumps lurk in their shadows, dipping their toes into stagnant pools.

Again, the stench of death fills the room. As our lights bounce over the surface of the water, I see why. Drowned rats. Decaying, bloating, and disintegrating. Bits of fur float along separate from the bodies. A chill skitters over my spine, and I look away, staring at Christian's feet as he leads us through the cavernous room.

At long last, we climb a set of concrete stairs and find our exit. The door seems tiny compared to the room, far too small for the behemoth machines contained within it. Following Christian's lead, we turn off our flashlights and tuck them away in the inner pockets of our jackets.

He pushes open the final door, letting in waves of fresh air and the orange glow of firelight. I drink the fresh air in, glad to escape the horrendous stench which plagues this room. We do our best to quiet our steps on three rusty metal stairs which guide us to the ground.

Then, it registers in my mind. The plant was built into a hill which rings the reservoir. Turning to stare at the building, I see the slope of the ground butted up against it, see the way The Wolf used it as a section for his wall.

If not for the stupid wall, it would have taken us mere minutes to walk from the door we entered through to the one we just exited, letting the downward slant of the earth speed us along our way. As it were, weaving through the treatment facility, it took nearly an hour, if not longer.

Sighing, I feel resentment build within me as I turn to face Breyerville.

My stomach plummets, dropping into my boots. Everywhere I look, buildings are caved in on themselves. A block away, clearly visible over the rubble that was once a thriving city, an apartment building burns. Plumes of smoke climb into the air, spiraling until they obscure the stars.

Garbage lines the streets, and the illusion of fresh air vanishes. Relative to the concentrated rot in the water treatment plant, it's fresh, but by no other standard does it come close. Bodies, left lying wherever they fell, send their filth into the air. Sewage lines have clearly broken throughout the city.

How can they live like this?

The sight humbles me.

Burnt out, abandoned cars litter the streets. Dumpsters overflow. Stray animals scurry about in the overgrown weeds, and bare branches rattle together. A single gunshot sounds in the distance.

I draw my own gun from its holster and thread a silencer into the barrel. Safety off, I pull the slide back to chamber a round and listen as everyone else does the same.

The burning building collapses on itself, sending up a shower of sparks. For a moment, the night sky gets brighter, playing host to millions of new stars until they fizzle, burn out. Bits of ash flutter, float to the ground, landing without a sound.

A lonesome woman screams in agony, buried within the burning rubble.

Chapter 29

Christian

Across town, another building goes up in flame, surrendering to sparks cast off by its neighbor. Bathed in the light of an inferno that may well consume an entire block by morning, Karen and Jesse's apartment building looks like a black hole. It drinks in the light, giving nothing back.

It strikes a cold and hopeless chord within me, even as I correct myself.

Karen and Tate's apartment. Jesse isn't there, now.

Two deep breaths and several seconds pass before I recover sufficiently from that thought to continue walking.

I try to estimate the time to distract myself. Having begun the hour-long drive at around 7:00, I guess that, even with the delays of broken trees and powerlines and the trek through the water treatment facility, it can't be later than 9:30. Even if Karen extinguished every candle and tucked Tate into bed early, the fireplace would still be burning bright to fend off the brisk night air.

Fear slinks through the shadowed corners of my mind, stirring panic in my heart and chasing adrenaline through my veins.

Every window is dark.

Am I too late?

My chest collapses under the weight of dread.

Some small, insignificant portion of my soul argues that they may have left to find some way out on their own. Or, perhaps, they merely went to bed early and forgot to stoke the fire.

But I know that part of me is a liar. It's the same part that once told me one more candy bar was okay, catering to my sweet tooth. The part that coddles and soothes, despite reason or logic.

Something is wrong.

Yet, I continue with the plan knowing that, without searching the apartment, I'll have no hope of finding them.

Once inside the building, our flashlights come to life, painting beams of color on the shadow world through which we walk. Garbage lines the walls, fills the corners. A portion of the banister on the once-beautiful staircase lies in pieces on the tile floor of the lobby.

After having been away in a place people cared to keep up, Breyerville is all the more depressing and decrepit by comparison. Stairs creak forlornly beneath feet, lamenting that they've been allowed to fall so far.

Every step fills my nose with a scent I've grown unfortunately familiar with since the fall. Death and decay. My heart rate quickens, as does my pace. Taking the stairs two at a time, I ignore the groan of crotchety old wood, impatient to let the disaster overhead reveal itself to me.

Is it them? Am I too late?

I quickly amend the trepidation and the train of thought which follows, aching to placate my conscience.

Maybe it isn't them. Maybe it's a bunch of rats. Or a random dead person in the hall…

Stamping down the guilt of wishing death on some other person, nearly *any* other person, I barrel down the hall. The stench of rot grows stronger with every step, as do the nightmare images of what may lie ahead. They tear at my heart, filling me with fear.

I can't lose them, too.

I can't fail them, too.

Dust motes float gracefully in the jerking, jarring beam of my flashlight as my arms pump up and down. All the while, my mind is a chaotic, tangling mass of serpents, each with scales painted to depict a new, more terrible scene of death. They writhe, bodies pulsing as they constrict around their prey, a single little mouse, squeaking over and over, "They can't be dead."

If they are…

The tiny mouse squeaks loudly as the serpents wrap tighter and tighter. My heart constricts painfully.

If they're dead, this building may as well crumble around me.

Guilt plagues me once more when the footsteps of Chloe, Jackson, and Grant somehow echo over the pounding of my heart. The tension within me builds, threatening to crush me, and I amend my thoughts, once more.

It can crumble once they get out…

After what feels like eons of running down such a short hall for so very long, I come to the door, left hanging open. The smell is stronger here, but not as bad as I expected. For a few, gut-wrenching moments, I stare in, looking at the small circle of mild disarray illuminated by my flashlight. The cushion of the futon is tugged partially over the edge of the metal frame, drooping lifelessly.

Behind me, Chloe skids to a stop, followed quickly by Grant and Jackson. Chloe's hand finds my lower back, but I barely feel it. The comfort she means to extend is lost in a roiling sea of misery, floating away as I sink into the black depths.

I feel my lungs expand, filling near to bursting, then feel the air rush out. My brows furrow of their own accord, twisting my face into a mask of disbelief.

"I came back, I came all this way, and I'm too late…"

I barely take notice of the mouse within the ball of writhing snakes in my mind. Its cries of, "They're alive!" seem so far away, muffled by the mass of twisting bodies surrounding it.

Grant meanders a short way down the hall, but the blood running wildly through my veins, screaming bloody murder right next to my eardrums, masks the sound of his footsteps.

Vaguely, as if on some far-off island, I hear Jackson ask, "What are you doing?" But Grant's reply is lost beneath the sounds of my own hoarse breathing.

I stand there, staring, unable to take another step, though I know I must. My muscles turn to stone, refusing to move or even twitch. My heart threatens to stop. My lungs struggle for air.

Eyelids fluttering, I force myself to move. A deep, shuddering breath forces its way down my throat. I lift one foot and cross the threshold. My free hand trails along the door, feeling each grain in an attempt to calm myself, but it doesn't work.

My feet drag across the floor, and I cast my light over the living room. The metal futon sits, lonely and worn down. No bodies materialize before my light, though. A few embers still glow in the fireplace, and a pile of wood scrapped from furniture rests nearby.

I wander to the kitchen, needing a bit more time to steady myself before I move down the hall. I check the cabinet but can't make sense of what I find. Stacks of cans. Rows of boxes. All full.

Why would they leave that behind?

It leaves a sour taste in my mouth.

They didn't leave by choice. Karen would have taken it with them.

Chloe drifts over to the fridge. She opens the door, and the rubber seal pulls away from the metal. A soft "hm" sneaks past her lips, and I look over her shoulder. More food.

Cases of bottled water are stacked, one atop the other. The shelves have been removed, to make room for them. Bags of rice fill the door. Boxes of cereal and long-stale baked treats, so processed they might still be good, rest atop the cases of water. Loose granola bars and protein bars fill the meat drawer. Bags of jerky fill the vegetable drawer. In the freezer, still more food sits, abandoned.

Most surprising of all, a few fresh vegetables rest in the freezer door. A precious commodity, certainly from The Wolf's own greenhouse.

But...

"I didn't expect to see this much food here," Chloe says.

"Me either." For a moment, my mind spins in circles, unable to wrap itself around the situation. "I don't know how she got it all."

A dark sickness creeps into my soul at the thought of what it must have taken. And then to just leave it all?

Finally, Grant and Jackson come in, closing the front door behind them. "One of your neighbors is pretty…ripe," Grant says.

Turning, Chloe asks, "Is that what that is?" She wrinkles her nose for effect.

I close the fridge and freezer, leaning my head against it. I try to quiet my heart so I might hear them.

Walking closer, Jackson says, somewhat more politely, "She killed herself. Poor thing looked like she was wasting away. She's in a better place, now."

Is she, though?

Yet again, I find myself questioning the afterlife, questioning a god that could allow Karen and Tate not to be here.

Outside, a crash sounds and sparks burst into the sky as another burning building collapses in on itself. The stainless-steel fridge glows orange with the reflection, and I close my eyes against it, not quite ready to allow light into my world.

Not yet.

First, I need to know.

"What did she look like?"

Was it Karen? Did something happen to Tate? Did she leave the apartment to finish herself off, unable to look at this place anymore without him?

My blood freezes in my veins as I wait, bones and flesh turning to ice.

"Um…pale. Skinny, little blonde girl," Jackson says, sparing us the details of how she looked after the ravages of death consumed her.

He goes on, but I don't hear the rest of his description.

"Thank God," I whisper. Sinking to my knees, I let my hands fall from the handles of the fridge and land atop my head. Cold metal presses into my face. Tears roll down my cheeks, and I don't even care that everyone is here, watching me unravel.

"It's not her," I breathe, voice faltering over the words. "They might be okay."

The little mouse in my mind pulls in a deep breath as one of the serpents gives up, slithering away with a single hissing taste of the air. It goes off in search of another meal, fully aware that too many are present, twisting and twining, to consume a single prey item.

Gentle hands find my back, rubbing and trying to soothe. Their warmth can't penetrate my jacket, but the intention is no longer lost on me.

"Come here," Chloe whispers near my ear. Her hands pull softly at me, urging me to turn around.

So I do.

She sits down next to me and wraps me in her arms. Pressing my head to her shoulder, she croons, voice low, "We'll find them. I promise."

Throwing my arms around her waist, I breathe her in, letting myself fall apart with temporary relief. I shove away my guilt, knowing that the death of that other girl is tragic but reveling in the knowledge that maybe, just maybe, Karen and Tate are still alive.

Somewhere.

Fingers clenching Chloe's thick wool hoodie, I breathe deeply, drinking her in. The soft, floral scent calms me, as do the gentle caresses of her thumb winding back and forth over the back of my neck. Gritting my teeth, I will myself to get a grip. I can't hope to find them like this, sitting on the floor, crying.

Figure this out.

Make a plan.

I nod and blink a few times to clear my eyes. After planting a single kiss at the base of Chloe's neck, I pull away. "Thank you," I whisper hoarsely, blinking against the reflected beam of a flashlight bouncing off the fridge.

She smiles and rubs her thumb over my jaw. Her eyes flick back and forth between mine, taking in every striation, every speck. "It's no problem."

My eyes fall to my lap, and I breathe deeply. Time to check out the rest of the apartment. Suddenly, it doesn't seem so daunting. With the door closed, the smell of the dead girl is faint, almost gone. No other such smells claw at my nose.

Whatever may have happened, I know that Karen and Tate aren't dead in the bedroom. Some small, foolish part of me hopes that they're cowering in there, afraid to make a sound, lest they draw the notice of the intruders in their home.

I push myself up and extend a hand to help Chloe. As we search, I don't hide the tear tracks which stain my face. I keep my shoulders firmly back and my chin lifted, even when every doorway leads to an empty room.

Their clothes still reside within their closets. Tate's toys lie spilled across the floor in his room. By the looks of it, they had just eaten, and Karen had been cleaning up when they left. She was fastidious and hated the slum they'd fallen into. Cleaning up trash was always done immediately so as not to worsen their living conditions.

But she didn't get to finish.

They didn't plan to leave. Something, or someone, forced them to go. A sick feeling slithers into the pit of my stomach, leaving a slimy trail in its wake.

I pace in Tate's room, eyes picking over the toys strewn about. Near the door, I find Tate's favorite, a fully posable raptor. It doesn't make sound anymore, but he still loves it. He carried the thing the whole way when we tried to escape, tucking it very carefully in his pack.

He would have taken it with him, given the choice.

Chloe looks in, leans on the doorframe. "Hey," she says, cutting into the silence that filled the apartment. "I'm sure they're fine. We'll just wait for them here. They'll be back."

The words sound like she's saying them only because there's no other logical course of action. There's nothing else we can reasonably do. But she doesn't believe it. She can't. There's no way to know they're ok, especially here. Especially now.

I know that, all too well.

She leans her head against the door frame and I pace over to her. With a small sigh, I resign myself to waiting and wrap my arms around her. She snuggles into my chest, pulling away from the wall.

Resting my head upon hers, I focus on our escape route and the amount of food we can reasonably expect to carry out of here. We'll have to eat what we can before going, to lighten the load and lessen the waste we leave behind.

Tipping Chloe's head back with my forefinger, I look into her eyes. The amber light of the freshly stoked fire glows upon her pale skin, dancing in her eyes.

"Thank you. For coming with," I say.

I shudder to think what I would've done had she let me go it alone, only to be greeted by this empty apartment. The path the neighbor girl took likely would have seemed appealing. That, or a rage-fueled rampage.

Chloe says nothing, choosing instead to kiss me gently on the lips. When she pulls away, my eyes drift to the strands of hair that the wind tugged loose from her ponytail on the ride here. They fall just beside her eyes, and I push them back behind her ear.

But then my gaze finds something else. On her temple, where she leaned her head against the wall, a patch of dark flakes decorates her skin.

My face scrunches, and I lean in closer to get a better look.

"What's wrong?" she asks.

Rather than answer, I turn to the doorframe. A small, dark smudge stares out at us, laughing at how long it took us to notice it. I click my flashlight back on to examine it better. All at once, I wish I hadn't seen it and hate that I missed it for so long.

Dried blood paints the wood trim. Not much, just enough to get a point across. About Karen's height, a few inches under Chloe's height.

Fury coils in my belly, poised and ready to strike. The target is obvious. The Wolf. Or Billy. Who else would have come here?

Nothing else makes sense.

Did she steal that food? Did The Wolf come to teach her a lesson? Did he drag her away to make her pay *for it? Why would she take Tate?*

The implications ooze down my spine, making me shudder. Nausea rolls over me in waves, threatening to drag me under as the horrors The Wolf could inflict upon Tate float in and out of my mind.

"No," I say, cursing under my breath.

Those bastards came for them...and they're going to...

I can't finish the thought, can't bear to hold it in my mind for more than half a second. Another shiver convulses my body and my gag reflex bucks. I hold down my gorge, though just barely.

"That son of a bitch," I spit, shaking my head. "Mother*fucker*," the word is a hiss, barely audible.

"Talk to me," Chloe pleads. With her hands on my shoulders, she turns me to face her. "What is it?"

"I know where they are."

"How bad is it?"

Terrible. As bad as it could *possibly* be.

"They're with The Wolf."

Jaw working, lips pursing, I shake my head as if that denial could somehow undo this. As if it could bring them back, unharmed. My hands ball into fists, and my nails bite into my skin, carving little, white half-moon divots.

Chloe nods, taking a deep breath. She chews at the inside of her cheek for a moment, contorting her face. Hands falling from my shoulders, she wraps them around my fists, instead.

Heart pounding angrily, I fume. My breathing becomes rushed and shallow, and my nostrils flare. For a minute, I close my eyes, trying to fight off the burning desire to smash The Wolf's face in.

But the image is there.

The satisfying crunch his skull would make as it caves in calls out to my fist, practically begging for it.

My muscles itch with the need to move, to go to them. To kill every Fang that gets in my way.

To kill The Wolf and that motherfucker, Billy.

"I'm going," I say, eyes wild with rage when I finally open them.

"What? Where?"

"That filthy, disgusting fucking brothel. That's where they are." I sidestep Chloe, making my way to the front door. Blood rushes behind my ears, drowning out the sound of my feet on the tile and the crackle of wood in the fireplace.

"You can't, though. There's bound to be a lot of them there. They'll kill you." Chloe follows me. She reaches out a hand and catches me by the arm.

Spinning on my heel, I face her. Voice low, I say, "They took Tate. To the goddamn brothel." I pause to fend off a wave of nausea. "There's only one reason for them to take him there, and I'd rather die than just let that happen."

With a tear in my eye, voice breaking over the words, I whisper, "He's just a kid. I can't let…" Clearing my throat, I try again. "I can't let them do that."

Chloe's lips part, but no words come out. Her eyes are desperate to find some solution that can save them, without sacrificing me. The flickering shadows of the fire hide too much of her expression, concealing her intentions.

"I'm going," I say, cutting off any argument and saving her the frustration of looking for a better plan.

Her eyes flutter, and she nods. A tear rolls down her cheek.

I wipe it away, mustering all the tenderness I can, what with the maelstrom of hatred whirling in my gut. I kiss her on the forehead. I may never see her again, after all.

I pull in a deep breath, then level my shoulders. My feet lead me to the door. For the first time, I'm glad the bastard took my house. Muscle memory will guide me there, even in the dark.

Behind me, I hear, "Come on. We're going on a road trip." Chloe's voice is strong and clear.

Jackson and Grant don't argue. They spring to their feet, leaving the warmth of the fireplace behind.

For Tate.

If not for the boiling blood racing through me, I might stop to hug them. As it were, I can't bear to stop. My hands find the doorknob and jerk the thing open. My feet pound down the hall, leaving the poor dead girl and her stench behind.

A small amount of dread trickles in as I barrel down the stairs. I don't really want to see what these animals have done to my house. All my hard work, all the effort, and care I put in to make everything perfect have likely been trashed.

That place is like an extension of myself. Seeing what they've done feels akin to an author watching someone burn their book.

But for Tate, I'll see my masterpiece destroyed.

Chapter 30

Karen

"Please, just let him stay in there. Please!" I pull at The Wolf's arms, rebelling against him for the first time in longer than I remember. "I'll do anything you want! I'll be here every day. Please, just leave Tate in there."

I squeeze between his tall frame and the closet door, utterly defenseless in just my old bra and underwear. With my heart screaming along faster than it's ever beat before, I beg.

A malicious glint shines in The Wolf's eyes as he watches fear shift my posture, warring with the defiance and maternal instincts driving me. His lips quirk into a smile and my insides fill with slime. I shiver beneath his gaze but keep myself firmly planted between him and Tate.

"Not good enough," he says, all too calmly. His eyes peer into my soul, and the scars on his face suck in the light like deep chasms. "You'll be here every day, alright. But he's coming out of there."

Then, dropping his voice to a sinister growl, he says, "Now, move."

He starts to shove me out of the way but stills when Billy speaks up. "Come on, man. Leave the kid out of it."

I freeze, stunned by the conscience concealed within the man who just five minutes ago beat the tar out of me and used me twice over.

"Excuse me?" The Wolf asks, turning to face his second-in-command. "You think *you're* going to tell *me* what to do?" He shoves Billy hard, but the big man barely moves. "After everything I've done for you? After I dragged you up from the pit your sorry ass was in? I fed you, gave you a purpose, gave you all the women you wanted, to hurt however you want."

Tone even and low, he continues, "I made you what you are. Without me, someone would have put you down years ago like the dog you are. But I made you more than that. I gave you power. I gave you control. Over yourself. Over them."

The Wolf jabs an unforgiving finger at me.

As The Wolf berates Billy and his upbringing, extolling the abuse Billy apparently suffered at the hands of his mother after his father's death, I watch the big man. A strange sort of sympathy grows within me, springing up alongside the gratitude I feel for him trying to spare Tate.

I watch fury build in him and hope he'll strangle The Wolf.

Wouldn't that be convenient?

Meanwhile, my mind busies itself calculating my odds of getting Tate to safety while The Wolf is distracted. I come up with nothing but dead ends.

Then, my eyes land on Billy's gun.

It sits, half-concealed by shadow and half sparkling in the candlelight, on the bedside table. Of course, Billy and The Wolf are partially between me and the gun, towering over my tiny frame. I need Billy to react, to punch The Wolf, to do something.

Anything.

But how badly whipped is he? What abuse has The Wolf put him through to gain his submission? Will he break those bonds?

Out of options, I rest my weight unsteadily on the thin ice of trust that has formed beneath me. Slipping and skidding, I try to balance upon it, hanging on the confrontation developing between these two monsters.

"He's just a kid, Robert," Billy says, squaring off.

A certain amount of power comes from knowing The Wolf's real name. It knocks him down a peg. The effect isn't lost on me.

Or on The Wolf.

I watch him bristle at the reminder that he's just an ordinary man, see the slight smile on Billy's face and the lift of one eyebrow into a smirk. He's just a touch shorter than The Wolf, but he has at least ten pounds on him. A fight between them would be fairly even.

It could drag on for a while…

A spike of hope surges through my veins.

Never one to back down from a challenge from a *lesser* opponent, The Wolf steps closer, staring down into Billy's eyes. Their noses nearly touch as he spits, "Get. Out. Now." Gathering up the tattered fabric of Billy's shirt, he adds, "Or you're done."

The Wolf shoves the shirt against Billy's chest.

"Hands off me," Billy says. The rows of fang tattoos scrunch together into a mass of black, extending the shadow around his right eye.

"Or what, you mangy fucking mutt?" The Wolf gathers up a wad of mucus in the back of his throat and spits it onto Billy's face.

The world stops. No one says a word. Even Tate stops whimpering in the closet, somehow sensing that our fates hang in the balance.

For just a moment, I can't believe what I've just seen or Billy's reaction.

He doesn't move, at first. When he does, he calmly wipes the disgusting mass off his face and shakes it onto the floor. He takes a deep breath, rasping through lungs marred by years of cigarette use, and the sound is like thunder.

Then, the world splits open, and Billy's bloody knuckles find The Wolf's jaw with a loud crack. It sends The Wolf careening backward into the wall, narrowly missing me and the closet door. Peeling bits of olive paint flutter softly to the ground.

Tate screams and I jump away. But Billy pays no mind, lunging after The Wolf. Still reeling, The Wolf doesn't stand a chance. He takes one punch after another, head snapping to the side each time. His eyes are wild, but they shine only for Billy.

I'm altogether forgotten.

My jaw drops as he reaches up, hooking his thumbs into Billy's eye sockets, pushing and trying to root out his eyes. It has the desired effect. Billy pulls back. The Wolf pushes himself off the wall, but Billy doesn't let him get any further than that, coming in with a fist to his master's stomach.

Snapping out of my fear-induced trance, I reach for the gun on the bedside table. Neither man sees me take it, so I tuck it behind my back. If Billy wins, I can take Tate back to our apartment. No harm, no foul.

No more Wolf.

If The Wolf wins…I have my back-up plan.

Repositioning myself between them and the closet, I wait. I try desperately to ignore the cries coming from behind me, much as they call to the very depths of my soul.

With one all-consuming effort, The Wolf shoves Billy off him so hard that the big man actually stumbles backward, falling onto the bed. Before he can get back up, The Wolf pulls his own gun from the back of his waistband and fires into Billy's chest.

Once.

Twice.

Blood wicks its way across the mattress beneath him, and his face goes slack.

"Mommy!" Tate cries, throwing his tiny body against the door.

"I'm fine, sweetie. Stay in there," I say quietly, pulling Billy's gun from behind my back. I aim it at The Wolf's back, not confident enough to aim for his head even at such a short distance. I've never fired a gun before and can't afford to miss.

With sweat beading on my forehead and The Wolf wiping blood from his jaw, I pull the trigger.

The gun clicks, uselessly.

The Wolf's head turns toward me as I stare at the weapon in my shaking hands, confused. I look at the safety and find it disengaged.

Red is dead, I know that much.

But why didn't it work?

I barely have time to realize I never cocked it, never chambered a round, before The Wolf's hand slams into the side of my face, open-palmed. Pain blossoms through my head and my vision cuts out for a moment. I topple over into the closet door, dazed and seeing spots.

Everything starts to fade out as I buckle under my own weight.

"Mom!" Tate screams, poor little lungs working overtime. His hand turns the doorknob, and he tries to push the door open. He isn't strong enough to move me, though. Tiny fists pound the door, and my head bounces painfully against it.

Billy's gun slips from my hand, landing with a hollow thud on the floor. Then, the world goes black.

Chapter 31

Chloe

Peeking out past an overturned ambulance, I stare at Christian's old house, awe-stricken. It looms a block ahead. The lights of a fireplace and a surplus of candles burn bright, casting flickering reflections on the windows. It was obviously a beautiful place.

Before.

Two stories with a quaint little porch, though only a few of the carved railings still stand. On the ground floor, dark shutters hang askew or lay broken on the ground. A few windows have been busted out and boarded up, letting out only small lines of light around the edges of the wooden planks. Graffiti mars the dark blue siding.

Christian's shadowed shoulders fall, slumping at the sight.

Taking a deep breath, I place a hand on his lower back and step up even with him, careful not to leave the safety offered by the ambulance. I look at him, see the way his face has fallen. I want to say something to repair the damage done to what must have taken him years to build but I know words could never suffice. So I allow him a moment of silence.

When I finally speak, he appears not to hear me at first. "Are all the Fangs irredeemable?" I repeat.

Lifting his jaw from the ground, he asks what I mean.

"Are they all scum? Or are some of them the 'wrong place, wrong time, just trying to survive' type?"

"No," Christian answers, shaking his head. "They're filth. The ones just trying to get by were killed off. You can't hesitate and expect to be a Fang."

I nod, glad to have been spared any guilt I may have had over taking lives here. Not that they're likely to give me a chance not to kill them.

"We're not walking in the front door, are we?" Grant pipes up.

"No. We'll go in the back," Christian says. Voice breaking as he continues, he adds, "I just had to see what they'd done to it."

A deep breath lifts his shoulders, expanding his ribs against my hand. My feet feel like stone, but we have to move. We can't stand here, staring at the guards on the front porch.

Sure, the guards don't exactly have their attention on the road, not with their backs turned and their faces pressed to the windowpane watching whatever horror unfolds within. But they'll turn around eventually. Staying here guarantees that we'll be spotted, at some point.

As if to illustrate the need for movement, a group of people bursts from a building down the street, one block further from Christian's old house. They yell loudly, clearly drunk.

On the other side of town, many blocks behind us, another building joins the fire, silhouetting the entire scene with tongues of orange. The smoke thickens, blocking out the moon.

"What level of hell is this?" I murmur.

Christian doesn't speak. He merely leads us around the block, darting between half-standing buildings, burnt cars, and decrepit-yet-still-lived-in houses. We pass piles of garbage and a few dead bodies, some clearly murdered, some starved.

Wild dogs and cats, once beloved house pets, now gnaw at the carcasses left to rot in the street. The tags and bells on their tattered collars jingle as they run, startled by the sight of humans who, in this place, are as likely to pet them as they are to maim or eat them.

At long last, we come to a wooden fence with a few panels missing. Several have been knocked over and one lays in a heap, crushed beneath a fallen tree limb. Christian turns and presses a finger to his lips.

This is it.

A million butterflies erupt in my stomach.

After a second's consideration, Christian steps closer. My skin grows warm as he reaches for me. The adrenaline singing through my veins finds a new source as his lips meet mine. I wind my free hand into his hair, pulling him in deeper and savoring the taste of him.

Just in case.

We separate, breathing quickly, and I put my off-hand back on the butt of my pistol. With my heart in my throat, I step through a gap in the fence, taking refuge behind a thick tree trunk. Christian follows, pressing close to me, and I peer around at the guard posted at the back door.

He sits, rather lazily, in an old, rusty patio chair. The rest of the set lies toppled nearby with the glass tabletop shattered and spread throughout the scorched grass. The light of the moon glitters on the shards. A black mark claws the side of the house with plastic siding shrinking away from the charred wood underneath.

Shaking my head, I decide to lure the guard away from the house. I snap a twig from a low branch and scrape it against the fence.

The Fang doesn't move, merely grunting, "Fuck off."

Rolling my eyes in frustration, I snap off a larger stick and smack it against the fence. This time, it's enough to warrant an investigation.

The large man hauls himself up from the chair, and it creaks in relief. Lumbering over, he growls, "I said. Fuck. Off. How hard is that to understand?"

Ears straining against the cries leaking out of the house like black water from old rusty pipes, I pick out each of his footsteps, gauging his distance carefully. Two more steps. One more.

His face appears beside mine, and I put the tip of the silencer against his forehead. I pull the trigger and watch realization fade from his eyes before he falls.

Nine more rounds.

Wiping at the specks of blood which now pepper my hands and face, I sneak a peek at the house. No one rushes for the back door. The silencer did its job.

Through the windows, beyond tattered curtains, I see Fangs in nearly every room, abusing these poor women in one way or another. My eyes drift to the second floor and I see a face I never wanted to see again. My blood freezes and my heart stops in its tracks.

"No," I croak, mouth suddenly as dry as a desert. A shiver of disgust rolls through me.

Christian follows my gaze to the second-floor window, sees the man with the scars dripping from his hairline, over his temple. Scars I vividly remember inflicting. I remember the feel of my fingernails catching and slicing through his skin. I remember clawing at him as I kicked and screamed, desperate to buck him off.

I remember the weight of him on top of me as he forced his way inside. The push of the nail, dragging its way through the skin of my stomach. The feel of the floorboards as my head slammed into them and the nausea rolling through me. I remember watching him murder my parents, remember the sound as they fell. The blood that leaked from them.

His coal-black eyes now fixate on another man, apparently squaring off, but I remember the way they tore through me as he fired a gun at me. I shrink back from the world, blinking it all away.

And I know it before Christian says it.

"That's him," he whispers, malice clear in his voice. "That's The Wolf."

"No," I say, brain struggling to comprehend the cruelty of it all. "Why is it him?"

"What?" Christian asks, careful to keep his voice low.

"That's…*him*," I say, lending my voice all the levity I can manage. My strength seems to have vanished, though. Even now, his mere presence robs me of everything I've built myself into.

Jackson hears my words though, really hears them, and steps through the gap in the fence. A gentle hand finds my back, and he looks around me to gaze up at the window. By now, *he's* barely visible, fighting with the other man in the room.

"Oh my God," Jackson says.

"Why is it him…" I whisper, barely able to get the words out. I look up at my brother and watch the world break into pieces in his eyes. Everything he thought he knew, all the hope he had, all the faith he held so tightly over these past years…All of it crumbles in an instant.

"I…don't know." His gaze falls, and he whispers, "How could God be so cruel?"

My eyebrows shoot up as if reaching for my hairline. Perhaps they, too, wish to run and hide from this horrible moment. The shock of watching Jackson forsake his faith, after everything, after all these years, jolts my system, forcing my brain to reset.

Rage floods me, chasing the fear from my veins. *No.*

That bastard took everything from me. He's not going to take it all away from Jackson, too.

I inhale the promise of revenge.

He ends, now.

Breathing deeply, I nod to Christian. My face is stern as I step out of cover. I make my way to the door, silently picking my way through the grass. I step onto the concrete patio, infinitely thankful that this property, too, has a slight incline. No stairs groan underfoot as they would have on the front porch.

At the door, I step to the side of the frame, allowing Christian to lead. Some small portion of him seems hesitant to cross the threshold. Yet, the rest of him surges onward, opening the door and slipping in quickly. I follow, surveying the room as I enter.

No Fangs lurk in the laundry room. Jackson and Grant join us in short order, and we take a moment to regroup.

We're in…We're here.

And so is he.

I do my best to still my galloping heart, to quiet the thudding behind my ears. But revenge is a powerful master, and it calls my name, whispering promises of closure.

Meanwhile, the sane part of me murmurs, "This is crazy."

Thoughts of certain death cloud my mind and I see them echoed on the faces of my companions. My heart hammers wildly in my chest, and my lungs panic.

But I know it's too late to turn back, now.

I'd never be able to live with myself, much less sleep peacefully, knowing he was still out there. The real, solid knowledge of it would eat at me like suspicion never could. Everywhere I went, I would expect him to turn up because true evil never leaves quietly. It has to be shoved out of this world with all the force you can muster.

Sometimes, that just happens to take the form of a .45.

Echoing my thoughts, the sound of a gunshot pierces the night, quickly followed by another. All eyes dart to the ceiling. All hearts stop.

A single word oozes from Christian, "No…" It trails off, hanging on the air around us.

All around me, in every other room, a cacophony of crying, begging, and brutality rages on. Several long seconds pass before anyone in the laundry room even thinks of moving and even then, it's merely to look at Christian.

Agony, pure and true, splays across his face. Eyebrows knitted tightly together, mouth agape, his eyes flutter as they fill with tears.

"He was fighting someone," I whisper, "some guy. Maybe they're okay."

Eyes vacant, Christian nods.

Then, a loud thud and a small child cries, "Mom!"

My eyes dart to the ceiling.

Same room as the gunshot.

In that second, all hesitation vanishes. Without a word, Christian pushes through the door into the kitchen. The air which rushes in to fill his wake reeks of chemicals, filling every breath, and I struggle not to gag. I pull my scarf up over my nose and mouth, filing through the door after Christian.

Two Fangs stand at the stove on the right side of the room, cooking some foul-smelling liquid down to a syrup. Cookie trays wait nearby to house the cooling liquid. Another Fang sits at the table in the dining room beyond, cutting a line of brownish-white powder from a pile.

The chefs go down with two headshots, sending a mess of blood, bone, and gray matter over the cabinets and the granite countertop. One of them knocks the pot off the stove on his way down, and steaming, sticky liquid spills over his slack form, creeping like molasses.

At the dining room table, the third manages a, "Hey! Who the fuck do you—"

Two shots, one center mass and one to the head.

Seven left in my magazine, eight in Christian's. One wasted round.

The man at the table slumps over the pile of off-white powder. His blood seeps out onto it, staining their vice and rendering it unusable before dripping onto the floor.

I look away, wishing I could see around the corner into what must be the attached living room. Anyone in there will have heard, or seen, the death at the dining room table.

Damn open concept floor plans…

Back to the wall, dangerously near the corner, Christian holds up two fingers. His gaze is locked on the outer wall, facing away from the living room. I don't get the chance to appreciate his use of their reflections in a massive, cracked mirror.

"Get up," a gruff voice says. A shuffling sound, then the thud of a body hitting the floor. "I said to get up!"

A zipper tears at my ears.

Stepping out from behind me, Jackson and Grant move into the dining room before the Fangs present can grab their weapons. They take them down with three shots. Another wasted bullet.

Grant rushes over to the door, jerking it open as the two guards rush in from the front porch. The one in front stumbles in, losing his balance as the door opens beneath his hand. All the force he'd intended to push into it topples him to the floor. His feet ensnare the legs of the other guard, bringing him down, too.

Two shots. One mine, one Christian's.

Six rounds left for me, seven for Christian.

Jackson drags the dead men away from the door frame, streaking blood across the scuffed hardwood floor, and Grant closes it. A sudden rush of cold air would alert anyone else in the house. No need for the risk.

Off to the right, reflected in the mirror, I see two ghostly forms. I turn around to find two barely-clothed women huddled silently on the living room floor, staring up at us. I hold my finger to my lips to silence them.

The older one, a curvy woman with dark brown hair cut short, wipes her lips and nods. She pulls the younger woman, barely 18 if I had to guess, into a hug. Smoothing the young girl's hair back in an overwhelmingly maternal gesture, she coos quietly into the girl's long brown locks.

Shuddering, the girl does what she can to keep her cries silent, not that she'd be heard over the screaming coming from a closed door just beyond the staircase which opposes the front door.

Christian jerks his head toward the screaming, and mouths, "We'll come back for her."

Though I hate the idea of ending up trapped upstairs, I know the sudden cessation of such obvious torment would draw attention. A sick feeling creeps into my stomach at the idea of using some poor woman's suffering as cover noise, but we have no other option.

Taking point once more, Christian starts a careful ascension. I step where he steps, trying not to coax a squeak from the boards beneath my feet, though the roaring of my blood would prevent me from hearing it if I did upset the tired stairs.

I barely make it up four steps before the screaming in the downstairs bedroom ceases. It turns to a soft whimper, muffled by walls and a door. My feet stop moving, as do Christian's. We wait.

The door opens, and a small, heavy object drops to the floor. "Take your stupid food, bitch," mocks a low voice, trembling on the edge of cruel laughter.

At the foot of the stairs, Jackson gestures for Christian and me to come back down and slip into the kitchen, but there's no time. Before we can move, the Fang has found his way into the living room. He begins yelling, immediately.

Grant puts him down, but not quick enough. Before I can even see how many tattoos circle his eyes, footsteps sound, heavy as thunder, overhead. Far more footsteps than should be up there.

A chill tramples through me as my mind assembles a few "group activities" they could have been involved in. I vault over the railing, taking what little cover I can while still allowing myself a shot.

Somewhat less acrobatic, Christian runs down the stairs and comes to kneel beside me just as Fangs start pouring from the rooms above. I try desperately to count the pairs of footsteps, but I may as well count the drops of rain in a storm.

Christian and I duck under the upper hall, passing the simpering woman, bloody and fetal with a blanket partially covering her on the bed. A can of green beans lies on the floor, three feet inside the door. I avert my eyes, trying to allow the woman a bit of privacy.

I pull the door mostly shut and gesture to the mother and daughter in the living room, sending them into the bathroom at the end of the hall. But the Fangs begin pouring down the stairs, all in varying stages of undress.

Grant peers around the corner, using the initial commotion and the distraction of the running women as cover, and picks two off. Their bodies roll loudly down the stairs, coming to a stop when one of them gets an arm caught in the rail.

A third man trips over them, landing with a crack at the bottom. His hand lays at an odd angle with both bones in his forearm clearly broken. Christian points and fires.

Six rounds left for both of us.

But I know that number is about to plummet.

Leaning over the rail, a Fang tries to aim for me, alerted to our presence by Christian's shot, but he can't balance properly. I fire once, a solid hit to the chest, and knock him back.

But not before he pulls the trigger. Without a silencer, the shot rings out, loud and brutal on eardrums straining to pick detail from chaos. Luck and my own bullet join forces, pulling his shot wide. The sleeve of my hoodie rips, but my skin remains intact. For now.

A great gust of air whooshes from my lungs.

Five in mine, six in Christian's.

I pull my thoughts away from the near miss, focusing on my count, reluctant to let myself be drawn into a panic.

The mother and daughter slam the door of the bathroom, and the lock bolts into place.

Taut silence shattered, all hell breaks loose. Gunshots ring out, splintering already desecrated walls left and right.

"Let's get this done," I whisper as a Fang falls from the hall above, landing with a sickening thud in front of me. I fire one into his chest, just in case, and pick up the knife now lying useless beside him.

Four and six. Then, reload.

I shout, "Cover!"

Grant and Jackson don't hesitate, leaning around the corner to fire over my head as I run up the stairs, ducking as low as I can. Christian follows behind, firing beside me as I shoot one Fang and toss him over the rail.

Three and five.

Chapter 32

Terror slices into focus as I open my eyes to the ceiling of Christian's old bedroom. Billy's blood is warm beneath me, soaking into the mattress. With a blurry mind, I try to roll from the bed.

Tight knots hold my hands to the side. The rope slips under the bed, tied to the rails of the frame. My feet are similarly bound, holding me completely immobile. Heart racing, I look to the closet.

The door is wide open.

A scream threatens to rip me in two, but the gag tied into my mouth strangles it. Head aching, I shut my eyes for a second, and the ringing in my ears eases.

Off to my right, small sounds of misery beg for my attention. I jerk my head to the side, mind whirling with echoes of the motion, and find Tate. A bruise smears itself across his beautiful little face, and tears roll over it. His eyes are scrunched up so tightly as he cries that he doesn't see me open my eyes.

But the monster hovering over his shoulder doesn't miss a beat. "Go on," The Wolf says, lips split in a smile made of chaos.

Only then do I see the knife held, white-knuckle tight, in my baby boy's hands. He wails, fresh tears pouring over his cheeks.

Patience long since worn away, The Wolf shoves Tate toward the bed, and my heart falters. He takes a few steps, but his footing is unsteady. He nearly slips, drawing my attention to the blood trail leading over the edge of the bed to the floor just behind The Wolf. Billy lies in shadow, eyes wide and vacant, in the floor.

Tate hesitates, and I try to reassure him. My attempts come out muffled.

Another shove knocks Tate into the bed, and my face contorts with rage as I try to scream at The Wolf. All my threats come out like so much garbled nonsense thanks to the disgusting cloth in my mouth, held firmly in place by a musty, silk tie. My hands ball up into useless fists.

Stooping to hiss in Tate's ear, The Wolf says, "Do you want to be pathetic like her? Do you want to be weak?" Grabbing Tate's tiny hand, he lifts it to poise the blade over my thigh. "Or do you want to be strong? To get what you want?" His voice drops lower, and he spits, "Do you want to live?"

Panic spills from Tate on frantic cries as he faces a dilemma far beyond his meager years. Lamenting the carefree boy he once was, I try to tell him to go ahead. Anything so that he lives.

But the gag stops me.

Little, blue eyes disappear behind lids, and he tries to turn away. Strong hands hold him in place, forcing his little fist to press the knife into my flesh. It bites hard, pulling tears to my eyes instantly, but I clamp my lips shut, determined not to scream. I won't fill his nightmares with my pain any more than The Wolf already has.

The knife slices through my skin easily and catches muscle as The Wolf uses Tate's hand to drag it down toward my knee. The disgusting smile on his face makes my gorge rise, and for a moment, I worry that I'll drown in my own vomit. I close my eyes, but the image remains, burned into my retinas.

The blood gushing from my leg and the agony tearing through my body mingle with Tate's cries to form a nightmare lullaby. It screams in my head, over and over, with each echo somehow louder than the last.

Until, somewhere in the house, the sound of a gunshot shreds my thoughts. My eyes open immediately with a desperate hope flooding me. I find myself praying that maybe Billy wasn't dead, a thing I never thought I'd wish for. Maybe he shot The Wolf. Or maybe someone else did.

But such fanciful notions are dashed, as quickly as they form.

The Wolf jumps, startled by the shot, and his smile turns to a violent sneer. "What the fuck are they doing?"

Shaking his head, he cuts his eyes at the door down beyond the foot of the bed but doesn't move. He resumes his torture after only the briefest hesitation, pressing Tate's hand down harder, digging the knife in deeper. I slam my eyes shut once more, and red bursts in firework patterns over the backs of my eyelids.

Only when a chorus of gunfire and screams plays in the hall does he stop. The Wolf rips the knife from Tate's hand, earning a cry of pain from the poor boy, and throws it across the room. It tumbles in the air, hitting the wall handle first, and bounces off.

"Fucking Christ! Can't they do a single, goddamned thing right!"

Leaning over Tate with a dirty, disgusting finger pointed in his face, The Wolf scowls. "Sit the *fuck* down and don't move."

Tate obeys without question, dropping to the floor amidst Billy's blood. I can tell he wants to disappear under the bed. I can see it in the slump of his shoulders. My heart breaks, a million times more agonizing than the pain radiating from my leg. His tiny body shakes as he sobs, and each jerking movement claws at my soul.

The Wolf stomps to the door and flings it open. "SHUT THE FUCK UP!" he shouts into the chaos.

For once, no one listens. The need to dodge bullets seems to have preoccupied them, and he takes a tentative step into the hall.

Working my jaw ferociously, I force the cloth out of my mouth and out beneath the tie. It takes time, precious seconds I can't afford to lose, but there's no way around it. "Baby, get the knife," I whisper beneath the screaming.

"Mommy..." he cries, hand snaking up to grip mine. "I'm sorry, Mommy! I didn't want to, I promise!"

"I know, baby. I know." Tears roll freely from my eyes, and my insides twist in agony. "Please, sweetheart, get the knife. While he's busy."

I glance at the door and see The Wolf clear the threshold, leaving us to cower. "Now, baby. Please. I need you to cut these ropes so I can get us out of here."

My mind turns to my leg.

I'll figure it out. Somehow. We have to go and this might be our only chance.

"Mommy, I'm sorry!" Tate cries, face buried in the side of the mattress just beside my hand.

"I know, honey," I coo, shushing gently. My fingers brush his scalp, just barely within reach. "Please, sweetheart. Get the knife for me, okay? I'm not mad at you. I know you didn't want to do that."

I strain at my bonds, arms aching to fold around him and cradle him to my chest. I want so badly to shelter him from all the evil in the world, but it's found him. At long last, the beasts of this world have found him.

"Please, sweetie, get the knife," I beg.

That's our only chance. I have to get out of these ties. I have to get him out.

"But he'll hurt me," he whimpers, finally bringing his eyes up to meet mine. His face scrunches up once more as fresh tears spill over at the sight of me. "He'll hurt you."

Shaking my head, I run my thumb over his jaw, considering the bruise on his face. "He won't get the chance."

Deep within me, something primitive calls out. I have to protect Tate. No matter what. Determination steals across my face.

Shakily, Tate nods and with a glance at the door, he rises to his feet. His steps are hesitant, at best, but he does it. He crosses the room, stoops beside the closet, and gathers the knife into his hands. Palms up and held away from himself, he carries it warily, afraid it could make him do something terrible, again.

My heart clenches. Tears cascade from my eyes.

Tate's gaze stays carefully away from Billy as he walks back around to where The Wolf told him to sit. He watches his feet, placing them gently near the blood streaks when he must, but never on them.

"You see this?" I ask, lifting my right hand to indicate the binding. "I need you to cut it, okay? Pull it tight with one hand and saw through it. Make sure you're cutting toward the bed, though."

Fear shines in his eyes, obscuring his fragile soul. But he trusts me. His movement is slow, but he places his hands how I told him. He starts cutting.

I watch the door, praying all the while that whatever is happening out there keeps The Wolf distracted long enough.

This will take a while.

Chapter 33

Christian

Firing up the stairs a few times, I hate my position behind Chloe. It feels cowardly, but I can't very well say, "Excuse me, pardon me, I'll go first." We don't have the time for things like that, and I have to admit, she's certainly more adept, as far as combat goes.

I shoot twice more, but the Fang I aim for is moving. The first shot misses. The second sinks into his thigh.

"Christian, reload," Chloe shouts, rushing forward to pull the man down onto the stack of bodies forming on the stairs. Off-balance thanks to my shot, he falls easily, landing face down upon the pile. She fires point-blank into his skull and ducks down behind the bloody mass.

How the fuck is she counting shots in this mess?

I hurriedly duck behind the pile, landing beside her. I eject my magazine and exchange it for a fresh one from my pocket.

She does the same, yelling out, "Cover!"

On cue, Grant and Jackson spring out from their shelter around the corner and spray several bullets upward. One of their pistols clicks empty, and they retreat once more, just as Chloe slams the new magazine into place. Their timing awes me, and I wonder, not for the first time, just who these people are.

I try not to think about how many bullets my nerves and the moving targets have wasted. I've already caught up with Chloe's usage, and I haven't taken down half as many. A little voice creeps up in the back of my mind to tell me that I'm not up to this, that I'll fail, but I shush it, shoving it as far down as I can.

Now isn't the time for doubts. The time for that passed the second I stepped out of the UTV.

Now, in the belly of the beast, the only option is to try.

At the top of the stairs, a deep voice booms, "SHUT THE FUCK UP!"

The Fangs still alive on the landing, few as they are, continue firing, raining bullets into the pile of meat protecting Chloe and me. It's enough to make me thankful that they aren't of a large enough caliber to pass through the dead men.

The voice stills Chloe's hands though, stiffening her spine. The Wolf. The devil who raped her, all those years ago.

My stomach drops now, just as it did outside when she saw him through the window. When I realized where I'd heard that name before. Robert Wolfgang Myers. His history of depravity reaches back farther than I imagined, but why wouldn't it? The evil which seethes within him couldn't have been contained by mere laws.

Reaching a hand out, I squeeze Chloe's knee. She looks at me, a hint of fear trembling in her eyes. But something else moves there, pulling her jaw taut and her shoulders back. Her chest rises slowly, then falls in a very controlled breath. Her fingers tighten around the grip of her pistol.

Something cold slithers in my soul. "Please, be careful," I mouth, begging silently, knowing that whatever place her heart has traveled to can't be reached by words.

Above us, The Wolf howls, "Get off your lazy, camping asses, and Fucking GET Them."

Confusion bursts across the landing as the Fangs question their leader's decision to send them behind enemy lines. A scuffle breaks out, and one Fang is shoved free from his hiding place around a corner.

"I told you to move!" The Wolf shouts, virtually tossing another Fang out of cover, this one a woman. The only female in the pack.

She trips and rolls down the stairs, knocking into the barricade of bodies. Her momentum carries her over it, and grappling hands find holds wherever they might. She pulls me and several dead men down with her, and we roll in a tumult of elbows and knees.

Ribs meet the edges of stairs, and fingers catch the rails. Grip iron-tight on the pistol, I try desperately not to send it flying, all the while keeping my finger carefully outside the trigger guard. A dead man settles on top of me and blood soaks into my pants. Finally, I stop rolling, but slide down a few more steps, abusing my back further still.

Another Fang is shoved down, though he retains a bit more of his balance. He never quite falls, running headfirst down the stairs. He leaps over the remainder of the pile, tries to leap over Chloe, but she seizes the opportunity. Her hands find his ankle, and she gives it a yank. His shoulder collides with the stairs next to my legs, issuing a loud crack, and the Fang screams in pain.

Two more Fangs lumber down the stairs, confident in the distraction The Wolf provided. Every muscle, every bone in my body cries out for a break, one I know will never come. As I watch two of the biggest men I've ever seen take one step after another, my heart threatens to check out early, beating wildly and packing its bags.

Apparently taking the relative quiet as a bad sign, Grant jumps out and raises his gun. Before he can pull the trigger, one of the big men fires, smiling from ear to ear. Rows of fangs underline bright eyes, dark beneath light. Tan skin shines with sweat, and he wipes it away absentmindedly, continuing his progress down the stairs as Grant falls.

I struggle beneath the weight of the bodies atop me, and horror lines Chloe's eyes as she screams, "Grant!"

Gaze drifting to his prone form, I see the gaping hole in Grant's stomach. Blood oozes out of him, pooling on the floor and trickling along the lines of grout like cars on congested highways, anxious to speed away.

The Fang tries to fire again, but his gun clicks empty. Panic floods me as I watch the Fang get closer and closer to Chloe, wondering if she'll be fast enough to defeat two behemoths.

I want to shoot the bastards, but my gun is pinned beneath yet another dead man. Beside me, the Fang who pulled me down rouses from an apparent blackout, bringing her presence screaming back into focus. Blood drips from her tan forehead. She turns, and it runs down into her eyes. A perfect opportunity for me, but hundreds of pounds hold me motionless.

Eyes darting upward once more, all the while shimmying free from the pile, I watch in helpless horror as the big man Sparta-kicks Chloe's barricade, sending her spiraling down the stairs.

By some stroke of luck, or perhaps thanks to some crazy, martial arts ninja shit that I can't quite comprehend, she lands with an elbow in the back of the living Fang next to me. A choked "oompf" coughs its way out of the woman's throat.

I continue pulling myself free and spare a glance at Grant. His hand shakes, but he tries to aim the gun. His other hand struggles to press his wound shut. He fires, and though it surely isn't what he intended, he knocks the leg out from under the man who kicked Chloe.

"Son of a bitch!" the Fang cries in a voice that doesn't quite fit his burly body.

Jackson steps out and puts the man down in one shot, then falls back behind cover. He fires around the corner into the Fang beside me and goes to Grant. Whispering, "Hang in there, bud," Jackson drags him out of view.

"Leave me," Grant says. The words are a burden, but he pushes them past his lips. "Go to the kid."

Pulling my arm free of the bodies, I lever myself up to sitting. "Fucking finally," I hiss, levering myself further out. "I'm so close. I'm almost to them. *So goddamn close.*"

Chloe springs to her feet, unencumbered by the dead, and launches up the stairs.

"What are you doing?" I scream, but she seems unafraid.

Meanwhile, ice fills my veins. Thoughts of losing her, of losing Tate and Karen, claw at me, trying desperately to pull me down.

Finally, I slip one foot loose from the pile, and far too much relief washes through me for such a small accomplishment.

Chapter 34

Chloe

Momentarily taken aback by my gall, the Fang freezes, dark eyes wide. I slam into him with a surprising amount of force, and he falls back onto the stairs. Bringing my hand up over my head, I slam the butt of my pistol into his nose. Blood gushes freely, warm as it splatters over me.

Dazed, he swats at my hand, hitting my wrist hard enough to send my gun flying. Force is an easy thing for him, considering his size. He must weigh at least 215 pounds. No matter. Before he can do any real damage, which he certainly could, I drive my elbow down into the center of his face with all my might.

His nose gives way, and the back of his skull splinters against the corner of the stair below it. He goes still, blood gushing out of him. It runs down the stairs, already slick with the end of so many monsters.

But not all of them.

My soul calls out for the death of one more.

Confident that no more lurk above, none except Robert Myers, I rush up the stairs. My arrival on the landing finds *The Wolf* fleeing.

Let him be afraid.

For the first time in his godforsaken life, let him be the one who's scared.

He looks back over his shoulder at me as he sprints through a door, and recognition flickers in his eyes.

Good.

I want him to know me.

I push myself harder, arms pumping and feet pounding. My blood rushes behind my ears, and a rib protests the movement, almost certainly cracked from my trip down the stairs.

But I don't care.

Slipping one of my knives from its sheath, I let rage and adrenaline push me through the door after *The Wolf.* Inwardly, I scoff at his pathetic moniker, using every bit of fury I can scrape together.

He spins on his heel and tries to raise his gun. I duck low and kick it out of his hand, spinning with my own momentum. As I come back around, I rise and drive my knife down into The Wolf's flesh, just behind his collar bone.

He pulls in a great gulp of air, croaking with the effort, and his pitch-black eyes go wide with terror. Hot blood flows around the knife, soaking his shirt, warming my hand.

"I've thought a lot about how you should die," I whisper.

Robert pries at my hand, trying to force it upward, to get me off him. I loop my other arm under his, bringing my hand up behind his neck and over his shoulder to hold the knife in place. His armpit serves as a leverage point. My face is inches from his, and every move he makes jerks the blade.

He stops moving, growing weaker with every second.

"You *should* have been in jail when the world fell apart. You should've been locked in that *fucking* cell to rot. You deserve to have been there. You deserve for the sewer to have backed up, flooding the jail with a few inches of sewage. You deserve to have had to listen to the other prisoners screaming as rats ate them alive, knowing your turn would come."

Something dark seethes within me, but there's no turning back, now. I have to let it out.

I hiss, "You deserve for those rats to nibble at your toes while you sleep. You deserve to catch one every now and then, just enough to keep you from starving to death, but not enough to ever feel full. You deserve to wade through *shit* to get to your sink for what little water still drips out of those pipes."

Robert gasps in pain, blood gushing from the base of his throat, oozing around the knife. Sweat beads on his forehead, and his dark eyes show true fear.

In the far corner of the room, barely slipping into my awareness, a woman stares on, bloody and holding a child to her with her only unbound arm.

"You *deserve* for infection to creep into those rat bites, for it to make you weak. Gangrene should've rotted the flesh from your bones, and fever should've boiled your brain. You should've spent your last days wondering which would claim you, hunger, thirst, or the toxic blood running through your body, only to writhe in pain and fall over the side of your filthy, *disgusting* little cot."

Two sets of footsteps creep into the room, clearly on edge. One leaves the doorway quickly, and Christian rushes into my periphery, dropping to his knees by mother and child.

Voice dropping even lower, I say, "You *deserve* to land face down, too weak to lift your filthy, *fucking* head out of the shit so you die choking on it." I pull the knife from his body, and he gasps.

"Lucky for you, I don't have the stomach to do all that. So, this…" I lower my hand and shove the knife up under his ribs, "…will have to do." The words are a growl.

His breath gurgles, and blood leaks from his mouth.

I twist the knife, breathing hard. The last of the darkness pours out of me as his blood becomes a waterfall.

I watch the life drain from his eyes. The man of my nightmares. The man who ruined so many parts of my life. The man who killed my parents…dies in my arms.

Stepping back, I loosen my grip and let him fall to the floor, a lifeless sack of leaking flesh. I stare down at him for several moments, tuning out the soundtrack of tearful reunions. A strange numbness settles over me as I look down at my knife, still sticking out of him.

I'm not taking it with me.

I decide this quickly, vaguely aware that my focus should lie elsewhere.

Several moments later, a gentle hand touches my back just between the shoulder blades. "Chloe, we have to move." It's Jackson. "There might be more of them nearby. There was so much noise…We can't stay here."

I nod, barely present.

I'll grab my gun on the way out…

The thought drifts through my mind, flitting free of my grasp when I reach for it.

Chapter 35

Karen

I hold Tate close, hugging him tightly when Christian frees my other hand. The poor boy shakes against me and his tears wash some of the blood from my face. I tangle my hand in his hair and press my lips to his forehead. Then, his cheek. Then, the other cheek.

Christian cuts my feet free and the man who came in with him looks at my savaged leg. Kneeling down, not caring about the crimson streaking the floor beneath him, he looks to me, hands hovering over the bloody ravine which splits my thigh in two.

"May I?" he asks.

I stop moving, letting Tate squeeze me tightly. I nod, shocked.

He's asking?

How long has it been since a man asked *if he could touch me?*

I don't know the answer.

His hands are gentle as they probe the gash on my thigh, trying not to cause any more pain than necessary. I watch him carefully, waiting for him to snap, to stab me, to pull at the cut to inflict more damage.

But he doesn't.

His bright green eyes meet mine, soft and gentle. "We'll get you fixed up."

He pushes himself up to standing, and I see the blood soaking his knees. A small line of blood drips from a cut on his cheek, perhaps from the riot downstairs, and runs down into the blonde scruff on his jaw.

He walks over to the redhead standing over The Wolf's dead body and says something to her about leaving.

But I can't walk...

Christian digs in the closet and comes away with a thick flannel shirt that he helps me put on. I shift Tate from one arm to the other, sliding my arms into the sleeves, and pull it tight around me. Every move hurts, and I do everything I can to not move my leg.

"They're good people, Karen. They stitched me up. They saved my life," Christian whispers.

With that, he leaves me to dig around in the closet some more, though I'm not sure why. There's very little in there.

Impossibly, he pulls a few guns from a hidden safe in the closet. A smile lights his face as he considers them, shoving the pistols into the waistband of his pants somewhat awkwardly.

A dark sickness settles into the pit of my stomach. I'd forgotten all about the safe he said he installed. The combination screams into focus. 18, 24,28.

Those guns have been there the whole time...I never thought to...

Guilt riots in my stomach, churning a fetid pool of filth.

Not that it would have done me any good to have remembered. I was never alone in this room. My eyes drift out of focus.

I couldn't have used them anyway, even if I'd gotten to them.

My ears replay the click of the gun aimed with shaking hands at The Wolf's back, and my heart plummets, unable to bear the weight of my own disappointment. The poor, tired organ lands in my stomach, lifeless and barren, sick of the bruises which adorn it. It barely beats, struggling to send blood through me and lamenting the flood which pours from my leg, rendering its work useless.

Slowly, the blonde man and the redhead walk over. The woman kneels over me and looks my leg over. She mumbles something, and I have to ask her to repeat it, though I'm not sure how much of the incoherence can be attributed to the fog in my own mind and how much is caused by the clouds hovering behind the redhead's eyes.

Clearing her throat, the woman says, "Is there a medkit here?"

I shake my head, moving it against Tate's head. His hair tickles my skin. "There's one at my apartment. My neighbor, she was a nurse. She…left everything to me."

Realization dawns on Christian's face, and I assume they've been to the apartment, already. They must have seen all the food. They must've smelled poor Lyla. But she couldn't be moved. The Fangs had to be able to find her if they came looking, which was obviously within their wheelhouse.

The blonde man nods and says, "Ok. Chloe, get the others. Tell them to follow us there. We can't carry all that food, and they need it more than we do."

"I can't walk, though. I'm dead weight," I whisper, covering Tate's ears. The fact that they're apparently doing well enough that they don't need a week's worth of food for everyone here is too shocking for me to register.

"I'll carry you," the blonde man answers. "If that's ok. Christian can carry Tate. Kid's been through enough, he probably doesn't want some stranger lugging him around."

Taken aback by his kindness, I nod. I'd assumed all the nice guys were gone. So many of them snapped when the world ended. Tons more were killed off by the Wolves and Fangs of the world.

Hell, I'd been certain Christian was dead, but here he stands, good as new. Apparently, thanks to these people.

Slipping free of his jacket, the blonde man drapes it over my legs. It stings on my thigh but I'll need it outside. Christian hands his rifle to the redhead, gathers my clothes from the floor, and coaxes Tate from my arms.

Cradling him like a baby, Christian kisses Tate on the forehead, closing his eyes to savor the moment. The gesture warms my heart.

"Ready?" the blonde asks.

"Yeah," I answer, voice creaking.

Exceedingly gentle, ever careful not to put too much pressure on my bad leg or pull the jacket tight against it, he slips one arm under my knees and the other around my back. I wrap them around his neck, trying to stabilize myself so he won't have to. We follow the woman out of the bedroom.

My eyes shift back and forth between Tate curled up in Christian's arms, held exactly like a baby, and the kind man holding me. On the landing, the woman who killed The Wolf disappears down the hall, beckoning the other girls to follow after us. Her voice is flat and strange.

Blood and bodies litter the stairs, and I crane my neck around to see if Christian has shielded Tate's eyes. The boy has his head buried in his uncle's chest, impervious to his surroundings, and I breathe easier.

At the foot of the stairs, the distant redhead calls more women from the other bedroom and the bathroom. As they dress themselves, she picks up a gun and threads her way through the bodies. Kneeling beside one, in particular, she closes her eyes.

I watch as her brows furrow.

Was that her brother? Her lover?

Just a friend?

She touches his face once and rises. "What are we going to tell Becky?" she murmurs.

A voice rumbles out of the chest pressed against me. "We'll tell her he did it for the kid."

The redhead nods. The other women emerge as clothed as they can possibly be, and we head out into the night. Cold air whips under the jacket draped over my legs, nipping at my flesh. I shiver, and the man holding me pulls me in tighter.

"I'm Jackson, by the way," he says quietly. Nodding to the other girl, he says, "That's my sister, Chloe."

Unsure what else to say, I introduce myself. Barely visible now that we've stepped out of the house, the smile in his green eyes stirs my heart in an unusual way.

"I assumed as much," he says, "Would've been weird otherwise, with Christian hugging you and all."

My lips lift in a smile just big enough to sparkle in my eyes.

***

At the apartment, Chloe stitches my leg by firelight while Christian helps Tate pack a few toys. The warmth of the fire sinks into my bones. A deep peace settles over me as I listen to him telling Tate about the other kids where we're going.

More kids!

My heart skips with joy.

Chloe wraps my leg and finally, speaks. "So, you were a teacher?"

Nodding, I say, "Pre-K."

"Mind teaching again? When we get home. Everyone has to pull their weight. May as well use the skills you had before to do it," she says, helping me slide on some loose-fitting pants.

Chest nearly bursting open, I wipe away the tears before they fall. "I'd love to."

In the kitchen, Jackson helps the other women from the brothel load food into plastic totes. A deep, sick greed tells me not to let so much food go.

Christian comes back in though, with Tate in tow. Seeing my expression, he guesses my thoughts. "You won't miss it, I promise."

I take a deep breath to calm myself, telling myself to trust them.

They just saved my life. They saved Tate's life. They saved Christian. This shouldn't be hard.

But it is.

I glance at Christian, remembering all the times he defended me against Jesse. I think of the hell he went through to get us out last time and the nightmare he put upon himself for Tate and me tonight. I can trust him, even if my heart hesitates to trust the other two.

"How far do we have to go?" I ask, mind drawn to the pain in my leg and the need to be carried. By Jackson. I shove down the strange little fluttering in my stomach, unwilling and certainly not ready, to acknowledge it.

"Once we're out of Breyerville, about an hour," Chloe answers, voice finally leaving its monotone state.

I gasp. "An hour! That's all? That's not far enough!" My mind fills with thoughts of The Wolf finding me, of the Fangs hunting me down.

Then, I remember his blood on Chloe's hands. His lifeless body on the floor. All their bodies, littering Christian's house.

"An hour's drive," Christian gentles as the other women sort food in the kitchen.

"You guys have a car?"

Coming over to kneel next to me, Jackson says, "Sort-of. Not really. It's a side-by-side."

"What?"

"A UTV. Off-road utility vehicle." He shrugs. "We used it on our farm, before."

"You guys ready?" Chloe asks.

After a chorus of "yes," Jackson lifts me up off the futon as if I weighed nothing. Tate practically jumps into Christian's arms with a backpack full of toys dangling off his little back and his favorite one cradled in his arms.

With one last look, I say goodbye to my home, watching the food Tate and I needed just hours ago be divvied up amongst others.

I take a deep breath and listen as Tate whispers, "I missed you," against his uncle's neck.

"I missed you, too," Christian answers, voice breaking.

Tears prick at the corners of my eyes, and a lump forms in my throat.

***

Loaded into the bed of the side-by-side, I hold Tate to me. My thigh aches and I wish for the pain killers of the old world.

By the light of the moon, I watch Christian approach Chloe. The strange woman slides her arms around his waist, and he smiles.

With a hand in her hair, Christian whispers, "Are you okay?"

She nods against his chest, "I am, now."

My heart nearly bursts, and my face splits open in a smile.

Jackson turns the key, and the side-by-side starts up on the first try, a feat that amazes me. Turning around, he asks, "You think you'll be too tired to eat when we get there? Or would you like some pizza and cookies?"

Tate's head shoots up, and a smile burns in his eyes, brighter than the stars could ever hope to be. "Really?"

"Yep. We'll make them while you guys get cleaned up. We'll even have some cold milk with the cookies. Sound good?"

"Mom, did you hear that?" Tate asks.

"I did, sweetie." My throat tightens, and tears fill my eyes. I smooth a few strands of hair out of his face. "I sure did."

He reveals this discovery to Christian, drawing his uncle's attention away from Chloe. I use the time to smile at Jackson.

"Thank you," I say. "I don't know what I would've done…"

"I wouldn't have been able to live with myself if we hadn't at least tried," he says, laying a gentle hand on my shoulder.

Chloe and Christian pile in, and we set off, heading home. A strange concept. I haven't *felt* at home in so long. But now, with Tate tucked under my arm and a safe place on the horizon…

Maybe it's possible.

Chapter 36

Chloe

After a long day spent working in the fields and caring for the cattle and chickens, I help Jackson prepare dinner. It's our turn this time, and Christian, Karen, and Tate will be over any minute. Tomorrow, we'll be over at their house, sitting at what used to be Mrs. Ableman's table.

The next night, we'll put Tate to bed on the couch here, and Holden and Calista will leave the twins with his parents so we can have our card night. It'll be the first since the babies came three weeks ago. The warmth of a routine with loved ones in a safe place soothes me, chasing tension from my veins.

I lift the hamburgers from the stove and settle them onto a plate. Jackson pulls the chips from the pot of oil and dumps them across a towel to dry. I smile at the familiarity of it all. The front door opens, and I listen as our guests arrive. Tate bounces into the kitchen first, excited to see what delicacy awaits him today, practically exuberant.

A rare sight.

The adults currently contained within these walls are the only ones he'll smile and laugh around. He was even shy around the other kids, at first, a thing which was apparently so far outside his normal behavior that Karen was an absolute wreck over it. But he warmed up to them, in time.

Considering everything, being mistrustful of most adults and slow to warm up to children is probably the best we could have hoped for. He's resilient.

Strong arms wrap around my waist, and I sigh contentedly, hoping he'll sleep over again tonight. It's hard to tell if Tate will insist on having his uncle around for the night. Christian kisses the nape of my neck, and a soft sound crosses my lips.

Karen walks in and immediately busies herself, taking plates and glasses from the cabinets. She starts to set the table and Jackson stops her.

"Why don't we eat outside? It's so nice, today," he says.

She smiles up at him, ample bosom swelling with a deep breath. Jackson helps her carry things out, even gets the door for her. As she passes by him, his hand finds the small of her back, the most progress I've seen them make since she came here a month and a half ago.

Jackson likes her, I can tell. My face splits into a smile watching them. I think Karen likes him too, but after everything she's been through…

Jackson has patience to spare, though. They'll be fine.

My eyes drift over to the window as I gather bread from the cabinet and cheese from the fridge. I see Becky dragging fallen branches back to the woodshed, ready to be chopped for firewood. Part of her community service.

She almost left when we told her about Grant. We almost didn't need to come up with a punishment for her.

We all knew leaving would have been a death sentence for her, though. She's never been an outdoorsy type and though she's come a long way since the fall, she still relies heavily on everyone around town. Which is really the point of this place, working together so no one is relegated to merely surviving.

After a town meeting and a vote, we decided on community service. There's no jail in Harville or she likely would have spent some time in there. This seems to be doing the trick, though. She's already apologized to Christian and me of her own volition.

She's been speaking with the Tevins, both social workers before, about her need for attention.

Yet, who's to say whether that's the work of her sentence or of the loss of the one person she had left?

"Aunt Chloe?" Tate asks. He's taken to calling me that, and I love it.

"Yeah, sweetie?" I answer, pouring the chips into a bowl.

"Are we having dessert, tonight?"

"I think I might have made some ice cream last night." I tap one finger against my chin, pretending to try to remember, but he knows it's an act. He squeals with delight and runs for the door, eager to eat.

"Hold up," Christian says. The boy skids to a stop and turns around. "Take these with you."

Tate runs back over. He takes the bread and cheese held out to him before scurrying along. With food in hand, Christian and I follow him out to the picnic table Christian built between our houses. The scent of honeysuckle sweetens the air and a light breeze rustles the branches overhead.

***

After dinner, I venture upstairs for the first time in years, slipping away from the group to do so. I glance

325

around at my parents' things, nearly untouched since their deaths over a decade ago.

The bed they slept in is still made, so tight you could bounce a quarter on it. Most of their clothes still hang in the closet and rest within the dresser, though they won't for long.

Jackson made the first trip up here the morning after we came back from Breyerville. He gathered up enough of their clothes to get by and left it at that. I wasn't quite ready for more than that.

Now, I trail one hand over the top of the dust-covered dresser, leaving clean streaks behind my fingers. I open the top drawer and feel Dad's shirts. Pulling one free, a black tee-shirt with the logo of Dad's favorite tractor brand on it, I press it against my neck, resting my chin atop my balled fists.

I'll keep this one.

I drape it over my shoulder and push the drawer shut.

Karen will need more clothes, and I know Mom's clothes will fit her with only minor alterations. Christian has already inherited clothes from Holden and from within the closet Mrs. Ableman kept for her son's visits.

But no one else in town is close to Karen's size.

With the sun's last rays floating in through the massive floor-to-ceiling windows, I pull open the closet. Mom's shirts are soft. I can almost smell her on them as I press them to my face. I run a sentimental hand over the sleeves.

I take a deep breath and pull them from the closet.

About the Author

As a busy nerd, Elexis Bell enjoys many hobbies, including reading, shower-singing, and playing video games and dungeons and dragons. She lives with her husband, their dog, and a small army of cats.